PENGUIN BOOKS

MATCHED UP

Also by Jenny Ireland

MATCHED UP

JENNY IRELAND

PENGUIN BOOKS

PENGUIN BOOKS

UK | USA | Canada | Ireland | Australia
India | New Zealand | South Africa

Penguin Books is part of the Penguin Random House group of companies
whose addresses can be found at global.penguinrandomhouse.com

www.penguin.co.uk   www.puffin.co.uk   www.ladybird.co.uk

Penguin
Random House
UK

First published 2025

001

Set in 10.75/15.5pt Adobe Caslon Pro
Typeset by Jouve (UK), Milton Keynes
Printed and bound in Great Britain by Clays Ltd, Elcograf S.p.A.

The authorized representative in the EEA is Penguin Random House Ireland,
Morrison Chambers, 32 Nassau Street, Dublin D02 YH68

A CIP catalogue record for this book is available from the British Library

ISBN: 978-0-241-72095-0

All correspondence to:
Penguin Books
Penguin Random House Children's
One Embassy Gardens, 8 Viaduct Gardens, London SW11 7BW

For Lyla and Rory. Thank you for the football. x

1

I tapped newly painted nails on my laptop impatiently.

'Can we turn over now? Barcelona–Sevilla is on.' I rolled my eyes and turned to my best friend with prayer hands.

'It's almost over. This is the best bit!' Megan watched the screen, hugging her tanned legs as her eyes welled up.

'You said that half an hour ago.' I gave an exaggerated sigh. 'Oh, and by the way, if you look at them when they're old, the height difference is completely off, so unless he's shrunk, I reckon he's actually talking to a complete stranger and it's not Allie at all,' I said. I loved finding inconsistencies in movies.

A pillow was pushed over my face. I threw it away and laughed. 'Hey!'

'Stop trying to ruin *The Notebook*. It won't work.' There were tears streaming down Megan's face now. I don't know why she did it to herself; every Sunday when she chose the movie, she picked something that made her cry, full-on heartbroken tears, like the trauma had just happened to her. It made no sense to me. But that was the deal.

I got up and paced around my room for about the tenth

time during the movie. I'd never been any good at sitting in the same place for extended periods of time, but since I'd agreed to movie night with Megan every Sunday in exchange for extra training, I'd actually been getting better at sitting.

'Don't you get enough football?' Megan asked. We trained twice a week with Westing FC and played matches once, and sometimes even twice, weekly. Sometimes I got a game, if they were a player short, but lately the whole squad had been showing up and the closest I got to a match was freezing my arse off on the bench. But it was all going to change this season. I knew it.

'Blasphemy!' I said, horrified. I gazed at the framed poster of Aitana Bonmatí on my wall. 'Bet Aitana doesn't lie around watching movies all the time.'

'Bet she doesn't eat these either.' Megan shoved a handful of Doritos in her mouth and a million crumbs dropped on to my bed.

'I'll kill you,' I said. I didn't add that of course Aitana wouldn't eat them. Sometimes I wondered if I talked about her too much, my idol, the Barcelona midfielder who I'd been obsessed with ever since I'd started playing. When me and my twin brother Niall had started watching Liga F, the Spanish women's football league, alongside the Premier League, Serie A and La Liga. Niall was as into football as I was. Maybe it was a twin thing, always liking the same stuff – I'd never really thought about it too much – but it was nice, always having him around. I mean, Megan was my best friend, but Niall was more than that, like he was almost part of me.

She laughed and brushed them off. 'OK, it's over. You happy?'

'Yes. You owe me a practice,' I said.

'Oh, come on, it's too late. And it's way too cold,' Megan whined, her huge brown eyes begging me to back down.

'Sorry. You promised. And who cares if it's cold? Bet Aitana plays in the cold.'

'Yeah, and I bet she's zero craic,' Megan said, pulling herself off the bed. 'OK, fine, I'm ready.' She looked in the mirror and tightened her ponytail. She was wearing her new lululemon shorts. The pink ones that barely covered her arse.

'Do you want to borrow some trackies? You'll be freezing,' I said, pulling on one of Niall's massive hoodies.

'No, I'm fine,' she said and spun round on one foot. 'Let's go before I change my mind.'

'Where are you two going?' Niall didn't even look up from the screen as we passed. But Hunter did. He was my brother's best mate, and because Mum and Dad were so chilled out about having people round to the house, and Hunter's parents were always fighting about something, he was always there. They were sitting in the adjoining living room to our bedrooms, the one Niall had turned into a games room.

'Practice,' I said.

'You serious? It's Baltic.' Both of them were looking up now.

'That's what I said,' Megan complained behind me.

'Why don't you stay in? We could even play *Mario Kart*?' Hunter said, smiling. He knew how much I loved *Mario Kart*; it was the only game I had any chance of winning against Niall. He also knew how much I liked to beat Niall, at anything.

'Sorry, can't. We've got work to do, haven't we, Meg?' I grabbed her hand and pulled her towards the stairs.

'Kill me,' she said, and I heard Niall and Hunter laugh.

We walked into the kitchen where Mum was drinking a glass of wine and watching some Scandinavian crime drama. I'm pretty sure that's all she ever watched.

'Isn't it a bit late to go outside, love?' she called when she saw where we were headed.

'Just going out to practise.'

'OK, but not too long. Sport isn't life, remember.'

I rolled my eyes. She loved to trot out that phrase at least once a week. She didn't know what she was talking about. She wasn't even into sport.

'And, Megan, love, I'll ask Niall to run you home after.'

'Thanks, Mrs Ryan.'

'*Inga problem*,' Mum replied.

I shook my head. 'She thinks she can speak Swedish now.'

Megan laughed and walked outside. 'Love your mum. Jesus. I still can't believe your mum and dad paid for this.' She did a backward whistle. 'You're so lucky.'

She was talking about the football pitch that Dad had installed just before Christmas. It wasn't a complete surprise because there were workers in our garden for weeks, but he told me on Christmas Day that he'd decided to build it after a conversation we'd had about how much I wanted to make the team and that he wanted to support me as much as he could.

'Not as lucky as you,' I said, opening the gate and switching on the little floodlights. 'Megan Evans, daughter of the NI team doctor!' I kicked a high ball to her, and she trapped it with her chest effortlessly.

'Apart from free match tickets it's not that exciting, you

know,' she said. 'I'd much rather have this pitch . . .' She kicked the ball back to me, hard. 'Actually, I'd rather have the money the pitch cost and go on a really expensive holiday.' She grinned.

'OK, let's do this,' I said. 'Dribbling drills?'

Megan pulled a face. 'OK, *Sadie.*' Sadie was our coach. The coach that everyone, apart from me, hated because she was so serious.

Then we were interrupted. 'You ready, Megan?' Niall's voice from the side of the pitch. I looked over to see Hunter standing there too, drinking a can of Coke, and watching us play.

'What? Go away – we've only just started!' I shouted back.

'Yeah, we've only *just* started,' Megan said, dropping to her knees and pretending to cry.

'Mum says I need to leave Megan home.'

'She's not ready,' I said, getting annoyed now. 'We'll be finished in an hour.'

'An hour?!' Megan screamed.

Niall and Hunter laughed. But it wasn't funny.

'I watched your stupid movie; you promised you'd practise with me,' I said, aware of the fact I sounded like a child. 'You can go now,' I said to the boys, who were still hovering at the side of the pitch.

They didn't go. 'Two versus two?' Niall called.

'I'm in!' Megan said before I could say no.

We were supposed to be doing drills. But I guess it was better than nothing.

'Fine,' I conceded.

Niall joined us on the pitch. 'Maybe we should split the teams? Make it fairer?'

5

'Yeah, right! Scared to lose to a couple of girls?' I always fell for Niall's wind-ups.

'Niall is,' said Hunter.

He crushed his Coke can and threw it over the little fence and I didn't even say anything. I was in football mode, where nothing else mattered.

'OK, fine, Ryans versus rejects,' I said, and walked over beside Niall. Niall and I had played together so much we made the perfect team.

Hunter scoffed. 'Hear what they called us, Megan?'

'Let's destroy them. Twins are going down.' Megan gave us her best evil stare, and Niall laughed.

'Let's go!' I passed the ball to Niall and we played for an hour. No breaks. By the end of the match, they were winning, and Niall had taken to holding back Megan, ignoring her half-hearted protests.

We sat on the pitch, exhausted, although when I glanced at Megan she barely looked out of breath. Unlike me she hadn't missed a pass, hadn't hit the ball wide and still managed to smile, when all I could do was try to get my breath back.

'You're such a cheater,' Megan said to Niall. But it was light-hearted.

Hunter walked over to me and offered his hand to help me up.

I took it. 'Good game,' he said, 'except for the fact Niall cheated.'

'I don't see a ref.' I grinned. 'Go get that Coke can.'

'Oh yeah, sorry,' he said, like he'd dropped it accidentally. And by the time he got back, Coke can in hand, Megan and Niall were standing up too, passing the ball between them.

'You ready to go *now*?' Niall asked Megan.

'I've been ready to go for an hour.' She stuck out her tongue at him.

'I can take her,' I said, between gulps of air. 'Meg, you don't have to go with them, don't worry.' I was looking forward to driving her home. When we were in the car alone, we'd turn up the music and sing-scream until our throats ached, then piss ourselves laughing at how bad we sounded.

'It's OK, Lex, I don't mind,' she said.

'You look like you need a shower anyway,' Niall said, jingling his car keys in my direction. 'Bet you've sweated all over my hoodie.'

'Good!'

'Bye, Lex,' said Hunter with a little wave, which wasn't like him. Usually, he and Niall were throwing jokey insults in my direction.

'Bye, Hunter,' I said with exaggerated enthusiasm.

'See ya tomorrow!' Megan called, and the three of them disappeared.

But I hadn't finished yet.

This was it. Final thirty seconds of extra time and Lexie Ryan, star defender of Westing FC, is taking it up the wing. What's this? She's beaten three of Crusaders' defenders. She shoots, she sc–

'Fuck sake!' The ball hit the crossbar and rebounded back at me. I kicked it as hard as I could against the fence. I bent over, hands on thighs, hot breath disappearing into the night like cigarette smoke. The shadow from the floodlights stretched me out, taller, thinner, like Megan. Megan who didn't have to train like this. Extra hours on top of practice, working on my touch, working on my fitness. She had it all. Naturally. I wasn't jealous. OK, I was. Even though I hated thinking bad thoughts about her, but come *on*. I booted the ball towards the net again, hoping I'd sink it into the top corner and it would be a sign from the gods that the talent was there, just hidden really, really well. But no. Wide.

I went back upstairs, had a shower, did my skincare routine, and put on the new Victoria's Secret pyjamas that Mum had bought me. Then I put on the football and picked up the Doritos that we'd left on the bed.

I stretched out my aching muscles, then opened the new leather notebook that Megan had bought me for Christmas. My heart swelled for her. How well she knew me. How she knew how much I loved to make lists. New Year, new list.

1. Practise for at least two hours every day.
2. Study for at least one hour every day.
3. Eat, sleep and breathe football.
4. Start on the first team.

Tick, tick, tick, no tick. But I was working on it. And I would work as hard as I had to until Sadie started me. I fell asleep watching Barcelona vs Sevilla, the sound of the chanting crowd infiltrating my dreams.

2

I got up an hour before everyone else to get ready for school, because my need to be flawless didn't just apply to football. Hair, make-up, uniform. And the Blackport uniform was so ridiculous that it needed its own thirty minutes. Sometimes I even re-ironed the shirts that Mum had sent out because I needed them to be absolutely perfect.

Dad was away for work, and this time Mum hadn't gone with him. Over the last year, since me and Niall turned seventeen, she'd started going away with him on his work trips, spending time walking around European cities. And shopping, of course. But occasionally, she stayed behind, and when she did, she was always up early, like she was scared we'd forget something if she wasn't hanging around the kitchen making sporadic comments about things that happened weeks ago in school. I came down to her making crepes in her satin dressing gown.

'Morning. No sign of Niall yet?' she asked over her shoulder and giving a little yelp as she turned a crepe.

'Nope. Not yet.' I got a saucepan out and filled it with water, putting two eggs in to boil.

'No crepes, Lex? You used to love them.' Mum sounded disappointed.

'Sorry. Protein for breakfast. I'm in training. But, sure, I'll take one as well.' I smiled and Mum's face lit up as she handed me a plate with a crepe on it.

Niall snorted as he walked in, tie wonky, shirt tails hanging out, hair sticking up everywhere. And this is where me and Niall differed. I couldn't leave the house like that, never mind go to school.

'In training for what?' He walked over to Mum, sliding the plate of just-made crepes across the counter before drowning them in maple syrup.

'I'm making the first team this year,' I said. I'd told myself I was going to talk about it. Put it out into the universe in the hope that would help make it come true.

'Oh really?' The food in his gob didn't hide the sarcasm.

'Yes, really.' I resisted the temptation to throw an egg at him.

'Fair enough,' he agreed with a nod, and I felt a flash of joy. 'Meg was saying Sadie's gone all boss bitch this season.'

Meg? Only I called her 'Meg'.

'Yeah, what's wrong with that? It's the way it should be. It's Westing FC not Ferndale United,' I snapped. I didn't get everyone's problem with taking things seriously. If you don't want to put the effort in, go to another club.

'Nothing. Harrison's the same; said there's some new kid joining this week too. Better keep his hands off my position.'

'Oh, I'm sure he won't be as good as you, Niall,' said Mum, Niall's biggest fan.

'Thanks, Mum.' My brother directed his smug smile right at me.

'Bet Yamal doesn't eat maple syrup,' I said, checking the time for my eggs.

Niall responded by shoving the rest of the syrupy crepes in his mouth.

'When's Dad back?' I asked. I needed my own cheerleader home.

'Not until Wednesday,' Mum said.

I rolled my eyes, took out my eggs and sat down opposite Niall. 'You missed the match last night. You should have seen the goal Aitana scored. Free kick.' I kissed my fingers. 'Where'd you go after leaving Meg home anyway?'

'Hunter's.'

'Oh, wow, proper bromance now,' I teased.

'Nah, he just wanted to show me his new football shirt. Venezia. Class.' Niall was scrolling through his phone. He smirked at the screen.

'What's so funny?' I asked, leaning over to see, but he slid the phone into his pocket.

He pulled a face then flicked my ponytail. 'None of your business.'

I sighed, fixed my hair, then lowered my voice so Mum wouldn't hear. 'Did you do the maths homework?'

'Shit!' Niall whispered. 'I meant to do it last night – completely forgot. Fuck.' Then he gave me his innocent begging look that worked for all the girls in our year. It also worked on me, but I had to at least hesitate before I said yes.

He was just lucky that I didn't want our name dragged through the mud any more than he'd already managed with his rubbish grades. Not that mine were amazing or anything, but they were better than his.

'You can borrow mine.'

'Thanks, I owe you. Best twin ever!' He disappeared to look for my homework.

After breakfast I looked in the mirror again, checking my slicked-back ponytail to make sure Niall hadn't messed it up. I'd added a last-minute hairband to match the berry lip gloss I was wearing. I smoothed down my skirt and picked some fluff from my jumper.

I never wanted to be a 'Blackport girl'. It's one of the only private schools in Northern Ireland and the only reason we went there was because there was no chance in hell that Niall was getting into St Anne's with his AQE score, and we hadn't wanted to split up.

It might sound like a kind of twin cliché, but Niall genuinely felt like an extension of me. I remember when he went on the school ski trip in P7 and I stayed behind because I'd wanted to study. I'd never felt so lost. I got no studying done and cried when we went to pick him up at the airport. So separate schools seemed completely unthinkable. And there wasn't anything inherently wrong with Blackport. It had better grounds and sports facilities than any of the other local schools, but it didn't even have a football team. Boys or girls. Whatever, I had Westing.

Niall stuck his head into the kitchen before heading for the front door. 'Right, done. Thanks, Lex. Oh, and I said we'd pick up Megan this morning, so drive by Meadowview too?'

'Bye, Mum!' I called, then followed him outside. 'She didn't say anything to me,' I said, confused. 'Are you sure?'

'Yeah, she just asked last night when I was leaving her home.' Niall got into the passenger seat of my car. The brand-new BMW 1 Series that Dad had bought us both on our seventeenth birthday, mine white and Niall's black.

When we pulled into Megan's drive, she was already at the window waiting. Weird. She was a late person. Always. No matter how hard she tried, she was never on time.

She got into my car in a cloud of Ariana Grande perfume.

'You smell good,' I said, pulling out of her drive.

Megan sat forward so she was pretty much sitting between us. 'Thanks.'

'Trying to lure a date for V-Ball?' I joked. Of course my best friend already had about five offers of dates to V-Ball, all of which she'd turned down. She said she was 'waiting for the right one', but from where I was standing, she could have her pick. V-Ball was Blackport's Valentine's ball, the insanely huge budget black-tie event of the year. Megan lived for it. I, on the other hand, couldn't care less about it. To me it was time wasted, when I could be practising football. 'I saw Hunter looking at you in a perverted way the other day,' I confessed.

'Hunter's always looking at me in a perverted way. And you. I saw him staring at your tits on Friday. Don't blame him, though – your mum did you a solid with those.'

Niall made a retching noise and Megan laughed. 'Sorry, Niall, but your mum and your sister are hot. Deal with it.'

'Please stop.'

*

At school everyone was congregating on the steps by the maths block as usual. Hunter was telling everyone about how amazing he was in his last football match, as usual. Zoe and Amina were looking at something on Zoe's phone. As usual.

I sat down beside Zoe. Megan and Niall were chatting to each other, ignoring Hunter.

'We're talking V-Ball, Lexie – who's your date?' Zoe was staring at me with her perfect almond-shaped eyes, her auburn hair tied up in a high ponytail with a white bow. She was smiling. Zoe was always smiling. I wondered if someone could smile *too* much. Like, do smiles become worthless if they're there all the time?

'Earth to Lexie?' Zoe waved her hand in front of my face, and Amina laughed.

'Sorry, em, nobody. Haven't had any time to think about it.' I shrugged. I mean, that wasn't entirely true. I *did* think it was a bit of a waste of potential football practice hours, but at the same time, it wasn't like I was drowning in date offers.

'Oh my God, let us find you a date. We'll get you someone really hot,' Zoe said enthusiastically. 'Oh, and you're coming to my party on Friday, yeah?' Zoe nodded at me, like I didn't actually have any choice in the matter. But it worked because I nodded back, even though it was the first I'd heard of a party and hadn't had a chance to think it through. 'But I *will* find you a date. I'm making it my mission.'

'No, it's fine, really.' I tried to laugh it off, but Zoe had already turned away to talk to Amina.

My heart was racing now. The one thing worse than not being asked by anyone, was Zoe Parker asking people on my behalf and being rejected. I glanced up to catch Niall sharing a look of sympathy with me.

I tried to get Megan's attention, throwing a 'save me' look across the steps to where she was sitting beside Niall. But she wasn't looking at me; she was laughing at something Hunter had said.

'You're going. Leave it to us.' Zoe turned back. She put her hand on my leg and grinned at me. 'Don't worry Lexie, we won't let you down.' She squealed and clapped. 'I just love playing cupid.'

Great.

3

Niall was striker for the boys' team at Westing. He'd been obsessed with being a striker ever since we were little kids, and when Harrison put him on the first team last year his happiness was contagious. His moods seeped into my bones. Like when we got our AQE results and I saw his score, it physically hurt. It didn't happen as much now, or as deeply, but it was still there. And I wasn't jealous. Not the way I was of Megan, how everything came so easily to her, how she walked on to the team without even thinking about it. I'd always just been happy for Niall. Proud even. And he was always the first person I wanted to tell good news to. I daydreamed about Sadie starting me on the first team and Niall would be the first person I'd tell. Well, Megan would know because she was already on the team, but then it would be Niall, and *then* Mum and Dad.

'You ready to go?' I asked him on Tuesday evening. He was playing Xbox.

'It's only five o'clock,' he said.

'I know, but we should get there early. Sadie likes it when people are on time,' I said, pacing the gaming room.

'Like, I know you're into being early, Lex, but that's way too soon.'

'Please?'

Niall sighed and turned off his game. 'Fine, but I'm choosing the music.'

I always drove to practice. In fact, I always drove everywhere. Which was fine. I liked to have the control of leaving whenever I wanted.

The club was empty when we got there. Only Harrison's car was in the car park.

'Lexie, what the hell? There's nobody here.' Niall thudded the back of his head off the headrest.

'Want to get out and do some passing?' I asked hopefully. I checked my hair in the mirror, then reapplied the lip gloss I'd brought with me.

'Nope,' said Niall. So we just sat in the car and listened to music.

'There's Harrison,' I said. Niall's coach was standing beside the pitch talking to someone. A boy. He wasn't in a Westing kit, but we were too far away to see who it was.

'Who's that?' Niall said, straining to look.

'Not sure,' I replied. 'Wait, must be the new kid. Didn't you say someone was starting?'

'Oh aye.' Niall leaned forward to get a better look.

Then Megan blocked our view when her dad pulled in beside us. She jumped out of the car, and I swear to God her clothes were getting smaller every week. It was *January* and she wasn't wearing any under-layers, just tiny shorts and a Westing top that clung to her body like a wetsuit. She got into the back seat.

'You're early.' I turned to her, confused. 'Again! Do you have a temperature?' I reached back to feel her forehead.

She laughed. 'Nope, just sick of rushing all the time.' She shrugged. 'Who's Harrison talking to?' But when we looked again, they'd gone.

'The new kid,' Niall and I said together.

Megan twisted her fingers in my ponytail. 'You know Zoe's going full on with this V-Ball thing. She's trying to get me too. And she's having a party after the match on Friday, so be warned, she'll probably try and set you up.'

'Ugh, yeah, she said yesterday.' I rolled my eyes. Then we got out of the car, leaving Niall in the passenger seat.

'You not coming to watch?' Megan asked him before she got out.

'Maybe,' he said.

I hoped he wouldn't. It was extra pressure when Niall was there.

Sadie was pulling footballs out of a net bag and setting them up for our first drill. I always tried to gauge her mood at the start of practice. Tonight did not feel like a good night. Her voice was clipped, and her blonde hair was tied back so tightly that there was nowhere for her frustrated looks or crow's feet to hide. The other girls were just standing around chatting, and laughing like it was school break time. How could you possibly be giggling about something one second, like Zoe and Amina, and then put in a decent session? You couldn't!

'OK, girls, big game on Friday. I want you to be sharp tonight – no lazy passing, no messing about. Got it?' She scanned us. 'And some news. We had to let Sophie go. I need full commitment if you want to be part of the team. Practice twice a week, no excuses.'

I felt sick. Even though it was nothing to do with me. The thought of leaving Westing was my worst nightmare, and if it was because of lack of commitment? I couldn't think of anything more humiliating.

I glanced over at Megan to share a look, but she was staring off at the sideline. She got distracted so easily. I noticed that Niall had actually come to watch.

'I still haven't decided on the final team for Friday, so if you want to be in the line-up, it would be in your interests to impress me. Right, Megan?' Sadie shot a look at Megan, who was still in her own little world.

'Hundred per cent,' Megan said and saluted, even though there was no way in hell that she *wouldn't* be on the team.

I *had* to be getting better. Since the start of the season, I'd been doing extra practice at home and putting in max effort at training. Every week I'd hope she'd pick me for the first team, but it never happened. Not yet. Always a sub, never a player. But things were going to change.

So that night I gave it my all, running so hard I wanted to throw my guts up, lungs burning, legs aching, concentrating on my touch.

'Nice feet, Lex,' said Sadie during a dribbling drill, and it spurred me on, filling me with hope. Maybe tonight would be the night.

When Sadie blew the final whistle, Megan came sauntering over to me. She was hardly out of breath, whereas I could barely breathe and could feel sweat dripping down the back of my Nike Pro shorts.

'The squad for Friday is as follows . . .'

Sadie's voice blurred into the night. Heartbeat in my ears, exhausted, desperate, scared to listen. But my name didn't come. And Sadie must have sensed my disappointment, because she held me behind.

'Keep going, Lex. Your effort isn't going unnoticed. It's just tough because you're competing against Zoe for right back, and at the minute, she has the edge.'

I winced but I tried to hide it. Clearly not very well because Sadie put her hand on my shoulder.

'That's not to say she always will. Look, keep putting in the practice. I know how much you want this, OK? Busting your ass for something you want? It's always a good look. For anything.' Sadie winked at me and I tried to smile back, but I could feel the pressure behind my eyes.

'Thanks,' I said, turning away and following the girls back to the changing rooms. I didn't talk to anyone. I ignored the chat about the Birch High Spring Formal and our V-Ball. I just wanted to be alone or with Megan. Where was she? I couldn't see her, so I walked towards the shower. Then I heard Zoe.

'Hey, Lex, you still coming to my party?' She smiled as if she hadn't been there when my dreams were stomped on by Sadie.

'Sure,' I managed to choke out.

She squealed. 'Awesome, and make sure to get Niall and Hunter to tell the boys' team too.' She let her red hair down from its ponytail. It sat in fiery waves over her shoulders, and it just added to the pang of jealousy after my conversation with Sadie.

I had a shower. In the disgusting shower block that had barely any hot water. Nobody showered there so I knew I'd be alone. I let myself cry silently, tears disappearing into lukewarm water. By the time I'd finished, the changing rooms were empty. I pulled on my spare under-layers and my Westing hoodie, with a woolly hat over my wet hair. I looked in the mirror. Red-rimmed eyes, lips dark pink from biting them. I reached into my bag for some make-up and did the best I could.

I walked outside into the freezing night, and it felt colder than ever because of my wet hair. The boys were almost finished, and there was Megan, watching from the sidelines.

I got there just in time to see Niall score. He was playing out on the left wing for some reason. At least Sadie had never moved me from defence. There was something I loved about being the last man before the keeper, the thrill of getting a last-second foot in to ruin their play.

I sidled up beside Megan.

'Oh my God, tell me you did not go into those gross showers?' She fingered my wet hair. 'You OK? Sadie doesn't know what the hell she's talking about; you're by far the best defender on the team, Lex.' Megan sounded like *she* was going to cry.

'I'll be fine.' I forced a smile and focused on the pitch. 'How's practice going?' I asked, changing the subject.

'Check it out.' She pointed across the pitch to someone I didn't recognize. The new kid, who'd been talking to Harrison, in a mismatched tracksuit, running rings round the rest of them.

And it was like someone had hit slow motion on the world. The way this kid played, it was beautiful. It was like he barely touched the ball; the tiniest move here and there and he was sending the other players completely the wrong way. Then he took a shot, hard and low – Fry was never saving it.

'Jesus.' I'm not even sure I closed my mouth. 'Did you get a name?'

'Shane something. He came from Ferndale United,' Megan said.

My eyes drifted towards Niall, who I could tell was raging by the set of his jaw.

'But Ferndale are crap!' I said, so confused that nobody had heard about this kid. Everyone knew the good players from all the local teams. The ones who stood out a mile and you half expected to see them on *Match of the Day* in a couple of years.

'I know. Well, all apart from this guy, anyway. And he's a striker.' Megan looked at me with concern because we both knew what this meant.

'Shit, Niall,' I said reflexively, that familiar lurch in my stomach when something bad happened to him.

'Yeah,' Megan agreed, as if she'd felt it too.

Harrison blew the final whistle.

I let my gaze fall back on Shane. He walked alone, ahead

of the other boys, and as he got closer, I could see his face properly. His features were delicate but masculine at the same time. His hair, shaggy, longer at the front and shaved up the sides, almost black, but it was hard to tell if it was really that dark or the shine of sweat that made it that colour.

One thing I did know? He was beautiful.

I had to drag my eyes away from him because he was getting closer and there was no hope of changing the expression on my face. I turned to see where Megan had gone, and just as I did, he hopped over the fence beside me and knocked into my arm.

'Don't believe in gates?' I blurted out.

He turned to me. More than a head taller. Lean, quarter zip, zipped up to his chin, black track bottoms skimming over *everything*. He smelled like sweat and body spray. I had to stop myself moving closer to smell him again because that would have been weird. But my God, he was gorgeous.

He smiled at me. His eyes were light. Blue maybe. 'There's a queue. And I'm going to miss the bus.'

'Zoe's having a party,' I said too loudly. 'On Friday.'

'OK,' he said, looking bemused.

'She's on my team. Said to invite the boys' team too if you want to go or whatever?' I tried to act nonchalant to make up for the embarrassing display of desperation.

'Where does she live?' he asked.

'Castle Hill.'

He whistled. 'Nice. But don't think I'd be very welcome. Not sure the team are too happy I'm here.' He looked back towards the road. 'I really am going to miss the bus.'

'OK, yeah, well, maybe see you at practice on Thursday then?' I dug my nails into the side of the fence. Mortified.

'Yeah, cool,' he said.

Just before he left, he looked at me again, his eyes searing right into my soul, making my heart race faster than it had all night.

And whatever this feeling was, I knew he felt it too.

4

I was dying to talk to Megan about Shane, but Niall was in a total rage the whole way home.

'Can I come back to yours?' Megan whispered. 'My mum's out and Dad's super grumpy at the minute; he's so busy at work and Marissa's not even here any more to share the tension.'

'Sure. Want to practise?' I offered. 'Take your mind off everything?'

She laughed. 'Absolutely not.'

Niall was sitting in the back seat in silence, but as we turned the corner into our street, he started an epic rant. 'He can't just fucking swan in here and take my position. What the hell was Harrison thinking? He's not even that good for fuck's sake.'

'You're right,' agreed Megan and I fired her a look. I'd only seen him play for five minutes and I knew that wasn't true.

'And did you see the end of that match, when he didn't even pass to Ben? Ball-greedy bastard.'

I could feel his angry black cloud closing in on me.

I was so relieved when we pulled into the driveway. There were loads of cars outside the house. Audis mostly, a Range Rover, a Lexus. Mum's 'book club'. I wasn't convinced they read the books at all; I think they just used it as an excuse to drink wine and gossip, then they'd leave their cars here because they'd all be pissed and doing karaoke by the end of the night.

Niall stormed straight up the stairs, while me and Megan loitered downstairs. I took off my trainers and hung up my bag on autopilot. Megan did the same. And she could have been talking to me, but I didn't hear her. I was thinking about Shane, about his maybe-black hair and maybe-blue eyes. The easy smile and the way he controlled that ball. My God.

Mum came into the kitchen and leaned on the island. I could already tell she was drunk. 'Hi, ladies. Would you like some champagne?'

'Mum!' I said. I couldn't believe what I was hearing. Dad *hated* underage drinking. His friend was killed in a car crash as a teenager, and he was always really strict about me and Niall not drinking until we were eighteen.

'A little bit won't do any harm,' she slurred. 'There's loads left over. Help yourselves.' She made her way back into what she calls the 'good room' and I watched Megan pour herself a glass.

'You're not joining me?' She took a sip and scrunched up her face.

'No thanks,' I said.

'Sure you don't fancy a run? Just a wee one?' I asked.

I needed it. The way I always did when I had to get rid of a feeling. The disappointment of not hearing my name in Sadie's line-up and Niall's position under attack.

'I can't think of anything I'd like to do less,' she said, sipping more champagne. 'But why don't you go? I'll wait for you in here, drinking your mum's expensive alcohol. I can even watch you from the window.' She smiled and held up her glass.

'I won't be long, I promise.'

I pulled on my trainers again, walked outside into the freezing cold and started running laps. And it was then, when I was alone, that all the disappointment came back, like a brick in the face. So I ran harder, pushing myself as much as humanly possible, so all I could feel was pain and I didn't have to think about the list of names that didn't have me on it. Then I started hitting balls into the net, getting as much power behind them as I could. But two out of three were going wide.

Fuck it. It was the football. It was flat. Niall kept the good ones in his room, the ones that cost like £100 each. I needed one of those.

I ran across the pitch, sprinting, legs already aching. But I liked the burn, the way the muscles screamed at me to stop and I wouldn't let them.

I burst into the kitchen where Mum was pouring herself another glass of champagne. No Megan.

'Still practising, Lexie? Maybe you should stop now; it's getting late.' She swayed out of the kitchen before waiting for an answer. 'There's such a thing as too much practice, you know.'

Mum didn't understand. Of course she didn't. The only sport she played when she was at school was tennis, and she'd told me she only played it because Grandad was chairperson of the tennis club, so she got on the team without a trial, and she liked the outfits. It wasn't even that late anyway, not even half nine, but she probably didn't have a clue because she was drunk. She didn't get the effort you had to put in to be the best. Or even just to get on the team.

I ran up the stairs and walked towards Niall's room. Music was blaring as usual. I called his name, but he didn't answer.

Then I opened the door.

And I wanted to claw my eyes out with a fork.

Megan screamed, her eyes so wide that it looked like they might pop from their sockets. Even after the scream ended, her mouth was still open. She moved it, like she was trying to say something, but no words were coming out.

I couldn't understand what I was seeing.

'Lexie,' Megan finally said.

Then Niall appeared from under the blanket.

'Lexie, what the fuck?'

I couldn't move. Why couldn't I move? Why was I standing there, staring at my half-naked best friend who had a matching horrified look.

'Why are you still here? Get out!' Niall shouted.

And whatever way he moved the blanket, I saw his actual naked arse. I wanted to throw up.

When my brain and legs finally reconnected, I legged it out of his room. I slammed the door, ran into my room, threw myself under my own blanket and tried desperately to erase what I'd just seen from my mind. Megan's face. Niall's arse. Jesus Christ.

I'd never understood the need for every bedroom in our house to have an en-suite. But right then I couldn't have been more grateful. I had another shower, desperately trying to wash away the thoughts of the two of them. And once the nausea had disappeared with the Sol de Janeiro suds, all that was left was rage.

Megan and Niall? What the actual fuck?

My best friend and my brother! Not only my brother. My *twin*! That word used to mean something. It used to mean that we told each other everything and we had each other's backs. It meant a pact: that if one of us was in trouble, the other one would do whatever they could to fix it. It was him doing one-on-ones with me whenever I asked, and it was me doing his homework for him because he got the looks, and I got the better brains. Did that not mean anything now?

I ran downstairs and straight outside, ignoring Mum's slurs asking where I was going. I was going to the beach. The beach that was connected to our back garden with a metal gate. I pushed it open and ran on to the sand, taking huge gulps of salty frozen air. I sat on a rock and screamed into the night, trying to expel the feelings that I couldn't get my head round. I'd felt bad for him, how Shane was taking his position, and guilty since I'd asked Shane to come to Zoe's party. How stupid. And Megan? How *could* she?

I stood up and kicked the sand. Hard. Then I just stared out at the raging sea for what must have been at least forty minutes with tears streaming down my face.

I was freezing by the time I went back inside. Mum was talking to Niall in the kitchen.

'Lexie!' she said overdramatically and walked towards me, her arms outstretched. 'I was so worried.'

'I was just at the beach,' I said, trying to hide the fact I'd been crying.

'I told her that's where you'd be,' said Niall.

His voice made my chest tighten. I pulled myself from Mum's hug and made my way past Niall, knocking into him with my shoulder as I walked through the door.

I went upstairs and got into bed, hair still wet, and opened YouTube. I watched the football highlights, Man United vs Arsenal. I don't know why I did it to myself, I knew the score. Highlights usually calmed me down, but this was just depressing. I should have put on Barcelona. Bonmatí. Poetry.

There was a knock at the door.

'What?'

'Can I come in?' Megan's voice.

'No.' I didn't want to see her. Ever again.

'Please?' She pushed the door open gently.

Megan was wearing Niall's Metallica T-shirt and a pair of shorts. She hovered in the doorway, trying not to make too much eye contact. 'We wanted to tell you,' she said quietly.

We. We was me and Megan. Or me and Niall. *We* wasn't them.

'But?' I spat.

'But we didn't know how you'd react . . .'

I slammed the lid of my laptop down. 'So you just decided to *not* tell me?' I didn't let her answer. 'What's the deal then? How long have you been . . . doing *that*?' My face twisted without me even telling it to. I cringed when I thought about all the times the three of us had been hanging out. Had they been dying for me to leave? I avoided eye contact.

Megan was still in the doorway like she was scared to come in properly. 'Just a few months,' she said; it was almost a whisper.

'*Months?*' I felt sick.

'Lex. We wanted to tell you. I'm sorry.'

Rage throbbed in my gut and I glanced up at Megan, whose eyes glittered with tears. And I almost softened, like I usually did when she cried. But I forced myself to stop. What they'd done? Unforgivable.

'Please just get out,' I said through gritted teeth.

And she looked like she was going to say something, then decided not to, before turning and closing the door gently behind her.

For the next hour I stared at my phone in a strange kind of daze, waiting for a message from Niall telling me it was all a joke that I'd fallen for.

But no message came.

5

The next morning the tension was back, and I hadn't even gone downstairs yet. I loitered at the top of the staircase, listening to Niall slamming cupboard doors and Megan talking in a low voice. I wondered if Mum knew. Did she know Megan had slept in Niall's room last night? What would she think of her favourite child then? Maybe I'd tell her. Did Megan's parents know? I'm sure they wouldn't be happy that their precious youngest daughter had a sleepover with her boyfriend on a school night.

I checked the mirror before I went downstairs, only feeling like myself if everything was perfect. And I looked good. I looked like me, even though nausea flooded my stomach and my head ached from the spinning thoughts and the horrifying replay in my head of what I'd seen last night.

Mum wasn't up yet after her drunken book club, and when I walked into the kitchen Megan turned to stare at me, and Niall just ignored me completely. I made my boiled eggs and ate them in silence. I could hear Megan whispering something to Niall, but I couldn't make out what she said. Not that I cared.

I felt tears welling as I tidied away my half-eaten breakfast, then turned to them before I left. 'I'll be in the car if you want a lift. But maybe you'd rather be *alone*.' I hated that my voice choked at the end.

'Lexie,' I heard Megan say, but I didn't turn round; I took my keys and went to sit in the car to wait for them.

Megan got in the front seat and Niall sat in the back. He had his earbuds in and spent the whole journey staring out the window. And I don't know what I expected from him. But not this.

Megan didn't stop talking the whole way to school. 'So, Daddy said there's a Northern Ireland match in a couple of weeks. Against Portugal. He'll send me the tickets like always, so d'you want to go?'

She knew the answer to this. Of course I wanted to go. We went to all the Northern Ireland matches. But going didn't mean I forgave them. And she didn't even give me a chance to answer anyway.

'Oh my God, Dr Fox's son was at the surgery the other day. Remember Finbar?' she asked, speaking too quickly. Of course I remembered Finbar. Megan had a *huge* crush on him, even though he was, like, two years older than us and at actual medical school.

'Yeah,' I said with a sigh.

'Well, he brought his girlfriend with him and she's seriously gorgeous,' Megan said. She sounded like she meant it. Like she wasn't seething with jealousy in the same way she would have been a year ago.

'That's nice,' I said, wishing I'd driven to school alone.

'And she said she liked my trainers, which was super nice. I was wearing my new Nikes. You know, the purple ones?' Megan was speaking ridiculously quickly.

I nodded.

'So are you going to go to V-Ball with Hunter then?'

'What?' I snapped. As soon as it came out of my mouth, I knew it was over the top.

'Well, Zoe just said . . .' Her voice tailed off.

'I don't care what Zoe said. You know I wouldn't go with Hunter,' I said, frustrated and driving more quickly than usual.

'Jeez, sorry, I just thought –'

'You just thought what?' I shot back. 'That because you and Niall are a couple, that everyone else should have to find someone? Like I'm not good enough on my own or I'm not good enough to find my own date?' I looked at her this time, challenging her to say something else to piss me off.

'No, Lex, I didn't mean . . .' Her eyes welled up.

'Whatever,' I said, pulling into Blackport.

Niall hadn't spoken the whole way here. Usually, our car rides were all of us taking the piss out of teachers or coaches, stomachs sore from laughing before we even got to school. And before Megan and I were friends it would just be me and Niall, inside jokes or easy silence. Not like this weird mash-up of awkward silence from Niall and Megan spewing meaningless words like she was on speed.

When we got to school, I got out first and stormed across the yard, only turning to lock the car when I heard them close the doors. My stomach dropped when I realized that soon the whole of our year would know about Megan and Niall and then there'd be nowhere to hide. Blackport kids liked nothing better than new gossip.

I kept my head down all day, avoiding Megan and Niall at break time, and at lunch I put on my PE kit and went for a run round the pitches. I ran hard, distracting myself from the now and focusing on the burning in my thighs and the cold air in my chest. I went over football drills, memorizing them so I'd be ahead of the game tomorrow night. Maybe Sadie would be so impressed that she'd play me. She'd see that I was fitter than everyone else, that I wanted it more than everyone else. She'd change her mind.

When I thought about football, it took up all the space in my head. It had been that way since I'd started at Westing FC four years ago. I knew if I was going to play for that club, I needed to be serious. There was no taking it easy. I had to put in the work. And I had. I'd done everything I possibly could so far. It just wasn't good enough. Not yet. But I'd keep going. I needed to stay focused.

But under the winter sun, rhythmic breath, racing heart and aching muscles, I wasn't just thinking about football. I was thinking about him. The way he moved with the ball, effortless, natural, like he'd been born on a football pitch. The sharp lines of his jaw and the way his cheekbones caught the shine of the floodlights.

'Lex!'

I looked up but couldn't see anything but the school golf course and groups of kids congregating on the path surrounding it.

'Lex!' I heard again.

I turned round, running backwards, reluctant to break my pace.

It was Hunter, holding a rugby ball and shouting in my direction. He threw it towards me and I slowed down, focusing on the ball that was being fired at my face. But I must have taken my eye off it because I missed it.

'Shit,' I swore, and I could hear Hunter laugh from across the pitch. I picked the ball up, thinking about throwing it back but not wanting to embarrass myself with a crap pass, so I held on to it until Hunter got closer, then threw it back to him.

'I knew you were dedicated to football, but this is taking it to a new level. Lunchtime jogs?' He widened his eyes and laughed.

'Yeah, so?' I was out of breath and glad of the break. 'What are you doing with a rugby ball anyway, traitor?'

'Jack of all trades,' he said. 'So Niall and Meg are out in the open then.' He threw the ball in the air and caught it, and my insides tightened all over again.

'You knew?' I stared at him and watched him realize that he'd said something wrong.

'Only for a couple of days. Niall told me that night after we left Megan home . . .' His voice trailed off and my heart beat even faster than it had been.

'Nice to know where I stand when it comes to those two,' I said. 'You know they didn't even tell me? I just found out by accident.'

Hunter pulled a face. 'Shit.'

'Yeah. Made me want to throw up.'

Hunter threw the ball to me. I threw it back. Hard.

'Wow, nice arm. You ever thought of playing rugby?' He walked over and squeezed the muscle of my triceps gently.

He got a laugh out of me. 'Nope. Football till I die,' I said.

'You know, if it's any consolation, I think Niall only told me because I saw a message Megan sent him as soon as we dropped her off.' He shrugged and spun the ball in the air.

I shook my head. 'Can we not talk about it any more?'

'Fair enough. Have you got a date for V-Ball yet?'

I looked at him, desperately trying to not look shocked. He'd grown his brown hair out and it stuck up at the back and then fell over his face like an anime character. He swooped it out of the way. Was Hunter nervous? I'd known him almost all my life; he was literally like family. And then, just in that moment, I knew it was coming. Other people might have guessed it before, the way he'd changed from acting like another Niall to someone who didn't take the piss out of me, and seemed genuinely interested in my life. But I'd always been crap at noticing this stuff. Football had been my focus for so long that boyfriends and V-Balls never crossed my mind. I just didn't have time. And even if I did, it wouldn't be Hunter. Going with nobody would be better than going with someone you didn't want to go with and only said yes because you didn't want to hurt their feelings.

'Nope,' I said. 'I mean, I probably won't go. It feels like a day wasted, when I could be training. What about you?' I shrugged and tried to act like I'd no idea what he was about to ask.

'No, not yet. I was just wondering, if maybe you weren't training, we could go together? I mean, I just thought it might make sense because Megan and Niall would be going together, and we could get the same car or whatever . . . ?' He trailed off when I didn't say anything.

I'd never seen Hunter like this. He was loud. Always had been. I couldn't count the number of times I'd come out of my room to tell him and Niall to shut up. I didn't know what to say. I'd never been good at coming up with stuff on the spot.

All that came out of my mouth was 'Oh.'

'Oh,' he repeated.

And we just stood there staring at each other until I flicked my gaze to the grass.

'It's not like I wouldn't want to go with you if I was going, I just don't want to waste a night I could be training, you know?' I lied. I was waffling. It made no sense. Of course I could take a night off. One night would make no difference, but did I want to see Niall and Megan all dressed up and all over each other? Hell no. The thought of being that way with Hunter made me squirm. Which felt kind of cruel because he was nice, he just wasn't for me.

'No, I get it. Yeah, that's cool. I'd better go – bell's about to ring.' He turned and jogged back towards the school.

'Shit.' I was going to be late. I sprinted to the changing rooms, glanced at my phone and realized there was no time for a shower. This wasn't me, Lexie last week wouldn't be caught dead unshowered at school. I stared at my red face and messy hair in the mirror, thinking about how a few days ago my life was normal, and now I didn't recognize any of it.

6

In my normal life, if Hunter had said something like that to me I'd be running to find Megan, bursting to tell her. Instead, I avoided everyone, focused on school, and thought about football in the car on the way home, dreaming about the day I'd get to go to Barcelona to see Bonmatí in real life. Nobody spoke. Niall sat in the back seat, earbuds in, and Megan scrolled through her phone. I could feel her glancing at me every few minutes, but it didn't faze me. When I was thinking about football, nothing else mattered.

I dropped Megan home and as soon as I got back, I got changed and went straight outside.

Our house overlooked Belfast Lough, so the air was thick with salt and the tang of the sea. It had always calmed me down. Running out there had always felt like a remedy for whatever I was feeling. Pissed off, disappointed, lonely? Fixed. Maybe it would work for betrayal too.

I ran across the grass, opened the gate and stared out at the water, taking deep breaths of salted air, before walking down the steps on to the sand. The wind was strong and blew my hair across my face. The waves smashed against the shoreline like they were as angry as I was. And I was about to scream into the wind, to let it all out, the disappointment of not being chosen for the firsts again, the pain of Megan and Niall being together, the awkwardness of Hunter asking me to V-Ball. All of it. It was all too much. But then I heard someone calling my name from down the beach.

'Dad!' I shouted, running towards him. 'When did you get back?'

'Just in time it seems,' he said, laughing. His eyes were twinkling. 'Looks like you were about to take a swim.'

I wrapped my arms round his waist. He was still wearing one of his work suits, minus the jacket, and he smelled of the same aftershave he'd always worn. Spicy and sweet at the same time. I breathed him in. I don't think I realized how much I still missed him when he was away. When I was a kid, I used to cry about it and Niall would make up stupid songs to cheer me up, but even though the tears didn't happen any more, the house kind of felt empty without him. A big man, with an even bigger presence.

'How are you, Alexandra?' he asked when I released him.

'I'm good, yeah. School's fine, football's fine.' I was speaking too quickly.

'And how's your brother?'

Niall's mission in life was to impress Dad. It always had been. And it was weird because I never felt like that. Maybe it was because I didn't have to work too hard for Dad to act like I was the greatest thing that graced the planet.

'He's fine too,' I said, hoping that would be the end of questions about Niall, because I'd never been able to hide my feelings very well, and there was no way he wouldn't guess something was wrong.

Dad was the only person I knew who loved the lough as much as I did. When he was at home, I could always find him staring out the kitchen window into the distance, where the lough disappeared into the Irish Sea.

I inhaled the salted air deeply and it slowed my heart.

'So why are you down here all alone?' Dad asked carefully.

'Extra training,' I said, followed by: 'I didn't make the first team.' Getting it out there before he asked.

He put his arm round my shoulder and pulled me closer to him. 'Keep at it, pet. If it's something you really want, don't give up.' He picked up a stone and threw it into the water.

'I'll get there. I know I will. I just have to work harder.'

'When's the next match?'

'Friday, up at the Dub.'

'Well, I might just swing by then.' Dad looked at me like he was going to say something else. 'You're my favourite daughter, you know.'

I laughed. 'When are you away again?'

He sighed. 'Next Friday. Stockholm this time.'

'Mum going?' I asked. 'Not sure she's been with you to Sweden yet. Then she could meet real-life Swedish people and see that they don't just murder each other and wear Fair Isle jumpers all the time.' I pulled a face.

Dad laughed and he looked like Niall.

'She is,' he said. 'You know, Alexandra, speaking of your mum, she thinks you're doing too much training. What do *you* think?' Dad looked straight at me, so I didn't have time to tell my face not to look so pissed off.

'Too much for what?'

'For your health. She's just worried about you,' he said, speaking louder over the wind.

I kicked the sand. 'Worried about me? What would Mum know about anything? The closest she got to a team sport was some snobby tennis club.'

'Your mum knows a lot about sports. More than I do.' He looked at me and raised his eyebrows.

'No, sure, you played football, didn't you?' I looked at him, confused. I'd always seen myself as a carbon copy of Dad. *Mum* wasn't into sports.

'I did, but I wasn't very good, and I certainly didn't have your work ethic. But, listen, I just wanted to check that you're not doing too much.'

'I'm not.'

'As long as you're sure, Lexie.'

'Positive.' I always liked the way Dad spoke to me like an adult.

'Race you home?'

OK, not always like an adult. And despite everything, by the time we'd run up the steps to the house, I was laughing.

Mum smiled when we walked into the kitchen gasping for air. 'You'll give yourself a heart attack running like that, Stephen!'

'I'm very fit, I'll have you know,' Dad said, walking over and pulling her into a hug.

She squealed and tried to pull away. Then they started kissing.

'Oh my God, please stop,' I said, but not too loudly. I was hoping that Niall would come in and have to witness it too.

And my wish was granted because he came in a few seconds later, saw what was happening, then walked straight back out again. Then my phone buzzed.

NIALL: Tell me when that's over

ME: No. Now you know how I felt. Except you don't because Dad wasn't . . .

NIALL: There's something very, VERY wrong with you. Why are you even still in the kitchen?

Why *was* I still in the kitchen, standing there like some kind of voyeur? I went up to my room, where I did my homework, watched more football highlights, and wished so hard that I'd never walked in on Megan and Niall. It was times like this I was going to miss the most. After-school gossiping, doing hair, doing nails, even Sunday-night movies. And it was like she knew I was thinking about her because my phone vibrated.

MEGAN: Can we be friends again yet?

MEGAN: I'm sorry I didn't tell you

MEGAN: I'm SORRY!

MEGAN: Please forgive me

MEGAN: I miss you ☹

And even though my heart broke for our friendship, I couldn't bring myself to message back. I stopped myself from writing something horrible in reply. But that was the best I could do.

7

Megan came back to ours after school the next day, like she usually did when we had practice. *Usually* she'd be in my room with me getting ready, but now she was with Niall. I turned up my music and put extra effort into looking perfect. It was all I could do. I couldn't train any harder, play any better, but I could put more effort into my looks, doing my hair, my make-up, wearing my most expensive under-layers and my new boots. I still might not look as good as Megan with her shiny dark hair and big brown eyes, but I could look like a better *me*.

I left before them without saying anything. I couldn't face another silent car journey. They could drive themselves.

The club was pretty much empty when I got there. The floodlights were on, and I felt immediately calmer. I walked into the middle of the pitch with a ball I'd found lying at the side and started to kick it into the net. Testing myself. Giving myself a target: top left, bottom right, whatever. And two times out of three I got it.

'Nice shot.'

I spun round. And just like the other night, the world stopped for a second. There he was, on the other side of the fence.

'Thanks,' I said, putting my foot on the ball to stop it rolling.

He jumped over the fence and on to the pitch. He was wearing all black again. Black zip-up Adidas top, black track bottoms and the same battered black boots from Tuesday night.

I passed him the ball.

'Sorry I had to go on Tuesday. If I'd missed the bus, it would have been ages for the next one and I needed to get home.' He kicked the ball back and I stopped it dead, one touch, then passed it back.

'Where do you live?'

I had so many questions and that was the first one that came out.

'Near Ferndale. You?'

We kept passing the ball between ourselves, getting closer and closer, so it would be even more obvious if I made a crap pass.

'Seaport. Close. *Not* Lane,' I added. Then realized how stupid it sounded. My house was pretty big, but not as big as the mansions on Seaport Lane, like the one Hunter lived in.

'Where's that?' he asked, flicking hair from his face at the same time as pulling the ball up on to his toe and doing keepy-ups.

'Just on the lough,' I said.

He passed it back and I had to bring it down out of the air.

'Very nice.' He smiled, but it was towards the ball.

'How come you're here so early?'

'Harrison asked me to come down; said he'd go over some stuff during your practice. It's pretty intense here.'

'Yeah, "intense" is one word for it,' I said. 'Where did you play before?'

'Ferndale United.'

'Ah, OK ... Well, yeah, definitely more intense than Ferndale,' I agreed. 'Hold on, what shirt's that?' I nodded at where I could see a white shirt beneath his track top.

He laughed. Maybe it was more of an exhale. He unzipped his top in one smooth motion.

'My eyes!' I covered them.

He laughed. 'Everton supporter?'

I shook my head in disgust.

'No, don't tell me it's United.' He squeezed his eyes shut, moved away with the ball, then turned back to me and passed it.

I just about stopped it. 'Through and through. Come on. Liverpool, really?' I couldn't help feeling the tiniest bit disappointed.

'Aye, my dad's a Scouser. So it's always been Liverpool for us.' He shrugged. 'Pass.' He nodded at the ball.

'As if.' I pulled it back. Then he ran towards me. I held out my arm and turned, blocking him from the ball. But I clearly didn't do a good enough job because he was doing keepy-ups beside me in less than five seconds.

'Something else my dad taught me. If you really want something, go get it yourself.' He smiled again, flicking his eyes towards me, but still keeping total control of the ball.

I lunged towards him, and he turned, blocking me. His back on my chest. I grabbed his arm to pull him back, the only way I'd have any chance in hell of getting the ball.

'Foul,' he said with a laugh, holding me off and moving the ball to his other foot.

I twisted his arm and he turned round, ball between us, so close that I could feel his warm breath on my face.

'Lucky there's no ref,' he said.

'Oh yeah? Or what?'

'Straight red.' He raised his eyebrows and grinned, his eyes shining in the glow of the floodlights.

'Ref didn't see it,' I challenged, my hands on my hips.

'Pretty useless ref then.'

He was so close I could smell him. Body spray, fabric conditioner. God, he was even more gorgeous close up, even in the dark. Square shoulders, lean, footballer's build, but it was his face that got me. The light eyes with eyelashes so dark it looked like he was wearing eyeliner.

'So what's the deal with your team? You playing in this league?' he asked, dodging my tackle.

'South Belfast Youth League? Yeah, we've a game tomorrow night, just before yours actually, up at the Dub. Cliftonville – it'll be a tough one.' My stomach lurched at the thought of the game, even though I was a sub.

'Oh shit. Good luck. I've no idea who we're playing.'

'Glentoran. Niall will say they're shit, but he always does that when he's nervous about a match; they're really good.'

Shane passed me the ball. 'Niall the other striker?' He looked at me, like he was trying to work out why I'd brought him up. 'He your boyfriend or something?'

I burst out laughing and flicked the ball to him, watching

him trap it dead under his foot. 'Boyfriend, no. Brother, unfortunately. Twin.'

'Ah, I see.'

'He's with Megan. She's on the team, midfield.' And I hated how it felt on my tongue. Bitter and wrong.

'Ah yeah, I think I saw her play at practice.' He passed the ball back and I tried to ignore the sinking feeling that always showed up when people talked about Megan playing football.

'She's had a couple of teams try to poach her, but she's stayed at Westing.' I never understood that about Megan. She had all the talent in the world. She could play for whatever team she wanted, but she had no interest in moving; it was all just fun for her.

'You love it then? Football?' He was looking right into my eyes now for the answer. But it was my smile that gave it away.

'More than anything. When I'm not playing it's all I think about, always thinking of the next game, always out in the back garden practising, watching it on TV. Football's my life.' I felt my face flush with embarrassment. 'I don't think I've told anyone how much I love it. It's like if you admit it, it's embarrassing if you're not the best player. I mean, it would be OK for Megan to say she loves it because she can back it up. But me?' I laughed, trying to hide the humiliation of sharing so much. But it felt easy with him.

He stopped the ball and looked at me deadly seriously. 'You shouldn't talk about yourself like that.'

My stomach flipped. 'Yeah, I know, just a habit.'

'What's your name?'

I'd forgotten that we hadn't even exchanged names, even though I knew his already.

'Lexie,' I said.

He repeated it, like he wanted to try out the way it felt on his tongue. 'Nice to meet you. I'm Shane.' He grinned as he held out his hand.

And that was all it took. A handshake that sent waves of electricity through my veins and I knew that this was only the beginning.

8

'Ready, Lexie?'

I turned to see Sadie and the rest of the girls walking on to the pitch.

'Oh shit, I'd better go,' said Shane, not breaking my gaze. 'See you later?' He smiled and winked before turning and jogging to the side of the pitch where he hopped over the fence again.

And it took a few seconds to come back down from whatever high I was riding, until the mash-up of nausea and excitement in my stomach calmed down and my breath went back to its usual rhythm.

'Ready,' I said to Sadie, trying to shake it off more quickly.

This didn't happen to me. Can't eat, can't sleep, crushing on people. That was a Megan thing. I was focused. I was eye on the ball at all times. Until now.

And it wouldn't leave me alone. The whole practice I was thinking about the way his eyes had skimmed over my legs and always ended by looking straight into my eyes like he could see my soul.

'Lexie, where's your head?' Sadie's voice was like a cold shower, as a ball flew past me.

'Sorry!'

At our water break Zoe came skipping over to me. 'Oh my God, were you talking to Shane? He's really cute, isn't he? I'm going to invite him to my party. Do you think he has a girlfriend?' She was looking at me in expectation, her trademark smile lighting up her face.

'I have no idea.'

'What are you wearing? Do you and Megan want to come early? Predrinks?' Zoe grinned.

'I don't actually know how we're getting there, but I'll let you know. Thanks, Zoe.' It took all my effort to be civil, when the way she talked about Shane made me seethe.

Just before we started back, I glanced over at the sidelines to see him standing there, leaning on the fence, watching our training. So I upped my game. I tackled harder, tried to make my passes accurate, and even though I missed a couple of penalties, I think I did an OK job. I heard the rest of the boys before I saw them. I was too focused on Shane and the way he rested his chin on his hand and smiled when I let myself make eye contact.

Hunter's voice broke me out of the other world at the end of practice. 'Nice job, Lex!'

I kind of thought he'd give it a rest now, maybe chill out a bit after I'd said no to V-Ball. But there he was, with a big encouraging smile, his eyes on me.

I pretended not to hear him and glanced to where Shane had been standing. But he wasn't there. He was on the pitch now, warming up by himself.

'You coming, Lexie?' Megan called from the sidelines,

probably wondering why I was hanging around when the boys had already started kicking the ball between themselves.

And because I was thinking about him, I forgot I wasn't talking to her.

'Yeah, coming now.' As I realized my mistake, I saw her grin like she'd just been awarded person of the match.

'So . . . what's he like?' she asked.

'Who?' I asked coldly, even though I knew exactly who she was talking about. I was looking at him now, weaving in and out of all the other players. Effortless.

'Shane. The really hot new guy you were talking to?' She couldn't hide the excitement in her voice.

I bet she thought if I had some guy to think about, I wouldn't care about what her and Niall had done to me. Well, I would care, and I'd *never* forget. I wasn't going to fall for her mind games.

'Yeah, he's nice, I guess.' I shrugged and didn't elaborate.

'He's amazing,' she said, and I side-eyed her to see that she was staring at him too.

I hated that I thought of Niall then. And how hurt he'd be if he'd heard her say that.

'Go, Niall!' she shouted, then looked at me like she'd heard my thoughts. And somehow that was worse.

We used to make fun of the girls who came to watch their boyfriends play and acted like their own personal cheer squad. Now Megan was one of them.

'Sorry,' she said, when she caught my look. 'You know he's really worried about losing his position.'

My stomach dropped.

She continued. 'Like he got really upset on Tuesday after practice.' Megan said it like it was a secret she wasn't supposed to share. It was something Niall would have told me . . . before. Was this how it was going to be now? Me getting a rundown of Niall's feelings second-hand?

And as if to make her point, Shane took the ball round Niall, sending him in completely the wrong direction and he ended up on the ground. He made it look so easy. Shit.

But Niall wasn't done. He jumped up, ran back after Shane and went in for a tackle. Hard, dangerous, illegal. I'd noticed it with all the boys; going in full on when they were tackling him, their passes strong and fast, like they were hoping he wouldn't be able to control them. But he always did.

'Fuck sake, man!' Shane grabbed his ankle, his face screwed up with pain.

Harrison blew his whistle. 'Watch it, Niall,' he said, walking over to Shane and bending down to examine his foot.

I glanced at Megan. She was biting her lip. I wouldn't have been surprised if she jumped the fence and ran to my brother. She caught me looking at her but didn't say anything.

'Bench, Niall. Ten minutes.'

'Poor Niall,' said Megan.

'Poor Niall nothing. That tackle was ridiculous. Isn't that how it works? New kids come along and you have to fight for your position?' At least Niall had a position. I was constantly fighting just to get off the bench. I shrugged despite the fact I couldn't ignore the hollow in my stomach when I studied Niall's face. Everyone else would see anger, rage, petulance even, when he slammed his fist into the fence, but I knew it was shame. That was how Niall worked. He didn't do regular embarrassment; he just got angry. I knew to leave him alone when he was like that; asking him what was wrong was the complete opposite of what was going to help. Pretending not to notice, that was how to do it. I kept my mouth shut. Why should I make life easier for Megan?

'I guess,' said Megan sadly.

'Oh my God, he's so hot.'

Zoe's voice was a welcome break from the tension between me and Megan, even if her words made me feel sick.

'Who, Hunter?' I asked.

She grinned. 'I knew you liked him!'

'I don't,' I said too quickly. 'He's just Niall's mate.'

'Who you think is hot,' she said quickly.

'But I don't.'

'Chill, Lex, I'm only joking. I was talking about Shane, obvs. Go, Shane!' Zoe threw her arms in the air like an actual cheerleader.

'Isn't that your mum over there, Zoe?' Megan cut in.

We all looked towards the car park. A woman was walking towards us with rapid strides, and she seemed pissed off.

'Zoe, *come on*! You've got cello practice.'

Zoe glanced at us briefly, then put her head down and walked towards her mum.

'Did you score in the match?' I heard her mum ask.

'At practice?'

'Yes, at practice.'

'Not tonight.'

'Why not?'

And then they were too far away to hear what they were saying. But for the first time I felt kind of sorry for Zoe.

'OK, that was intense,' Megan said, and we shared a look.

'Yeah,' I said simply.

'What are you wearing to the party?'

I had to hand it to her; she didn't give up.

'Don't know yet,' I said.

This is usually when Megan would give me a full run-down of her outfit, right down to her underwear, but all she said was 'OK'. And I didn't tell her that Zoe had asked us to her house early just in case she thought I was her friend again.

We watched the rest of the boys' practice in silence, and listened to the swearing and the thud of shoulder on shoulder.

I kept my eyes on Shane the whole time.

And the feeling was back. The way he played did something to me. It took me out of myself, away from Megan and Niall, away from Sadie and the team list, away from Zoe, and everything that made my guts twist. Watching him play was like looking into another world.

A world where I didn't care about football. A world where all I needed was him.

9

School the next day was a blur. I was thinking about the match. Not just mine, but Shane's. And the rest of my brain was thinking about what I was going to wear to Zoe's party, and hoping that Shane was going to be there. I didn't even care that Niall was moping about the house. I shoved his feelings out of the way to make room for mine, the ones that were burning and aching to see the boy I'd just met.

I spent ages getting ready for the match. Perfect hair, perfect make-up and my favourite perfume, the one that was just the right side of sweet and lasted all day. I made sure to do extra stretches and sit-ups, even though I was on the bench. Just in case they needed me. I did them in my bedroom because doing them outside would just be asking for comments from Mum and Dad, or worse, Niall, and they all knew I wasn't actually playing tonight.

Dad drove us, and all his attempts at conversation fell flat. I was in another world and Niall was in a mood. I thought about telling Dad about Niall and Megan then and there in the car, in the traffic jam through town. Then I could watch Niall squirm, and it would be payback watching him explain to Dad that he has a girlfriend. I knew how awkward he felt about all that stuff. When Mum tried to talk to him about puberty when we were younger, he locked himself in the bathroom and wouldn't come out until she promised to stop trying to talk to him. And he was the same about girls, except with me. He used to tell me who he had a crush on.

Used to.

I stared out the window, willing the traffic lights to change. I let my eyes lose focus and concentrated on the blurred, multicoloured streaks that turned the night into an abstract painting. An attempt to stop thinking about Niall. But when we pulled into the Dub and I stepped out of the car, I didn't have to try. Something changed.

I was in it. Hypnotized by the Friday-night lights. The atmosphere. The pitch lit up like a stage in the darkness. And I suppose it was a stage, a performance. And I couldn't wait for Shane's show.

We walked over to the pitch and left Dad with the rest of the spectators. The whole team were there already, warming up with Sadie on the pitch.

'Come on, Lex.' She waved me over and I started warming up with the other girls but scanning the crowd for Shane.

'This is going to be a tough match. I want you all to give it one hundred per cent. Midfield – Cara, Lola, Megan – do not stop running. Do not stop looking for passes. Wait, where's Megan?' Sadie looked at her watch then back to the entry gate to see Megan running across the pitch. 'Megan, we're about to kick off!'

'Sorry, sorry.' Megan didn't even have an excuse, and it

didn't matter; it wasn't like Sadie would ever put her on the bench.

Megan pulled off her hoodie and grinned back at Niall, who was standing with Dad at the side of the pitch.

And then I saw him. Standing by himself, hands in pockets, staring right at me. I tried to stop myself smiling, but I couldn't. So I looked down at my feet, Sadie's words a blur.

'Go Westing!' The girls shouted together, but my head was too full of Shane.

I held his gaze as I walked back to the bench and sat down.

The match was intense. The last time we played Cliftonville they beat us three nil. But this time? We were putting up a fight. Nil–nil at half-time. I tried to look like I didn't care if Sadie put me on or not, but inside I was begging for it. Zoe wasn't playing *that* well. I could do just as good a job as her. I looked at her as she wiped her brow, and wondered if Shane noticed how good she looked tonight. How her hair swung in a perfect ponytail and how long her legs looked in the Westing shorts.

'OK, same team. Come on, girls, let's win this,' Sadie said, then walked back to the sideline. I went back to the bench and sat down beside Amina and Penny, who were complaining that Sadie wouldn't let them have their phones.

'We're supposed to be watching the match,' I said, stating the obvious.

Amina sighed. 'Ugh, can you be bothered? We won't be playing; I think they just *have* to have subs or something.'

'You don't know that,' I said. 'Yes, Lola!' I stood up as she travelled with the ball into their box. She passed it to Megan.

Sadie was screaming 'hit'. And she did. Hard and low, bottom-left corner; it was perfect. I cheered without thinking about all the other stuff. Sadie cheered, the whole team cheered. And then I felt stupid. When it all died down and Cliftonville had possession again, the crowd silent, I just felt pointless and pissed off at myself for cheering. Amina and Penny were right.

The match ended two–one to us, and I should have been happier, but sitting on the bench all night in the freezing cold with Shane there to witness it, had dampened my mood. I picked up my bag and started to walk away from the team when I heard my name.

'Lexie.'

I looked up and scanned the other side of the fence. And there he was. Staring at me, waving me over to him. And all the other stuff? White noise.

'Shane,' I said. 'Hi, how's it going?' I didn't know what else to say.

'Meet you behind the pavilion in five?' He raised his eyebrows and flicked his eyes towards the big white building. The boys match didn't start for another thirty minutes.

'Sure,' I said, trying to tone it down so he wouldn't hear the excitement in my voice.

I ignored the shouts of my name from Megan and tried to hide behind people as I passed Dad.

And there he was at the back of the pavilion, standing against the wall, looking at his phone, one foot resting on the brick.

'Hey,' I said.

He turned round, smiling, and all the disappointment from not playing in the match just disappeared into the night.

'Hey,' he replied. 'Good match.'

'Yep,' I said, walking over and standing in front of him.

'You know what would have made it better?'

I looked up. 'What?'

'Seeing you out there.'

I tried to swallow the lump in my throat when he said it. It was like all the feelings came back at once. The disappointment. The fact I was just a sub, that I'd never be as good as Megan.

'Hey, you OK?'

He took my hand. But it wasn't just my hand; every nerve in my body was on fire.

I looked up at him. 'Yeah, I'm OK.' I whispered, moving closer, so close I could feel the heat of his body.

And then something happened. Something I can't explain because it wasn't conscious. It was primal.

I turned into him, so he was pressed against the wall. Right there in the dark I stood on my toes and reached up to kiss him. And he kissed me back. His mouth tasted of Coke, sweet and warm, his hands on my hips, finding the bare-skinned space under my shirt and just above my shorts. My whole body tingled. I ran my hands through his hair, then they were on his face, pulling him closer to me. I let my hand explore underneath his tracksuit top, feeling lean muscle and zero per cent body fat. My mouth was aching when we stopped. Out of breath, we stared into each other's eyes.

'Holy shit,' he said.

'Sorry,' I said on an exhale.

I couldn't believe what I'd just done. Not that I regretted it. I wanted to do it again. I wanted to do it forever. It wasn't like I made a habit of kissing boys I didn't know. I'd barely kissed anyone. Like one other guy at some house party last year. But this just felt right.

'Don't apologize,' he said, taking a deep breath. 'I've wanted that since I first saw you. Can I ask you something?'

'Anything,' I replied.

'Why do you stay here? If you're not getting game time? There are other clubs, ones where you'd get to play way more.' He looked into my eyes, and I didn't feel shame. There was no taking the piss, just genuine curiosity.

'I really want to make the team,' I said. 'It's like a challenge I've set myself. To see if I can make it this year. But it hasn't worked out yet. I train *so* hard, but I just can't seem to get off the bench.' I ordered myself not to cry but I could feel pressure building behind my eyes.

He scanned my face, taking it in. 'Can I help?' Our faces were centimetres from each other. He wiped a rogue tear from my cheek with the sleeve of his top. 'What about if I help you train?'

Something lifted.

'You would do that?' I couldn't help smiling.

'Yeah, I would. I mean, I don't have that much free time, but what are you like with early mornings?'

'Any time suits me. Literally any time.' I tried not to sound too excited but I failed.

He pushed a bit of hair behind my ear. 'OK, meet me at the club tomorrow, six a.m.?'

'Saturday? Don't you want to sleep in?' I mean, I didn't ever sleep in, but I assumed most people did. Niall didn't get up until midday at the weekend. I felt a wave of heat rush through me as I thought about Shane in bed.

'Ah no, I'm a morning person.'

'Same. Oh, are you going to Zoe's party?'

'The redhead? Yeah, she text me about it actually; not sure how she got my number.' He shrugged, and I tried to keep my face neutral, a desperate attempt at hiding the jealousy that was so strong it made me feel sick. 'I'll be there if you are,' he said when I didn't say anything. It was the perfect answer. He reached down and threaded his fingers through mine, reigniting tiny fires in my veins.

I grinned. 'I'll be there. And I'll be at the club tomorrow.'

He nodded. 'Good.'

I moved so it was me against the wall. And this time I pulled him by his track top towards me and he kissed me again, slower. Our tongues in perfect sync. When I pulled away, I saw Shane glance towards the pitch where the boys had started to gather. 'Are you staying to watch the match?'

'Of course.'

'I'll try and score for you . . . But, Lexie?' he asked awkwardly.

'Yeah?'

'Can you go on? I need to fix something and it's not going to get any better with you being here.' He eyed his trackies and I laughed.

'Good luck.' I reached up and kissed him again, long and gentle, before I walked back over to the pitches with a smile on my face, going over and over the kisses in my head. And it surprised me how easy it felt. I'd thought about it before, kissing new people, how I'd do it then getting scared about how awkward or embarrassing it would be. But this was none of those things. It felt like it was supposed to happen.

'I've been looking for you. Where've you been?' Dad put his arm round my shoulder, and I leaned into it.

'Just went for a walk.'

He stopped and we both moved out of the way of the crowd that had started to gather for the boys. 'Cliftonville wouldn't have scored if you'd been playing.'

'Thanks, Dad,' I said, even though it wasn't true.

'Do you want a hot chocolate, pet? I saw a van selling coffee over there.' He nodded to the other side of the pitch.

'No thanks.' I wanted to keep the taste of Shane in my mouth forever.

We watched the boys walk out. Niall included. I'd half forgotten that Niall was on the team too. What was happening to me? Usually, I'd have guessed the boys line-up and I'd be waiting to see if I was right. Maybe Niall would be on the bench now that Shane was here. I glanced up at Dad, who was on the phone, wondering if he'd regretted coming altogether.

Niall wasn't on the bench, and as pissed off as I was at him, I breathed a sigh of relief. Harrison had put him on the wing. *Left* wing. He was fast but his left foot was his weaker one. He was not going to be happy; he'd have to cut in.

'Isn't that Megan? Hello, Megan, love. Great game, incredible goal!' Dad held up his hand to high-five her and I wanted to die.

She didn't leave him hanging. 'Thanks, Mr Ryan. Could

have done with Lexie in defence, though.' She glanced at me as she said it and I pretended not to hear. Zoe was standing next to her sipping a hot chocolate, Westing hoodie sleeves pulled down over her fingers. She looked annoyingly good.

Glentoran were around the same place as Westing on the table, so it was always a good game. Last time they played it was a three–all draw. But they didn't have Shane then. And it didn't take long before Shane made himself seen.

I hadn't taken my eyes off him since he'd stepped on to the pitch and Zoe and I gasped at the same time. Hunter crossed the ball and Shane hit it first time. A volley off the crossbar and into the net.

'Bloody hell,' said Dad.

Unlike Niall or any of the other boys would have, Shane didn't celebrate. He just jogged back down the pitch with his head bowed. Then just before he turned, he locked eyes with me and I saw the tiniest smile. A split-second curl of his perfect lip before it disappeared again and the ball was back in play.

'Oh my God, I'm going to video the rest of the match so I can send it to him, then he can watch it back and see how good he is.' Zoe was right beside me now, gazing at Shane and biting her lip, holding her phone through the gaps in the wired fence. She looked at me like she was checking I'd heard what she'd just said.

I laughed and wished Zoe wasn't here. 'Who wants to watch themselves back?'

'He has no confidence. Like, I was telling him how good he was and he was all, "No, I'm not." This way he can see it for himself.' Zoe smiled a self-satisfied smile into the night. 'And I found out he doesn't have a girlfriend.'

I squeezed the fence in front of me and bit my tongue instead of telling her yes, actually, he sort of did. I mean, it might not be official or anything, but we'd done *a lot* of kissing, like, twenty minutes ago. *And* he was my coach now *and* I was going to invite him to my house when my parents went away. That thought surprised me. Because it came out of nowhere. It wasn't something I did or even thought about, but it was like he made my brain wire differently.

I forced my face to relax the tension that was desperately trying to make me frown. 'Oh really?'

'Well, not that it matters really, and I'm not bragging, but when I want something, I usually get it.' I didn't even have to look at her to imagine the stupid smug smile. I hoped she could sense the stabby vibes I was sending her while pretending not to hear. I think Dad was pretending not to hear too.

'Well, just keep your paws off Niall,' said Megan seriously.

Dad looked at me in confusion.

I shrugged. I wasn't in the mood to explain anything right now.

Zoe wasn't fazed at all. She laughed. 'Oh, Megan, did Lexie tell you about predrinks?' Zoe looked between us and now Megan looked confused.

'No? What predrinks?'

I nudged Megan and eyed Dad. 'Keep your voice down.'

'OK, but what?'

'Zoe asked us to come to her house early, but I said I didn't know.'

'Why didn't you say?'

'Forgot.'

'Well, straight after the match is fine if you can make it,' said Zoe. 'Mum's always telling me to invite more people round.' She smiled, then turned back to the match and Megan glanced at me, puzzled.

Then Shane scored again. And this time I saw him looking at someone else. I followed his gaze to a woman in a coat and scarf standing alone. And this time his smile was full-on and all for her.

10

Even though his team had won, Niall's mood had turned to rage now. And I got it, I really did. Before he got into the car, I watched him kick the ground, digging his foot hard into the grass that we walked across to get to the car park. Dad didn't even notice. He was pointing out some building work that was going on across the road. But I hadn't seen Niall this angry in a long time, if ever.

'That new kid's good, isn't he?' Dad said on the drive home.

And as pissed off as I was at Niall right then, I had to fight the urge to tell Dad to stop. I tried firing him a look, but he didn't catch it. 'Yeah,' I agreed so Niall wouldn't have to.

'Good game, Niall.' Dad glanced in the rear-view mirror to try to get his attention.

But nothing.

'So what are your plans tonight?' Dad had clearly given up with Niall and asked me instead.

'A party at Zoe's,' I replied.

'Are her parents *mad*?' Dad laughed. He would *never* let us have a party in the house.

I smirked at him. 'I think they're just out. They *trust* their child.'

'And I trust mine too. I just don't trust the other teenage tearaways that would show up. I will *never* consent to a party in that house. Unless me and your mum are there.'

'Oh God, no thanks,' I replied, my face screwed up in disgust. Not that I wanted to have a party anyway; houses always ended up getting wrecked, someone would throw up on a carpet somewhere or there'd be cigarette burns in curtains.

At home I went straight upstairs to get ready. My tightest jeans, my lowest-cut top. Hair down, make-up that looked natural but actually took ages to do.

I looked in the mirror, happy with what I saw, but as much as I wanted to, I couldn't ignore the fact that I missed Megan. Getting ready was so much more fun when she was with me.

I shook it off and thought about Shane again. And there it was, the feeling that made my stomach flip and made me smile without telling myself to.

A knock on the door shook me out of my head.

'Lexie?'

'Niall?' I replied, confused.

'Will you drive us tonight? Megan too?'

I knew what this meant. Niall wanted to drink.

I rolled my eyes in the mirror. 'Whatever.'

'Thanks,' he muttered.

'What's this your dad told me about you and Megan?' Mum asked when we walked in downstairs, her question directed at Niall.

I could almost see his shoulders tensing.

'What do you mean?'

'I mean, is she your girlfriend?' Mum asked outright.

I loitered by the kitchen island, holding my breath.

'Megan just made a comment that sounded that way,' Dad started to explain.

'Yeah, so?' Niall said defensively.

Mum held up her hands in surrender. 'I would just appreciate you telling us these things, Niall, especially when she's sleeping over here,' Mum said gently.

'God, Mum!' Niall screwed up his face and walked out of the house, leaving me standing there with Mum and Dad staring at me.

'You picked a terrible night to bring that up,' I said, and walked towards the door after Niall, like it was a reflex.

'Why? What happened?' Mum asked, concern in her voice.

'New kid at football took his position.' I shrugged and started walking again.

'Of course, *that's* it,' Dad said, the penny only dropping now.

'Lexie?'

The soft tone of Mum's voice made me turn round.

'What?'

'Are you OK? Niall and Megan? It's a big deal for you too.'

I didn't expect for anyone else to even notice, or care about how it was for me. But if I started talking about it, I wouldn't stop. 'I'm fine. See you later.' And I walked out the door.

Niall had taken some of Dad's beer with him in a backpack. I didn't know how he had the balls to take it, because Dad would go mad if he knew.

Silence until the end of the driveway. Then I decided to break it, because this wasn't how we were.

I sighed. 'Why didn't you tell me?'

'Tell you what?' he snapped.

Now my back was up too. 'You know what.'

'About Megan? Lexie, it's nothing to do with you.' He stared out the window as we drove to Megan's house.

'Except it is. She was my best friend and you're my brother, don't you think I'm owed some kind of honesty?'

'That's not how it works. You think next year when we're at uni, I'm going to phone you up and ask you if it's OK to go out with someone or if it's going to hurt your feelings?' he spat.

It was like a football to the stomach. I had to compose myself because my words were stuck, and there was a lump in my throat. 'I didn't say that.'

'We were born on the same day, Lexie. That's it. It doesn't mean any more than that. There's no special connection, no magic twin thing that you seem to think we have. I have my life and you have yours. It's not my fault they overlapped. You're just going to have to deal with it.'

I gripped the steering wheel and my jaw clenched. 'You're just pissed the new kid took your position,' I said quietly, because I didn't want him to hear the weakness in my voice.

'Fuck off,' he said.

He'd never said that to me before, never seriously. And it hurt.

We pulled into Megan's driveway, and he got out of the front seat and into the back, but he didn't take any of the tension with him.

Megan got into the passenger seat wearing Nike shorts and a baggy jumper. She looked great. Not that I was going to tell her. Normally we'd dissect the match. Well, I would. Megan would want to talk about the party.

'Wow, frosty,' Megan said, looking at me and then twisting round to look at Niall. Neither of us said anything. 'OK then.'

Zoe lived in a mansion about ten minutes away. One of those really modern houses that looked like something out of a sci-fi movie. We pulled into her humongous driveway and I parked the car. I'd barely stopped when Niall got out, taking his bag of beer with him, leaving me and Megan behind.

And I almost cracked. Shane was on the tip of my tongue. I had so much I could tell Megan, and I knew she'd be happy for me. But I couldn't. She'd made her choice, and it wasn't me.

I got out of the car and Megan followed.

Zoe was at the door. She was wearing a tiny green dress and her red hair sat in waves over her shoulders. She looked gorgeous. Then I remembered what she'd said about Shane. How she wanted him, how she'd been messaging him. How she always 'got what she wanted'. I squeezed my hands into fists at my sides as she showed us through to the massive kitchen. I fixed my hair in a mirror, and Megan went to talk to Hunter and Niall, who were lining up shots on the counter.

'Hey, Lexie!' Amina slung her arm round my shoulder. She was wearing a tiny skirt and a skin-tight T-shirt, her black hair down for once and almost touching her waist. She was drunk. Someone clearly hadn't bailed on predrinks.

'Hey, Amina, how are you?'

'I'm so good. Here, have a drink. I don't like this one. Sex on the beach.' She giggled and I took the glass from her before she spilled it over us both.

'I've never had sex on the beach, have you?'

I shook my head and put the glass down on a table. 'Nope.'

I heard a laugh. Loud. Exaggerated. Zoe.

'Zoe totally wants sex on the beach with him.' Amina pointed towards the corner of the room.

I followed her drunken finger towards a cream-velvet sofa in a low-lit corner of the kitchen. There he was. Same top from earlier, different track bottoms, different trainers. Smiling at whatever Zoe had said. Her leg was touching his. Then she was *whispering* something to him. That bitch.

I almost forgot Amina was hanging on to me as I moved towards them. She stumbled and I had to catch her, but her other arm knocked a pint of beer all over the kitchen floor.

'Shit,' I said, seizing my moment. 'Zoe,' I called loudly, 'is there something we can use to clean this up?'

Zoe got up and a flash of *pissed off* clouded her face, but it had disappeared by the time she reached me, and the trademark smile was back.

'I'm so sorry,' Amina said.

'Don't worry. I'll get the mop. Go, enjoy yourself.' She smiled at me. 'Such a shame you couldn't come earlier Lexie. Shane ended up coming an hour early, so me and Amina got to know him a bit, which was cool.'

I couldn't tell if she was trying to rub it in my face or if she was genuinely disappointed I couldn't make it. But by the time Zoe and Amina had disappeared for a mop and I looked back at Shane, Niall, Hunter and Megan were standing in front of him. Shit.

I walked over, dreading to think what Niall was saying.

'Why don't you just fuck off back to Ferndale?' Niall said, his tone harsh and cold. I cringed.

'Your coach asked me to come to Westing,' Shane said, sipping from a can of Coke, seemingly unfazed.

'Harrison? Big fucking deal. Remember the last kid he recruited?' Niall laughed and elbowed Hunter.

'Lasted a week,' replied Hunter. 'What do you reckon, Niall? Bet on it? That he doesn't last the season.'

'He won't last the month,' Niall scoffed, and I couldn't make any excuses for him this time. I hated what he was doing. I watched him empty half a bottle of beer down his throat.

Megan was standing by his side looking awkward. She didn't even tell him to stop.

'What's happening?' Zoe was back, looking at Niall and Hunter.

I couldn't speak. Humiliated that my own brother could act like that.

'I'll take that bet.' Shane held out his hand and stared at Niall.

Niall took his hand, no doubt squeezing as hard as he could.

I saw Megan tugging at Niall's arm. Hunter had been distracted by Amina walking past in her mini-skirt, and as he moved he put Shane in my eyeline. I hadn't noticed that about Hunter, the way it was like he couldn't help himself staring. At Megan, at me, at Amina, and it made my stomach lurch. And as if he could sense me thinking about him, he looked up and winked. I glared back, hating myself for not saying anything.

'Oh my God, Shane, are you OK?' Zoe was all over him now.

He laughed. 'It's fine. I didn't expect it to be a walk in the park.'

'I can make them leave if you want?' Zoe said. She was hanging on to his arm now and I needed her to stop.

'Nah, it's fine. I reckon that would make things worse. And I'll have to head soon anyway.'

'You're so right. Clever too. Amazing. Let me get you a drink.'

Then she disappeared. So I took my chance.

'Hey, I'm really sorry about that,' I said, moving close enough that I didn't have to shout over the music.

'It's not your fault. And don't worry. I can handle it. Want to sit?' He glanced at the seat behind him.

'No,' I replied instantly.

'No?' He looked confused but was trying not to laugh.

'I mean, it's a bit loud in here. Crowded. Do you fancy going out the back for a bit? There must be a football out there.' I hoped there was a football.

'Sure.'

He stood up and suddenly, I was nervous.

'I think it's out here.' I walked towards the only door that could have opened to the back garden. We walked through it and into darkness. Another room. I couldn't find the light. The sweet floral smell of fabric softener made me think it was a utility room.

I banged into something hard. 'Shit.'

'Are you OK?'

I felt him touch my waist. Electricity.

'Yeah, I'm OK,' I whispered.

Then he was beside me, so close I could feel the heat of his body.

'I feel terrible,' I said quietly.

'Why?' He sounded genuinely curious.

'Because of Niall. You shouldn't have come, I should have known it was going to be like this,' I said, shaking my head.

He tilted my chin up so I was looking at him, even though I couldn't see him clearly in the dark.

'Lexie, I came because I wanted to see you. That shit's just noise.'

Then his mouth was on mine, warm, sweet, slow. I relaxed into him, letting everything go. All the stuff Niall said, swallowed by a cloud of euphoria that exploded when Shane touched me. His body was hot against mine and he found the space between my top and jeans, like he'd done at the pavilion. He grazed my skin gently and I found myself gripping on to his shoulders, like I never wanted to let him go.

Whatever way we moved, Shane banged into something else. He pulled away and laughed. 'Ah, *here's* the garden.'

I moved round him and pushed the handle, and a blast of cold air made me gasp as I walked outside. 'You coming?' I turned towards Shane, who was standing so close to me that the hairs on my neck stood up all over again. Part of me wanted to turn back into him, feel his hands on me and touch the hard muscle of his stomach again, but I'd already committed to the garden.

'Lead the way,' he said.

We walked into the January night. I was definitely not wearing enough clothes for this. But, like I said, I'd committed.

'Jesus, it's huge,' Shane said, scanning the property.

It *was* big and I was embarrassed that I'd barely even noticed. It was separated into different sections by little paths, and evergreen trees everywhere.

'Yeah, it is. Let's find a ball. There's bound to be one somewhere.' I held out my hand to him without thinking. A second of cringe before he took it, lacing his fingers through mine, his smile half covered by the track top that was zipped right up to his chin. We walked down the first path we came to that twisted and turned, lit up by tiny little flower-shaped lights. We walked in silence until we reached a clearing that had a fountain in the middle.

Shane stopped and pulled me back into him, looking down at me in the moonlight. 'This is nice,' he said.

'I don't do this all the time, you know,' I said, embarrassed. 'In fact, I never do it.'

'Don't do what? Take walks in posh gardens at night in January?' He unzipped a few centimetres of his top so I could see his mouth. My stomach flipped as I remembered how those lips had felt on mine.

'Kiss boys I don't know,' I admitted.

'I don't kiss boys I don't know either.' He shrugged and I laughed.

OK, there was this one time when Niall was driving so I decided to see what the big deal with vodka was and I did kiss some guy at one of Hunter's house parties. But both of us were drunk, and all I remember is that there was way too much saliva.

He kissed me again. Slowly, not hungry and desperate like at the pavilion, but gentle and deliberate. I kissed him back, slipping my hand round his waist and standing on my toes. He had his hand in my hair, then both hands on my face, cupping my cheeks that were flushed with heat. And then the panic set in. I inhaled and looked back towards the house, looking through the trees to see if anyone else had come out. That was the last thing I wanted. To be seen. For Niall and Hunter to find out and cause even more drama. But it was more than that. Being with Shane would be the ultimate betrayal for Niall, and even though he'd hurt me more than I thought he ever would, I didn't want to do the same to him.

'You OK?' Shane looked down at me and I turned to him, letting my eyes settle into his gaze.

'Yeah, just freaking out in case someone sees us.' I gave a small laugh. 'Stupid.'

'Your feelings aren't stupid,' he replied, and it made my heart swell. I was shocked at how easily he said it, with no hint of embarrassment. Like I couldn't imagine Hunter ever saying something like that.

'Yeah, it's just complicated with Niall, you know?'

He reached down and pushed hair behind my ear, like he'd done at the pavilion.

I closed my eyes and the voltage surged through my veins.

'Complicated families? Yeah, I get it. But you know what? I don't usually do this either. So maybe it means something?' he mused.

I smiled. 'Can we not tell anyone about us? I just can't be bothered with dealing with all the drama.' I tried to keep it light.

'Sure, of course.'

I looked straight up through the trees to the sky full of stars. 'Have you heard of binary stars?' I asked him. I'd read up about them when we did this random module on astronomy in physics, and I'd wanted to impress Mrs Lee.

He shook his head.

'Stars that are gravitationally bound to each other, they orbit round the same centre of mass, and if they get too close, they can gravitationally distort each other's atmospheres.' I looked away, embarrassed.

'You've definitely gravitationally distorted my atmosphere,' Shane said with one of those smiles that wasn't full but wanted to be. And it was something that would have sounded ridiculous if it had come from anyone else. 'Whatever that means. You must be really clever.' He stepped back and turned away before coming back to me with a football at his feet.

'Hey, where'd you find that?' I asked. I'd been scanning the grass when we'd started walking. 'And I'm not. I just work really hard.' I kicked myself for not just leaving it out there that he thought I was super clever.

'Can't you be both? It was under that wee bench over there.' He held the ball on his toe and started doing keepy-ups.

'How many can you do?' I asked.

'Never counted,' he said. But judging by how easily he bounced the ball up and down on both feet, I guessed about a million. My efforts capped at seven.

He passed the ball to me, and I moved back to the other side of the fountain so I could control it. I concentrated, trying to impress him.

'OK,' he said. 'If you have the ball, you have to answer questions. 'What school do you go to?'

'Blackport.'

I passed the ball back just shy of his left foot.

He grinned. 'Terrible pass. We'll work on that in the morning. Blackport? Of course.' He cocked an eyebrow and laughed.

I put my hands on my hips. 'What's that supposed to mean?'

'Posh school. Posh girl?' He shrugged and waved his hand around the garden as if to make his point.

'Not necessarily ... Do you not like posh girls?' Because right then, I'd be anything he wanted me to be.

'You're the first one I've met, and I like you ...' He looked up from the ball and gave me a slow half-smile. I was glad he couldn't see me blush. We were getting closer to each other again, and closer to the fountain, the stream of water drowning out the thud of my heart.

'What school do *you* go to?' I asked, ignoring the ball that was at my feet again.

'St Anne's,' he replied.

'Why'd you move to Westing FC?'

'Better club,' he said.

'Yeah, but why now and not when you were, like, six?' I asked, genuinely curious, because usually if you're really into football, you start young, and if you're as good as he was, you go to the good clubs.

'I really liked it at Ferndale,' he said, closer again.

And then we were sitting on the fountain, legs touching, freezing water splashing the exposed skin on my back.

'I watched you train the first night I got there.' His breath twisted into smoke beside me.

'Oh God.' I thought about the faces I pulled when I was concentrating, the sweat, the things I said when someone tackled me.

'You look so hot when you play,' he said.

I relaxed, unable to hide the smile that came so pathetically easily with him. 'Oh yeah? Why is that?' I asked, fishing. I let my hand rest on his leg.

'I liked your wee shorts,' he replied.

I laughed. 'My shorts?'

'And I liked how angry you got when your coach gave the other side a corner. Passion. I like that.' He smiled, closer to me again.

'It *wasn't* a corner.' I tried to sound serious, but I was still smiling.

'It was.' Even closer.

'What else did you like?' I whispered into the disappearing space between us.

But I didn't hear his answer because we were kissing again, and my body was aching for him, in a way I'd never felt before, in a way I'd only read about in books or seen in movies. And it was *everything*.

But we were interrupted by a buzzing phone.

He pulled away, then stood up and slid it out from his pocket, walking a few metres down the path to have his conversation somewhere I couldn't hear.

Except I could.

'Hello . . . ? I'm just at practice, coach kept me late . . . Won't be long.' He put the phone back in his pocket.

'Everything OK?' I asked, thinking he might explain the lie.

And I half expected him to assure me it was nothing.

But he didn't.

'I have to go,' he said.

'Oh, OK.' I didn't know what else to say.

'Can I have your number?'

'Sure.' I took out my phone to see messages from Megan. I swiped them away and handed it to him, and he typed in his number, then I phoned him.

I stood up from the fountain, really feeling the cold now for the first time that night.

'See you at the club tomorrow morning?'

'How could I forget!' I said, the disappointment of him leaving diluted.

'Here, you look freezing.' He took off his top and handed it to me. I slid it over my shoulders and breathed in the smell of him. Fabric conditioner, heat. I hugged myself.

'Won't you be cold?'

'I'll be grand,' he said.

I didn't believe him, but he'd already turned away, like he was in a hurry, so I sat back down on the fountain, football at my feet, wrapped his top round me tightly and smiled into the darkness. My heart exploding.

11

It wasn't long before I heard Megan's voice, dragging me out of the quiet frozen bliss.

'Lexie? Are you outside?' She sounded a bit panicked, so I stood up and walked back along the path that I'd shared with Shane thirty minutes ago.

'Hi,' I said, emerging from the trees.

'What the hell are you doing out here? It's Baltic!' Megan said, shivering.

And the way she looked at me, with genuine concern, was touching. So much that I thought about telling her about Shane. I imagined how excited she'd be for me. I was desperate to share it with someone. Maybe I could just let it go, all that stuff with her and Niall.

'Just went for a walk with –'

'Niall's kind of drunk,' Megan cut in.

I don't know why it shocked me. It made sense. They didn't care about anyone else, just themselves. And I was glad she did it; it made my decision for me. I didn't need her, and I definitely didn't need Niall.

'He's an idiot,' I said.

'Ugh, I know, but he's freaking out about this new kid and has been really sad.' Megan looked distressed, but it didn't affect me at all.

'You mean the one he just told to go back to Ferndale?' I winced at the memory. The vitriol in Niall's voice.

Megan tried to defend him. 'He didn't mean it.'

'He did. Where is he?'

'In the fancy room. The one with the chaise longue.'

The heat from the kitchen was intense – radiators, bodies pressed against each other – the noise like nails on a blackboard. I wished I could go outside again. Megan grabbed my hand and pulled me through groups of people into the hall and then into the good room.

There was Niall, slumped on a chaise longue, leg hanging off the end. Hunter perched on the edge, drinking a beer. Zoe and Amina on the other seat, whispering to each other.

'Jesus, Niall,' I said. 'How much have you had to drink?'

Niall looked up through a mop of blonde hair, eyes glazed. 'Lex, is that you?'

'Yes, it's me, you dumbass.'

'I had too many shots.' He was slurring.

'You think?' I sat down beside his head. 'Get up.'

He dragged himself up and draped his arm over my shoulder. Megan went to his other side, and he leaned on her too.

'Here, let me help.' Hunter took the weight of Niall from me. Megan talked to try to keep him awake, but he kept closing his eyes. Hunter looked at me. 'This doesn't mean you have to leave too, does it?'

'Yep, designated driver,' I said, glad of the excuse.

'That's a shame,' he said with a grunt as he heaved a slipping Niall back on to his shoulder. 'I was hoping we could catch up tonight.'

'Sorry, gotta go,' I said, unsure what exactly he wanted to catch up on. I wished he'd just move on, to Amina or Zoe or something. Why did he have to go and make everything so awkward by asking me to V-Ball?

'Maybe we can catch up next week?' he asked with a smile that was usually reserved for Niall's rubbish jokes. It was like he'd forgotten about what had happened earlier, what he and Niall had said to Shane. Either that or he just didn't care.

'Yeah, maybe. But maybe you and Niall should be nicer to the kid who just joined your team and doesn't know anybody,' I added, burning with rage all over again.

He stared at me for a second, like he didn't know I'd seen.

'It was just a joke, Lexie. Chill out. If anything, he'll play even better now, just to prove us wrong. So it's win-win for him.'

'That's fucked up.'

'Come on, Lex, we didn't mean it.' He turned on the charm, smiling under the weight of Niall.

I shook my head and rolled my eyes. 'Let's just get him out of here.'

'Do *not* tell Dad about this, OK?' Niall slurred as Hunter walked him towards the door.

Amina laughed, and I looked over to see Zoe staring at me like she was trying to work something out. A tension that hadn't been there before. Was she wondering what I'd got up to with Shane? Did she recognize the jacket I was wearing? Part of me hoped she would, especially after what Amina had said about the sex on the beach.

'Let's go, Niall – you are not puking in Zoe's lovely house,' I said, making sure she heard me.

Hunter dumped Niall in the back seat, and Megan got in the front beside me.

'What's the deal with the trackie top?' she asked. 'How did I not notice that you were slumming it in Puma?' She stroked my sleeve.

I wondered how long she was going to keep trying to pretend that nothing was wrong.

'I was cold, so I found it in Zoe's house. Must be her brother's or something,' I said. I hoped she was drunk enough not to question me any more. I didn't even know if Zoe had a brother.

'Do you reckon Hunter got his teeth done? I don't remember them being *that* white. Or *that* big. Did he go to Turkey recently? I don't know, maybe I'm just forced to look at him more now because of Niall.' Megan rested her head against the window.

I couldn't believe she wasn't saying anything about what had happened between Niall and Shane.

'You need to tell Niall to lay off Shane,' I said.

She peeled herself away from the window. 'He was just letting off steam. He's really upset about it.'

'So what? It's hardly Shane's fault, is it?' I said, getting angry again.

'Well, he kind of did just walk on to the team and take Niall's position,' she said, like this was a good explanation. But she was drunk, so there was no point in arguing with her. She probably wouldn't even remember it the next day anyway.

'Whatever.'

'Whatever,' she sang. And then fell asleep.

Mum and Dad must have been in bed when we got home because the lights were off, except for the hall, and nobody said anything when we walked in. I actually wished Megan had come back with us just so she could give me a hand up the stairs.

Eventually I got Niall on to his bed. Even though part of me wanted to leave him in the living room, drunk, so Mum and Dad would find him, the tiny part of me that was Niall's first friend, first confidante, just couldn't do it. And it made me feel pathetic, that even though he'd been so horrible to me, and so horrible to Shane, I couldn't just say 'fuck him' and drop him in it.

This used to be the part where Megan would come with me, into my room, into my bed, where we'd talk about school and football and boys all night. But I shut the thought down. I had better things to think about.

I had been desperate for some time alone since Shane had left. His number in my phone, screaming out at me.

I left Niall and walked into my bedroom, going straight to the window. I opened it so I could hear the ocean. I looked out at the moon, the shimmering crescent that made the dark water glitter. The same stars and crescent moon that Shane and I had been standing under a couple of hours ago.

I reached for my phone and sent him a message before I gave myself any time to think about it. To convince myself that maybe he left because he was bored of my company or that maybe he was lying about not having a girlfriend. I felt brave. It felt like something with too much potential to just sleep on.

ME: Hey

SHANE: Hey, are you still at the party?

ME: Nope. Niall got drunk so got him home before he started a fight with someone else. Still really sorry about that . . .

SHANE: It wasn't your fault. Let's not talk about him anyway. What are you doing?

ME: Just standing at my bedroom window. You?

SHANE: Just getting into bed

Suddenly the image of Shane taking off his clothes was in my head, and I was glad he couldn't see the colour of my face.

SHANE: I had a really good time tonight

ME: Same

SHANE: What can you see out the window?

ME: The sea. Our house is on the lough

SHANE: Nice. What's it like?

ME: Pretty. There's this one streak of light from the moon that's made the water all sparkly

It was like magic.

SHANE: I wish I could see it too. My window just looks out on the street and more houses.

ME: You should come over sometime. There's this bit of the beach that's not ours, but it's basically private because it's so hard to get to from the road

SHANE: I'd like that

I shimmied out of my clothes and put my pyjamas on, trying not to interrupt the flow of conversation. Then I lay down on my bed, phone above my face, jaw aching from smiling.

ME: So what's the deal then? Do you want to go pro? Do you want to get scouted at Westing?

SHANE is typing

He stopped and started at least three times.

SHANE: I don't know . . .

ME: That's a pretty big thing not to be sure about . . .

SHANE: I've never said it out loud before

ME: Do your family want you to?

SHANE: Sort of. What about you?

ME: I just want to be on the first team. I need to work harder

SHANE: I think you're pretty great

ME: I will be

SHANE: You know what you're missing?

Him. I was missing *him.*

ME: What?

SHANE: The most important part of football

ME: Which is?

I was waiting for him to tell me some technique I'd never heard of.

SHANE: Fun

And I laughed out loud even though he wasn't there to hear it.

ME: I don't do FUN when it comes to football

SHANE: Maybe that's something we need to change

ME: I'm not sure about that . . .

SHANE: I am. Are you ready for your first training session?

ME: Yes Coach

SHANE: Get some sleep. I'll see you tomorrow x

ME: xxx

And of course I didn't get any sleep. But I didn't care, because no dream could be better than this.

12

I set my alarm for five fifteen. I jumped out of bed and pulled my hair into a high ponytail, before putting on my Nike Pro shorts, football socks, Man United shirt and Shane's track top. Mascara, lip oil, highlighter. And perfume. Always perfume. The same one I'd been wearing last night: sweet, musky, me.

I tiptoed out my door, and when I got downstairs I carried my boots outside so I wouldn't wake anyone up. Then I drove way too fast down the icy road to the club.

And when I arrived, there he was. My breath caught in my throat as I took him in. He was leaning against the locked clubhouse in a black hoodie, black track bottoms, the black boots, foot resting on a ball.

I jogged over to him, looking at the ground in case I accidentally gave him a huge smile and scared him off. I stopped a couple of metres from him. 'You're early,' I said.

'I'm always early,' he replied with a smile that made my stomach jump. 'Is that car yours?'

I followed his gaze to the car park. 'Yeah, got it for my birthday last year,' I said easily, then was immediately embarrassed as his mouth fell open.

'For your *birthday*? I got a football for my birthday last year.' He laughed. 'Posh school, posh girl, of course.'

I pushed him playfully. 'Shut up.'

'You ready?' he asked.

'Born ready.'

'We'll see,' he said, and walked in the direction of the grass pitches.

I looked longingly at the synthetic grass pitch behind us. 'Grass? Why?'

'Softer to land on. That one's frozen.'

'Are you expecting me to spend a lot of time on the ground?' I asked, laughing.

'We'll see,' he said again.

I followed him down the banks and into the middle of the pitch. I watched him flick the ball into the air then volley it into the net. Top-left corner.

Jesus, he was hot.

'Teach me how to do *that*,' I said.

'I will. But not yet.'

He passed me the ball. And then walked towards me. He fingered the logo on my – *his* – top.

'Nice top.'

I shrugged. 'Thought it might give me baller vibes.'

He laughed. 'Hope you're not tainting it with whatever's underneath.'

I pulled the top over my head to reveal my new Man United away shirt.

He covered his eyes. 'No. God, no, put it back on.' He

laughed. Then he looked at me seriously. 'Or maybe you should just take that off too.' One corner of his mouth turned up.

'Nice try. I'm actually here to train. *Some* of us are serious about football.'

'Remember what I said last night?' He raised his eyebrows.

'Fun, blah, blah, blah,' I teased.

I put my top back on and as I brushed hair from my face, he kissed me out of the blue, his lips cold, his tongue warm. Then he pulled away.

'OK, maybe I'll rethink ...' I bit my lip to stop myself grinning at him. 'I could get used to *this* kind of fun.'

'Sorry, I got distracted. You shouldn't show up looking like that ...' His hands were in his pockets now and he was scanning me up and down in the darkness. It was like he was tracing me with his fingertips.

'Like what?'

'So hot.'

And this time it was me who kissed him, closing the space between us, my hands on his face, tasting him, breathing him in. I was out of breath when I pulled away.

He smiled and arched an eyebrow. 'Maybe we should have a rule. No kissing during training?'

I mock pouted and sighed. 'That's a terrible rule. But makes sense, *I suppose*.'

He made me do drill after drill after drill until I really did have to take the top off again because I was sweating so much. But I was laughing too. Which was new for me when it came to football. He took the piss out of every crap pass or soft tackle, and it made me want to try harder. The opposite of Westing training sessions in every way.

Then we practised marking. He showed me how I should stand when the other team have a corner. One of my arms round his back, the other across his front. And it was hard to keep my focus then, to listen to him as he explained where and why and what that would mean for the rest of the game. It felt like I'd already learned more from Shane in thirty minutes than I had from Sadie in four years.

'Want to take some shots?' he asked eventually.

'I thought you'd never ask.' I took the ball and lined it up on the penalty spot as he stood in the nets.

He couldn't be a good keeper too. He was a striker, and goalkeeper was a very specific skill. Low and hard, that's where I needed to put them. And it was still dark too, he'd never save my shots.

My first shot was low and hard into the left corner, just like I'd planned. But I didn't score. His reflexes were insane. He threw himself on to the ground, left and right, jumping for the top corner ones.

He didn't let me score *once*.

'Oh my God, are you serious?' I laughed and he grinned back at me.

'You'll never get better if I go easy on you.' He stood up and wiped his hand across his forehead, pushed his dark floppy hair back and locked eyes with me. Then he looked at his phone. 'I need to go.' He sounded disappointed, which eased the sting.

'When?'

'In fifteen minutes.'

'So that leaves . . . five minutes?' I asked, walking closer to him.

'For what?' He put his phone down on the grass on top of his hoodie.

'For this.' I pulled him towards me and kissed him hard, my hands under his shirt, tracing the warm muscle. When I pulled away, I noticed his phone light up. I looked down and saw a message banner with the name 'Grace'.

My stomach lurched as he picked up his phone and his hoodie. Who was Grace?

We jogged back to the car park, and he kissed me goodbye. I walked to my car, and he walked to the bus.

I reminded myself to go round the back of the house when I got home, pretend I'd been out at our pitch all the time. If Mum knew I was going to the club before sunrise on a Saturday, she'd probably freak out completely.

I ran round the side of the house and slipped in through the back door to see Dad staring at me, a cup of coffee in his hand.

'Dad!' I said, closing the door behind me.

'Where were you?' he asked, his tone serious.

'At the club. Training,' I said. No eye contact. I walked towards the door.

'Lexie, now *I'm* starting to worry. This time on a Saturday morning?' He looked at the clock and then back to me.

'Do you not think Aitana Bonmatí or Simone Magill train this early on a Saturday?' I said defiantly.

'Just be careful, Alexandra, that's all I'm saying.' Then he sighed. 'What happened last night?'

I froze. 'What do you mean? Nothing happened last night.'
I tried to work out what he meant.

'Niall. You can smell the drink as soon as you walk up those
stairs. Were *you* drinking last night?'

'No,' I said so quickly that it sounded like a lie. 'I was
driving.'

'And Niall?'

And there was that pull. To protect each other. But then I
remembered what he'd said in the car before the party. He had
his life and I had mine; it wasn't up to me to make excuses for
him. Not any more. And then I remembered what he'd said to
Shane. But still, I couldn't.

'I didn't see him that much. I don't know what he was
doing.'

'Don't lie to me, Alexandra.'

I think Dad hated lies almost as much as he hated teen
drinking.

'Yeah, he might have had a bit, but everyone was doing it.'
I couldn't help trying to take the edge off the trouble Niall
was in.

'That's no excuse.' Dad raised his voice, then remembered
who he was talking to. The one who *drove*. 'Sorry, love, this
isn't to do with you.'

'I'm just going to . . .' I pointed upstairs and he nodded.

I went to my room and lay down on my bed, giving myself
permission to lie there and think about Shane and nothing
else, forcing myself to push intrusive Grace thoughts out
of my head. And as if he was thinking about me too, my
phone buzzed.

SHANE: You looked really hot this morning 🙈

ME: Thanks Coach x

Then I heard Dad coming up the stairs and flinched when he started shouting at Niall. I felt sick with guilt. I covered my ears and pulled open my laptop. Rosengård vs Barcelona. Aitana, goddess. I put on my headphones and turned the volume right up.

I got lost in the football almost as deeply as I got lost in Shane's blue eyes. I let it seep into my bones and through my veins. So much so that I didn't notice that Niall had opened my door. I glanced up just as he was turning away, his face tear-stained, the door slamming behind him.

13

Niall wasn't allowed to do anything all week. No Megan at the house, no going to Hunter's – just school and football practice, that was it. And if I thought our relationship was bad before, it got even worse.

But I didn't care. I had Shane. We had another early-morning training session and spent most of it with our tongues down each other's throats, despite the no-kissing rule that we'd made. It was like it was impossible to keep apart. But we had to at practice; Niall could not find out about us. I heard him on the phone to Hunter having another rant about Shane, how he wasn't that good and how they were going to make sure he didn't stay.

Niall didn't speak to me at all until Thursday, when his car was in the garage, and he needed a lift to school.

'Can't believe you told Dad I was drinking.' He'd never spoken to me with such venom.

And that hurt. Because I hadn't meant to.

'You know what he's like,' I replied.

'What kind of excuse is that?' he said.

I snapped. 'You know what, Niall? It's your own fault. You

were the one who said we had our own lives, that being a twin meant nothing, so you can just deal with it. And that shit you said to Shane? What the hell was that about?'

'Oh, you on first-name terms?' Niall said. 'What's got you so defensive? You know you'd do the same if someone came to take your position. Oh wait, you don't have a position.'

At a red light I hit the brakes harder than I needed to. 'Fuck off, Niall! When did you turn into such an asshole?'

'Whatever, Lexie.'

Despite Niall being grounded, Dad *and* Mum were still going away to Sweden tomorrow. They'd decided not to cancel, because Mum had planned this insanely detailed itinerary. They'd made Niall promise to stay in the house all weekend, except for football, but I hoped to God that he'd actually made plans with Megan so I didn't have to look at his miserable bake for longer than necessary. And I needed him out of the house, so I could have Shane over.

Niall looked out the window with his earbuds in the whole way. And because he hadn't been seeing Megan outside school, actual school was hell. I don't know whether they were doing it to piss me off even more, but they couldn't keep their hands off each other. It was disgusting. And something else had changed. Megan wasn't talking to *me* any more. There was no more of her chat in my ear, trying to act like things were normal. She completely ignored me.

'What's the deal with you and Megan?' Zoe asked me at break time when I was walking across the yard, intending to go for a dander around the pitches.

'What do you mean?'

'You're usually with her all the time.'

'She's busy with Niall.'

'Isn't that really weird for you?' Zoe was smiling when she asked. I didn't know if she just couldn't help it, or she was trying to be extra annoying.

I shrugged. 'I guess.'

'Well, you can hang out with me and Amina if you want?' She offered me a Tic Tac.

I shook my head to both. 'Thanks.'

'Did you have fun at the party? I hardly saw you all night. Hunter was looking for you.' She elbowed me and grinned.

'Yeah, it was great. Shame I had to leave because of Niall,' I added.

'Oh I meant to say, I saw you talking to Shane. You never said you were into him.' My stomach lurched and I stopped walking to look at Zoe, who wasn't smiling any more. As I turned round, she burst into a grin and waited for me to answer.

'Shane? No, I hardly know him.' I shook my head and looked away, I couldn't risk her seeing the look on my face that would out me as a liar. 'But I think he's seeing someone,' I added.

'Yeah maybe, but not at this school.' She smirked. 'I think I'm going to ask him out. He's really hot, don't you think?'

I shrugged and hoped she wouldn't notice the flash of heat that was spreading across my cheeks.

'I'm just going to go for a walk,' I said, hoping that would make her leave me alone.

'Oh good idea!'

Ugh. Zoe followed me as I walked.

'So things are shaping up really well for V-Ball. You know the way it's an enchanted garden theme?' Zoe was head of the school council, and she treated the job like it had been prophesied.

I didn't. 'Yeah.'

'Well, there are going to be flowers everywhere, and fairy lights, and it will be so romantic. And Amina's mum is hiring a photographer to go to her house, so we're all going to go there first, so you *have* to come. Yeah? Will you come?'

'I don't know.' I left it at that, unable to think of an excuse quickly enough. I was too busy thinking about Shane and how good he'd look in a tux.

She looked at me, horrified. 'You have to. Seriously, Lexie, you can't not go to V-Ball.'

'I'll see.'

'I wonder if you can bring someone from another school,' she said, and shook her Tic Tacs like it would help her think.

My chest tightened and my breath got quicker. I knew who she was talking about ...

'Shane. I might ask Shane. Don't you think we'd look really cute together?'

What was I supposed to say?

'Yeah, really cute,' I said, the words feeling like poison on my tongue.

'I have to tell Amina. I'll see you later, Lexie.'

Zoe ran off, back to school, and then the bell rang.

At the end of school, I drove home without Niall. He could get the bus. I wasn't waiting around for someone who hated me, and anyway, I needed all the time I could get. I was going to look hot for practice tonight. Hotter than Zoe.

As soon as I got home, I jumped into the shower and used all the expensive stuff Mum had bought me. I shaved, exfoliated and put on fake tan. I even straightened my hair before tying it up in a high ponytail and putting on more make-up than I'd ever worn before.

'Lexie! You need to eat something,' Mum called from downstairs when I hadn't even finished getting ready.

I wasn't hungry but the last time I went to training on an empty stomach I could barely run.

'You have to eat before training,' Mum said, then I heard her say something to Dad.

'OK, fine!'

'Take a banana at least,' she said.

'OK, I will, I promise.'

I studied myself in the mirror. My cat eyeliner was perfect. Even my eyebrows looked good. I smiled at my reflection, then toned it down, finding the perfect smile.

When I got downstairs the three of them were eating dinner. Dad in silence, Mum talking about some crime show she'd just seen, and Niall sitting there with a face like thunder.

I grabbed a banana from the bowl. 'I'm leaving now if you need a lift,' I said in Niall's direction before going outside to sit in the car. I would have left him to drive himself, but I still had it in me to want to impress Dad.

He joined me five minutes later and I noticed him do a double take when he got in.

'What is that smell?' He forced himself to cough.

'You *know* it's perfume.'

'Did you drown in it or something?'

I didn't dignify that with a response.

'OK, girls, big match next week.' Sadie clapped her hands and scanned the squad. 'Linfield. Everyone is going to have to play their hearts out. And what's the point if you don't? Right?'

'Right,' I said, swept up in trying to impress her.

Everyone except Megan turned to look at me.

'Good. Glad one of you is on board anyway,' said Sadie, saving me. 'So, I want to see you train like you mean it tonight. Fitness, then matches. Impress me if you want to see your name on the team list.'

Then we dispersed. My heart swelled, as if I'd already made the team. That's what it would feel like.

And it helped me push myself even harder than usual, imagining what it would feel like to tell Shane I was playing. I ignored the twinge of longing that showed up when Niall flashed in my head. Before all this, he would have been the one I wanted to tell.

I shoved him out of my head and thought about Shane again. Then we were playing matches. And I marked players the way Shane had shown me.

'Nice, Lexie,' Sadie called from the sidelines when I blocked a shot.

I thought I might burst with pride.

Me and Megan were on opposite teams. And when I went in for a tackle, I went in hard. But just as hard as I'd tackle anybody.

'Lexie, what the fuck?' Megan was on the ground holding her shin.

'I got the ball,' I said with a shrug. Which was true.

But she got me back. Took the ball round me like I wasn't even there, and scored, top corner like it was effortless. And although she'd been ignoring me, she made sure to look over me before turning to the sidelines with a swing of her chestnut ponytail, to smile at Niall.

'Yes, Megan!' Sadie cheered. 'That's what I need next week.'

I wondered what it would feel like to hear that from Sadie. I would. I *would* hear it. I just needed to do more.

By the end of practice sweat was dripping from my face and I had to double over to catch my breath. I pulled on my hoodie and sat in the stands, waiting for the boys to start.

As the boys' squad flooded the pitch, I looked for Shane. But I couldn't see him anywhere. Why wasn't he at training? Then I looked up towards the clubhouse. There he was, leaning against the wall, talking to Zoe.

And I felt sick.

14

I stared at them, trying to work out what they were saying. But they were too far away and the boys on the pitch were too loud. I needed to know what she'd said. What *he'd* said.

I watched the boys' practice but wasn't paying attention. I was trying to calm myself down. We had a thing; there was no reason he was going to fall for Zoe, even if she was gorgeous. But I relaxed a bit at the end of practice, when he looked up to the stands and smiled at me. Until the name 'Grace' flashed in my head again.

I sent him a message.

ME: Meet me behind the clubhouse?

It wasn't until the boys had gone back into the changing rooms that I got a reply.

SHANE: OK

A one-word reply? What if Zoe had won him over? What if he'd told her about us?

Megan and Niall were kissing against the fence when I walked past, and I was almost at the clubhouse when I heard Niall's voice.

'Let's go, Lexie!' he called.

'Just need to do something,' I said without turning round, and he didn't say anything else. Probably went back to kissing Megan. I had a quick look to make sure nobody was watching, before walking to the back of the clubhouse.

And there he was. Leaning against the wall, hands in pockets. He looked over slowly. I hadn't even said anything, it was like he sensed I was there.

'Hey,' he said.

'Hey.' And the panic began to subside.

I jogged over, standing in front of him, between his legs, and leaned my head on his chest. His heart was racing.

'Hey, are you OK?' he asked, prising me away gently.

I looked up at him and forced tears back from where they came from. So embarrassing. I couldn't *cry*. But he did something to me, made all my feelings so much bigger than they'd ever been. He made them rise to the surface where they erupted like lava. He made me feel *everything*.

'Yeah, I'm fine,' I lied.

He tilted my chin up to look at him, then pushed hair behind my ear. 'You sure?'

I nodded, scared of speaking.

'You look amazing when you play, you know.'

That smile. Suggestive and warm at the same time, making his blue eyes shine.

'Thanks. So do you.'

And it was true. He was such a natural. Beautiful to watch.

'I don't know about that. I also think your brother might kill me soon. Harrison has made me starting striker now, like confirmed.'

'Yeah, he won't like that. But it's not your fault you're better.'

'Ah, he's a great player; probably suits the wing better, that's all.'

And it made me want to kiss him right there, how nice he was, even though Niall had been such a dick. It made him even hotter. But I didn't, because I had something to ask him.

'My parents are away this weekend, and Niall will probably go to Megan's, so if he does, do you think you'd maybe want to come over? I could show you the beach?'

I was nervous now, looking at the size difference of my boots next to his. He was taking too long to reply . . .

'I'd like that,' he said eventually.

I smiled so hard it hurt. 'Yeah?' I looked up again and he was smiling too.

'Yeah,' he said.

I reached up to kiss him. Our mouths were warm and salty, and we fell into a perfect rhythm before he pulled away.

'Maybe I could cook for us?' he said.

That was a shock. 'You cook?'

'Yeah, just something I picked up.'

'You get more impressive every time I talk to you,' I said.

He laughed. 'I wouldn't say that. I just like it, you know?'

'I can't wait. I'll text you and let you know when Niall's gone.'

'Sounds good.'

And it was only then I remembered he'd been talking to Zoe. I couldn't ask what they were talking about, how could I? I'd sound ridiculously jealous. Which I wasn't . . .

On the way home I didn't even care that Niall was giving me the silent treatment. In fact, I was happy about it.

And just as we were getting out of the car, he said the most beautiful words I'd ever heard.

'I'm going to Megan's this weekend. So don't be running to tell Mum and Dad.' Megan's parents weren't even away. They didn't mind having Niall sleeping over, even though Megan preferred our house. They were taking Niall and Megan up the coast. I guess I was kind of jealous how easy it was for him.

'Whatever,' I said, using his favourite word against him. I forced my face to hide the fireworks, the butterflies and the very best kind of racing heartbeat at the thought of Shane coming over.

'Why are you being so helpful?' Niall asked me with a *tone* in the house later on. I'd been helping Mum pack for her trip to Sweden, suggesting clothes that looked good on her. And now I was upstairs, looking for my Chanel bag to lend her, which meant I had had to walk past him gaming.

'Why are you still playing *Roblox*? You know how cringe that is? Isn't that like P5 stuff?'

'It's ironic.'

'You don't even know what ironic means.'

'Can't wait to go to Meg's this weekend. Make sure the serial killer doesn't get you,' Niall replied. He didn't take his eyes off the screen once. And that was a new thing. Well, a since-Megan thing. A few months ago, I would have sat down beside him, and he'd have handed me the controller to take over. But now he barely looked at me.

'Dick.' He knew I had a thing about serial killers. We shared a bedroom until we were ten because I was convinced that a serial killer would come and get me in the middle of the night. I made Niall sleep in the bed closest to the door, so they'd kill him first when they got there, in the hope that I'd have time to escape while he just lay there in a heap, soaking the thousand-pound carpet in blood.

'I can't wait for you to go to Meg's either.' I sighed, taking my bag downstairs to Mum.

'Thanks, love,' Mum said as she packed. 'Do you think I've enough?' She looked genuinely worried, even though she'd packed enough clothes for two weeks.

'I think you'll be OK, Mum.' I picked a jumper out of her suitcase. One I hadn't seen before, wool, Fair Isle. Not Mum's style *at all*.

'Do you like it? Like Sarah Lund from *The Killing*.' She smiled. 'But *The Killing* is Danish ...' She tailed off in thought. 'Never mind. I've also been practising my Swedish on Duolingo.'

'What can you say?' I asked, actually interested.

'*Hej. Tack. God morgon.* Hello, thank you, good morning. Oh and *obduktion*!' Mum timed the zip of the suitcase with her new word.

'What does that mean?'

'Autopsy. But I learned that one from my shows.'

I laughed.

'It's nice to see you so happy, Lex.' Mum put her hand on my shoulder. 'This last couple of years, I don't know, you haven't seemed like yourself. But that smile? *That's* the Lexie I know.' She smiled at me warmly. I thought about hugging her, but decided against it. It would be too out of character.

'Who knows, probably just hormones or something.' I shrugged. 'But I'm away to bed anyway, and you'll be gone before I wake up, so have an amazing trip!'

'Thanks, pet. There's money in the kitchen if you want to order food. And not too much training, promise?'

'Promise,' I said, and I was glad I wasn't lying to her. I wasn't thinking about training this weekend; I was only thinking about Shane.

I studied for an hour before I went to sleep. I hadn't been keeping up with my list. Ever since Shane, my head had been all over the place.

I hardly slept. How could I? Tomorrow night there'd be no parents and no Niall. Just me and Shane.

And I couldn't ignore the fact that I was scared. Would he expect me to do *stuff*? I'd only got to grips with kissing him. I don't think I was ready for anything else.

Mum and Dad were already gone by the time I got up. Only Niall was in the kitchen.

'You know I'll know if you have a party,' he said, eating a Pop-Tart.

I poured porridge into a bowl and rolled my eyes at him. '*Not having* a party.'

'Mum and Dad have gone, you don't need to suck up with your healthy eating.'

I shrugged. 'My body is a temple.' I sent a message to Shane.

ME: Want to come over at 7? 7 Seaport Close

SHANE: Can't wait :)

Niall didn't say anything after that, but he left the rest of his Pop-Tart on the counter.

The rest of the day was the same. A fuzzy daze that nobody, not even Zoe, could dissipate. Any time I remembered her talking to Shane or the name 'Grace' I just thought about the fact he'd be with me in a few hours.

When I got home, I inspected the house. The cleaner had done a pretty good job, but I still went over all the counters again. I needed it to be perfect. I dimmed the kitchen lights, lit candles on the island and put my favourite Spotify playlist on low in the background.

I couldn't wait for him to come. I showered, wore my nicest underwear, the pink lace that Megan had bought me from Victoria's Secret. Not that I had a clue about any of that stuff, but I remember Megan saying you should always wear nice underwear *just in case*. She said it was in case you get knocked down by a car and the hospital have to cut your clothes off. Or if you accidentally take your clothes off in front of someone hot. I'd laughed so much at that because I could totally imagine her doing it. And then I felt sick as the image of her and Niall haunted me.

Even though it was early February, I wore a dress because I knew it looked good. A summer dress dotted with flowers that grazed the tops of my thighs and sat low on my chest. I pulled a chunky cardigan over my shoulders and I was careful with my make-up, lining my eyes with kohl, applying highlighter and contour in all the right places. I even straightened my hair until it fell over my shoulders in a shiny caramel curtain. Nike socks and trainers. Just so he'd recognize me.

I must have looked at the clock on my phone about a million times that afternoon. Finally it was seven, and I was so excited I thought I was going to explode.

The doorbell rang and I had to compose myself before opening the door.

Then there he was. Standing in his tracksuit. One I'd seen before but one he looked so good in.

'Lex. You look . . .' He exhaled and pushed back his dark hair. 'I didn't know we were dressing up. I should have worn something . . . I mean, it's not like I have anything fancy . . . You look, incredible.' He scanned my body and I laughed at his reaction.

I reached into the freezing night and pulled him in by the hand, planting a kiss on his lips. 'You don't need to dress up. And anyway, I have a serious thing for tracksuits.' I smiled and turned, leading him into the kitchen.

'Your house is insane,' he said, looking around.

'Yeah, it's a bit ridiculous. It's too big,' I said. Embarrassed.

'It's amazing.' Shane slid a backpack off his shoulders and opened the zip. I moved to his side of the island to look inside, but before I even got close, I could smell it.

'I hope you like risotto,' he said, pulling out a container.

'Oh my God, I love it.' It smelled incredible.

'Are you vegetarian? Because there are mushrooms in it, but scallops too. I can take out the scallops if you don't eat fish.' He was rushing his words as he pulled out container after container.

'I'm not vegetarian and, sorry, what? You cooked scallops?'

'Yeah,' he said quietly. 'And chocolate pudding for dessert.' He pointed at another container.

I could not stop smiling. 'This is perfect.'

And it was. We sat beside each other at the island, legs pressed together, eating the beautiful food that Shane had made. I had to make myself slow down. It was so good, and I'd forgotten to eat all day because I was so excited about seeing him.

I asked him questions in between mouthfuls.

'So tell me about you. Was that your mum who came to the match last week?' I asked.

He hesitated. 'That was my aunt actually.'

'Oh, that's so nice; she must be so proud of you!'

'She is. Loves football. She's my dad's sister and they were both mad into it growing up.'

He smiled when he mentioned his dad.

'She's from Liverpool too then? Does she live here?'

'Yeah, she moved over when . . . when I was wee.'

'That must be nice. Your dad couldn't come to the match?' I asked, reaching over to touch his hand that was resting beside his plate.

'Nah, couldn't make it. But, you know, my dad had a trial for Liverpool when he was nineteen.'

'What the hell?' I let go of his hand and turned round so I was facing him properly. 'Are you serious?'

He laughed. 'Yeah, he was an amazing footballer. Didn't get there in the end, but I've always been so impressed. He's brilliant, my dad.'

'And that's obviously where you got your talent. Oh my God, Shane, I'd be shouting that from the rooftops if I were you. So cool. What does he do now?'

Shane swallowed some risotto and took a drink of the Coke I'd left out. 'Ah, loads of stuff. What does *your* dad do again?' he asked, gazing around the kitchen.

'I don't actually know, you know. Some tech thing.' I hoped he wouldn't ask any more questions and we could go back to talking about his dad.

'So did your dad teach you everything you know?'

'I guess he did.'

'Can I meet him sometime?'

Shane looked at me, a flash of panic taking over his face.

I put my hand over my mouth. 'Oh Jesus, I didn't mean it like that. It's too soon. It's just the Liverpool trial thing is unbelievable.'

'I'm sure he'd love to meet you,' he said, then got up and opened another box that he'd brought. 'Dessert?'

The chocolate pudding was amazing, the perfect balance of

sweet and chocolatey. 'Where did you learn to cook?' I asked. 'Wait, don't tell me, your dad too?'

He laughed. 'I guess you could say that, yeah.'

'I'm sorry, Shane, but you've told me too much, I'm running away with your dad.'

He laughed. 'Will you show me the beach? The one you talked about the other night on the phone?' Shane looked at me, his blue eyes twinkling in the candlelight.

'Of course,' I said softly. I found his hand and twisted my fingers into his. 'I'm so glad you came to Westing.'

'Me too.'

As soon as we walked out the back door, Shane saw the football pitch.

'Are you serious?' He looked at me, open-mouthed.

'Yeah, they built it for me and Niall so we could practise,' I said, feeling stupid.

'Are those actual floodlights?'

'Maybe,' I said and pulled him in the other direction, down the garden and towards the beach.

The wind was strong, and the waves curled into wild peaks before collapsing with a hiss to the shore.

'This is so cool,' he said, helping me balance on the rocks.

'Me and Niall used to come down here and make boats from all the rubbish that had washed up.' I smiled at the memory.

'That sounds fun,' he said. 'My dad would love it here.' He stopped and I leaned into his side. We both looked up at the moon. 'He had depression a couple of years ago. It was really tough, on everyone, but eventually he came out of it. Mum says it was the sea air that fixed him, but I think it was just a coincidence that we'd gone up the coast and it was the first time we'd seen him smile in a really long time. But anyway, he loves the sea.'

'Oh, Shane, that must have been so hard,' I said. 'I'm sorry you had to go through that.'

'It was. But he's been OK for ages now, so fingers crossed it won't come back, but it's not his fault, so if it does, we'll just deal with it again.'

I squeezed his hand and then he broke the moon's gaze to look down at me. 'Aren't you cold?' I hugged myself, wishing I'd worn something more than a cardigan and a summer dress.

'Wee bit,' I lied, my chattering teeth giving me away.

'You can have my clothes,' he said.

'What do you mean?'

Shane stepped back from me and took off his shirt. He threw it into my arms.

I laughed. 'What are you doing?'

He didn't answer, just smiled, then bent down to take off his shoes, socks *and* trousers until he was standing on the beach in his boxers.

I hugged his warm clothes. 'What the hell! Are you crazy?'

'Come with me.' He held out his hand.

'What? In there? No chance. It's Baltic.' I shook my head. 'No, nope. No way!'

'You're missing out.'

He jogged towards the water and inhaled deeply as it splashed around him. But he kept walking until it was up to his waist. The moonlight caught all his angles, the smooth dips of his abdomen and the sharp set of his jawline.

'Shane!! What are you doing?' I shouted, still laughing.

'Lexie, come in. It's warm, I promise.' He turned and held out his hands, trying and failing to hide the fact that he was gasping for breath.

'Liar!' I shouted. Then: 'Fuck it.' I put down his clothes, dropped my cardigan and pulled my dress over my head, thanking myself silently for my choice of underwear. I squealed from the cold and ran towards the lough, towards Shane, and even though I knew it would be freezing, the temperature still shocked me. This wasn't me. I didn't do stuff like this, not without planning. It was Shane, pulling me willingly out of the cage I locked myself in. My feet were numb, and my skin was covered in goosebumps. I was almost beside him.

'I can't, I can't, I need to get out,' I said, turning back towards the shore.

'Wait,' Shane said.

Then I felt his hand on my arm pulling me back. He put his arms round me as the waves swelled around us.

'This is insane,' I said.

'Doesn't it make you feel alive?' he shouted into the night.

I leaned against his shaking chest and looked up at him, how happy he seemed. And it was contagious.

'You make me feel free, Lexie Ryan.'

But before I could ask what he meant, Shane had my face in his hands and we were kissing in the freezing salty water, warm tongues colliding, skin against skin. And either my feet were numb, or he took away the pain, because all I felt right then was him.

'Maybe we should go before we get hypothermia,' I whispered.

We picked up our clothes and ran back to the house, rinsing the sand from our feet before Shane followed me upstairs, my body still shaking from the cold.

'In here,' I said, pushing open my bedroom door and walking into the bathroom.

I switched on the shower and my bathroom filled with steam.

'I'll wait out here,' Shane said, barely audible because he was shaking. He was standing awkwardly in my room in soaking underwear, looking cuter than ever.

'Come with me,' I said. And I don't know where it came from. It just came out. But I didn't regret it. And it was weird because I didn't feel awkward or like I needed to cover myself, even though I'd never had so few clothes on in front of a boy before. Shane made everything feel so easy.

I stepped into the shower and he followed me. I slid my arms round his waist and stood on my toes so I could kiss him again. The taste of salt was still there, diluted by the streams of piping-hot water that washed away the grains of sand that were stuck to our bodies and to the underwear that clung to our skin.

When I turned off the water we stood there in silence, unsure what to do next.

'I'll get you some of Niall's clothes. Yours got wet sitting on the rocks.'

'Thanks,' he said, grabbing a towel and drying his hair with it.

Wrapped in my own towel, I brought back some sweatpants and a T-shirt and left him to get dressed, while I pulled on my checked pyjama trousers and a strappy top.

He came out with his hair towel-dried and Niall's clothes hanging off him.

Then there was a noise. A door opening and chatting downstairs. Niall's voice. It was unmistakable.

I looked at Shane in panic. 'Shit.'

15

'Lexie?' Megan's voice.

Shane and I were just staring at each other. Then I heard footsteps on the stairs.

'Bathroom, go!' I hissed.

Shane did as he was told and closed himself in. I walked into the games room, planning to keep Megan out of my bedroom, where Shane's clothes were still lying on the floor.

Megan had just reached the top of the stairs.

I feigned shock. 'Oh my God, you scared me. What are you doing here?' I asked, forgetting again that we weren't speaking.

'Niall left his charger here,' Megan said.

I shrugged. 'Oh, right.'

Megan walked into Niall's room. I stayed where I was.

'Meg, help me find it,' Niall called from downstairs.

Megan rolled her eyes as she came out of his room and didn't even look at me as she went downstairs.

I followed her, in the hope I could keep her there and then they'd both leave.

'Where are you?' Megan called, irritated.

'Kitchen,' he said.

Shit. I hadn't cleared up after dinner. There were still dishes sitting everywhere. Two plates, two glasses. Maybe they wouldn't notice.

'Did you tell her?' Niall asked Megan.

'Niall,' she hissed, annoyed.

'Tell me what?'

Megan stared at the table. She didn't say anything, but after a few seconds, she turned to me. 'Sadie phoned me earlier. There are Northern Ireland trials next week and she wants me to go.' She said it like she was talking about a holiday or a night out.

I couldn't speak. My mouth felt dry and my chest tightened. And it felt worse because it had been prompted by Niall.

'Oh,' I said. It was all I could get out because nausea-inducing disappointment was seeping through every single one of my veins like poison. Which was stupid. As if Sadie would ask me to do NI trials. I could feel my hands shaking, so I put them in my hair.

'It's on the same day as V-Ball,' she said.

'And?' Surely V-Ball wouldn't even come close to the excitement of this.

'It's in Fermanagh, so by the time I get up there, do the trial and get back again, I'll be wrecked and in no mood to party at all!'

Something snapped. 'Do you *know* how lucky you are?'

She shrugged. 'It's only lucky if you actually want it.'

I willed the tears to stay behind my eyes. 'Do you know what I would give to go to an NI trial?'

'Well *you* go then.' Megan seemed to expect me to agree with whatever she said, like usual. But not this.

123

I narrowed my eyes. 'Anything. I would give *anything* to have been invited.'

'I told you we shouldn't have said,' Megan hissed at Niall.

Niall was staring at us, looking guilty. He changed the subject. 'Lexie, what's the deal with all the plates? Who'd you have round?'

'None of your business,' I said, trying to ignore Megan's beautifully confused face trying to work it out.

'Well, it kind of is. It's my house too,' he said.

'It's *none* of your business. OK?' I shouted.

But he was ignoring me, looking at the leftovers. 'Risotto? Where'd you get this. *You* can't cook.' He snorted.

'Zoe. It was Zoe. We've got kind of friendly lately, so I thought I'd invite her over.' I shrugged.

Megan scrunched up her face. 'Zoe?'

'What's wrong with that? She's really nice.'

'Since when?' Megan said but didn't wait for an answer. 'Whatever, I don't care.'

She was clearly hurt. And the worst part? I was glad.

'You're on a date with Zoe?' Niall looked over at me, totally confused.

'It's not a date; we were just hanging out. But I want to go to bed, so do you guys have somewhere to be?' I wished they'd leave.

'Let's go, Meg. I found it,' Niall said.

I stayed in the kitchen until they'd left, my hands on the counter, breathing in deeply and trying desperately to get rid of the resentment before I went back up to see Shane. But it hurt how much she didn't care when all I did was care. And why had

Niall told her to tell me? So he could see me be upset about it? I never thought he could be so cruel. But then I'd seen how he was with Shane. Maybe I didn't really know him at all.

My phone buzzed.

NIALL: I thought you'd be excited for her

I wanted to tell him that I didn't care. But I couldn't type out the lie. So I didn't write back at all. Niall knew how much football meant to me. He knew how much I wanted to be on the team, to be better, how an NI trial would be a dream come true for me.

I was embarrassed to go back upstairs. Shane would know I was upset. I imagined what it would be like to tell him it was me that Sadie had phoned. How excited he'd be for me, how amazing I'd feel.

But I couldn't leave him in the bathroom.

'Shane?' I called when I got into my room. 'They're away.'

He came out smiling but his expression immediately changed when he saw my face.

'What happened?'

I burst into tears. It was so pathetic.

He didn't ask again; he just walked over and wrapped his arms round me and let me cry into Niall's hoodie until I'd stopped. Then he led me by the hand over to the bed, where we sat down.

'Want to talk about it?' He reached up to wipe away a leftover tear that had escaped.

I shook my head. 'It's stupid.'

'I bet it's not.'

'Megan got invited for Northern Ireland trials.' I forced myself not to cry again.

'That's great,' he said. '*Not* great?'

'It would be if she *wanted* to go. She doesn't care. Because V-Ball is the same day, she's actually thinking about not going so she can go to some stupid formal. It's crazy!' The rage was building again.

'Is it?' Shane asked and I turned to him.

'Em, yeah? She's super talented. Why would you want to waste a gift like that?' I asked, knowing I was right and there was no good answer.

'Maybe she doesn't love it? And if you're going to put your whole life into something like that, you have to *love* it,' Shane said simply.

'So you think she's right? To ditch this once-in-a-lifetime opportunity for V-Ball?' I couldn't believe what I was hearing.

'If that's what she wants to do? Yeah, one hundred per cent.'

I exhaled in anger.

Shane took my hand. 'Don't be angry, Lex. It makes no difference to you. And at least she's brave enough to say no,' he said, lying back on the bed, his hand still attached to mine.

I lay back too. 'What do you mean?'

'I didn't want to leave Ferndale United. I was having a great time there, and Raj, our coach, he didn't take anything seriously. Lost? Didn't matter; we just had a laugh about it. And football was so much fun. But then Harrison spotted me after one of our games and asked me to join Westing. My dad thought I should go, and I didn't want to let him down. I mean, don't get me wrong, I'm glad I came because I met you. But I don't love it either. I wish I had the balls to tell him I was happier at Ferndale.'

I didn't know what to say, but I wasn't angry any more. I listened to him explain it, my heartbeat slowing as he spoke.

'But you're so good,' I said.

'It doesn't matter how good I am. I don't think I want football to be my life. And actually, I respect someone who can stand up and say that instead of doing what I'm doing and just going along with it for someone else.'

'I guess that makes sense.' I turned it over in my head, and even though I still couldn't fully understand Megan, I felt sorry for Shane. I shrugged. 'Not wanting to let your family down? I get that.'

'Yeah, and it's not like my dad puts loads of pressure on me or anything, I've always just kind of wanted to impress him, you know? Is it the same for you?' He looked at me, genuinely curious. How could I tell him it was the same for me, except it wasn't my parents, it was Niall I wanted to impress. But he'd been such an asshole to Shane – he wouldn't understand.

'Sort of yeah, but maybe we shouldn't talk about families any more.' I gave him a tiny smile and moved closer, reaching up to push *his* hair back this time.

'Good idea.'

I kissed him, my hand still in his hair, and I felt all the tension leave my body.

He smiled. 'So tell me about V-Ball then. Is it really posh?'

I laughed. 'I suppose it is. It's all tuxedos and floor-length dresses.' I rolled my eyes. 'Would you want to go maybe?' I forced Niall and Megan out of my head and didn't think about the huge fall-out that would happen if I showed up with Shane.

He looked at me and hesitated, something obviously on the tip of his tongue. And then he exhaled and gave in to it. 'Zoe asked if I wanted to go with her. Like, a while ago, and I said no, that I was sort of seeing someone. I thought you should know.'

I shot up to sitting and he did the same. 'Zoe asked you to V-Ball?'

I couldn't believe what I'd just heard. I tried to keep calm, even though my insides burned like my organs were about to spontaneously combust.

'Yeah, but she asked and I said no, and that was that.'

He was right. She'd asked and he'd said no. It was fine.

'Anyway, I don't have a tux.'

'I can get you one. My mum and dad put money in my account every month and I have way more than I can spend.'

Shane breathed out and looked at me. 'This is just a different world,' he said with a laugh. 'I bet you're one of those girls who plays a million instruments and went to speech and drama classes too.'

I gave him a side-eye and let him follow my gaze across the room to my clarinet in its box.

'Flute?'

'Clarinet,' I clarified.

'And? What else do you play?' he teased.

'Piano.'

'I *knew* it! Will you play something for me? Please?'

'Oh my God, no, I haven't played it in ages.' I put my hands over my face.

'Please?' he begged. 'I never played anything. I think it's amazing when people can play instruments.'

'How am I supposed to say no to that?'

I put my clarinet together, turning away as I wet the reed. Then I played. It was amazing how much I remembered even though I hadn't touched it in years. It was out of tune, but it still sounded OK. I closed my eyes, getting lost in the music, and when I opened them, Shane was staring right at me. I was on the last few bars when he stood up and walked behind me. He planted tiny kisses on my bare shoulders right up to my ears, making me shiver with pleasure.

'Don't stop,' he whispered.

So I kept playing, he kept kissing, and soon after I'd played the last note, I'd forgotten all about the stupid NI trials, because now we were lying on my bed, Shane's body pressed against mine, and I wasn't thinking about Megan or Niall or football any more, I was only thinking about him.

16

We'd fallen asleep, twisted in each other, breathing in sync. And those minutes before I drifted off, I was drowning in happiness.

When I woke up Shane was still asleep, sheet over him, winter sun pouring through the window on to his perfect face. I got up to close the curtains and he stirred. Gently at first, then his eyes sprang open, and he reached for his phone on the bedside table.

'Fuck.' He threw himself out of bed.

'What's wrong?'

'I need to get home. I shouldn't have stayed over. I didn't mean to stay.' It was like he was talking to himself. He shook his head and pulled on his clothes frantically, the ones that were still covered in sand from yesterday.

'Can I drive you?'

He was putting on his socks, hesitated, then nodded. 'Yeah, please. I really need to get home.'

'Is everything OK?'

'Yeah, it's just complicated,' he said. *Again* he didn't elaborate on whatever it was he wasn't telling me. And because I didn't want to ruin last night even more, I didn't push it.

'OK,' I said. I got dressed too, pulling on sweatpants and a hoodie before tying my hair into a high ponytail.

He barely said anything. And neither did I.

I'd had visions of us sipping tea together in the morning before going for a walk on the beach. Instead, I drove out of Westing and towards Ferndale, all the way through and out the other side.

'Just down here.' Shane directed me to a run-down estate. I cringed when I thought about the size of my house and then kicked myself when I realized that he'd probably seen my face contort in embarrassment.

We twisted and turned down a million different roads, then he asked me to stop outside a mid-terrace. And just as he was about to get out of the car, he looked at his phone that had just buzzed and lit up. I didn't even have to move to see it. There was that name again, loud and clear. *Grace.*

'This is me. Thanks for the lift, Lexie.' Shane sounded formal. Like I was his coach giving him a lift home after practice. And as amazing and beautiful as he'd made me feel last night, this was the opposite. I felt empty. Worthless. I waited for him to turn and kiss me goodbye. But he didn't. He just got out of the car and disappeared into the house, leaving me in the driver's seat, hating myself, wondering what I'd done wrong and desperately needing to know who Grace was. Why couldn't he just tell me? I couldn't ask; he'd think I was crazy. So I sat there staring at his house, hoping it would magically give me some answers. But there was nothing. Just weeds up the driveway and a fence that could do with a few coats of paint.

I couldn't get my head around it. We'd been so open with each other. He'd talked about his parents, his dad's depression, and they were clearly a really supportive family if his aunt had come to watch his game. It just made no sense. Maybe he'd thought about my reaction to Megan's news and decided he couldn't deal with it. Not my finest moment, but I found it so hard to keep my feelings hidden when something like that happened. But he was so kind, and he'd made me feel so much better.

I spent the rest of the drive going through our conversations and thinking about what I'd said, desperately trying to figure out where I'd gone wrong. But I couldn't think of anything except the name 'Grace'. So when I got back home, I tidied up to distract myself from the thoughts that twisted in my head.

When I'd finished, I still felt horrible. So I did the only thing that had worked to keep myself out of my head for the last few years. I trained.

Out the back, I ran laps until I was drenched in sweat, I kicked ball after ball at the net, as hard as I could, getting out all the frustration, about Megan, about Niall, and about Shane.

Why couldn't anything be simple? Why do people have to hide things and have secrets? Even then I realized I was being a hypocrite. Before, if I phoned Megan and told her everything, she'd be straight over to see me. She'd probably have some decent advice too. But now? She was barely speaking to me. And even though I missed her, I'd committed to being pissed off about them being together. Then I remembered about the

NI trials and my mind was made up again. So I just kept running and dribbling and shooting until my legs turned into jelly and I felt like I wanted to throw up.

I went down to the beach and looked out at the sea, at the exact spot we'd stood the night before. I shivered, remembering how cold it had been, remembering how happy I'd been. So fucking happy.

I checked my phone. Nothing.

I wished we had a game today, that would have taken up a few hours. Instead, I had a shower and got back into my pyjamas, deciding to torture myself by watching love stories on Netflix all day. The kind Megan loved. I cried at the happy endings and pretended to relate when their boyfriends treated them horribly.

But Shane hadn't been horrible, and he hadn't actually done anything wrong; it was just the contrast of a night that had been so beautiful, ending like a plaster being ripped off.

ME: Are you OK?

SHANE: Yeah, thanks. Sorry about earlier. Just had to get home

ME: Do you want to come back over?

SHANE: Sorry, I can't, but I'll see you at training tomorrow? 5 a.m.?

ME: Wouldn't miss it

ME: Did I do something?

SHANE: No! It was nothing you did at all. Please don't think that. It's just family stuff

ME: Oh, OK. What's going on? Can I help?

SHANE: Don't worry, it's fine. But thanks

No explanation. I hated that the thought flashed in my head of him and Zoe, like they were having some secret relationship and *that* was the reason. But it didn't make sense. He'd said no to going to V-Ball with her. Then my head filled with the made-up image of some girl called Grace. But those thoughts hurt too much, so I let my head float back to Megan and the NI trials, the nausea in the pit of my stomach turning to anger again.

Niall used to understand. A few years ago, we'd come home from school and talk about everyone in the year, trading gossip and pissing ourselves laughing about the stupid stuff that the teachers said. I told Niall everything and I thought it was the same for him, but clearly not.

My sadness took me to Dad's study. I pulled open the

bottom filing cabinet and took out a box. There it was, the memory stick. This is where the old me and Niall lived now, on this tiny piece of plastic and metal, hidden away in a box.

I brought it down to the massive television in the living room and plugged it in before going to get some popcorn from the kitchen. I came back to see the screen burst to life. I hovered over 'play', knowing I wasn't in the right mental state to watch. But I did it anyway.

Winter five years ago, skiing in Banff. We were twelve. Dad was holding the video camera and he zoomed in on me and Niall at the top of a slope. He was showing me something. Then I remembered. I was scared to go down that slope, even though we'd been skiing every year since we were five. I'd fallen the year before and hit my head, so I was terrified in case it happened again. Niall stood with me at the top for ages, not rushing me, waiting until I was ready, giving me instructions and telling me he'd ski behind me the whole time in case I fell, even though he was miles better, and faster than I was.

I watched myself come down the hill, Niall, like he said, right behind me.

Dad cheered when I got to the bottom, but it was Niall I was watching. He came right over to me, threw an arm round my shoulders and said, 'See, said you could do it!'

And I remembered how much love I had for him then. For my family.

I watched videos all night. Holidays in France, Costa Rica and that one in Mexico where the video switched off two days in because we all got sick. I stayed up late deliberately. I wanted to fall asleep as soon as my head hit the pillow. I couldn't bear any more of my own thoughts.

It worked. I woke up to my alarm screaming at me and the sound of the waves crashing outside. When I got to the club, Shane wasn't there yet, so I went down on to the pitch to warm up, doing laps with the freezing air burning my chest.

Ten minutes later, it was like I sensed him. I looked across the pitch to see him jogging towards me. Grey hoodie this time.

'I'm sorry about yesterday, and I'm sorry I'm late,' he said, and he looked right at me when he said it. It sounded so genuine.

'Is everything OK?' I asked. 'At home?'

'Oh yeah, everything's fine; my mum and dad just like knowing where I am.' He smiled and then rolled his eyes, but something about the way he said it made me think he wasn't telling the truth. 'Will we start?' He flicked a football on to his foot.

'Yeah,' I said, knowing I wasn't going to get any more of an explanation.

'Hey,' he said, and I looked up at him.

He came close to me, took my face in his hands, and kissed me gently. 'It's just my weird family, OK?'

I smiled, the doubt in my chest fading. For now. 'OK.'

He took my chin and kissed me briefly on the lips, then turned and walked towards the net where there were two footballs. Even from behind he looked amazing. Square shoulders taking me back to the other night when I had my hands on them, holding on tightly as he kissed my neck.

I yawned. 'Maybe at the weekend we don't need to be here at five a.m.' I laughed. 'What d'ya reckon?' Recently I was finding it harder to get up in the mornings with all this extra training.

He hesitated for a second before he picked up the football. 'I kind of like it this early. Before the world wakes up, you know?' He turned and looked at my confused face. 'And sometimes I help out my dad really early . . . with work, so it's kind of perfect. But we're running out of time.' He threw the ball in the air and caught it.

At the end of our practice, we were both sweating and dehydrated.

'I forgot to bring a drink – you think the clubhouse is open?' He wiped sweat from under his hair.

'Shit, me too.' I'd been in such a rush to get out the door to see him I'd completely forgotten. 'But I know where there's a key,' I said. 'Come on.'

I grabbed his hand, and we jogged over. I lifted the plant pot and there it was, where I'd seen Sadie sliding it once, a little silver key. I opened the door, and we were hit with a musty smell as creaks echoed through the building. I followed him down the corridor to the water fountain and watched him drink, remembering the lips that were on mine, and feeling heat in my face as I imagined other things.

'You want some?' he asked, wiping a hand across his mouth.

'Yeah.' I flicked my hair out of the way and tried to look attractive as I bent over and sucked water from the fountain.

When I finished, I looked at him. 'How much time have we got?'

He looked at his phone. 'Twenty minutes before the bus.'

I wasn't wasting any time. I grabbed his hand and pulled him into the girls' changing room, leading him to a bench where I sat on top of him, legs either side, and we got lost in each other, tongues pressed together, my hands on his cold face pulling him harder into me, his hands everywhere.

We were completely and utterly consumed by each other, so preoccupied, that we didn't hear the clubhouse door creak open. But we did hear the footsteps that squeaked across the lino in the corridor.

And when the door into the changing room was pushed open, I was there, on the floor, after losing my balance trying to detangle myself from Shane, while he was round the corner in the shower block.

17

'Lexie?' Sadie's voice. Shocked, from the doorway.

'Jelly legs,' I said, standing up and trying not to make eye contact.

'What are you doing here?' she asked. She looked at her watch. 'It's six thirty.'

'Just wanted to get some extra training in. I was down on the pitches running laps. I need a change of scenery from the back garden sometimes.' I laughed for no reason, hoping it would distract her and she wouldn't see the extra clothes that were lying around.

She nodded. 'Lexie, I'd actually wanted to have a chat with you. Should we sit down for a minute?' She motioned to the same bench I'd just been sitting on with Shane.

'Sure.' I glanced towards the shower block, willing him to stay out of sight.

Sadie stretched her leg and groaned.

'You OK?' I asked.

Sadie never talked about her injury. There were rumours that she'd made a bad tackle, and some girl had got her own back and taken Sadie out entirely.

'Ah yeah, just gets a bit stiff if I'm standing too long. I'm fine. But, Lexie, I meant it when I said that all this extra work of yours isn't going unnoticed. I want you to start in our match on Friday.'

I couldn't help myself. I threw myself at her. The least open-to-hugs person I'd ever met. She exhaled, and I panicked, wondering if I'd somehow hurt her leg. So I let go.

'Thank you, Sadie, thank you so much. I won't let you down. I promise.' I was buzzing inside about everything this meant. I was part of the first team. Me!

'You remind me a bit of me at your age, Lexie. All I wanted in the world was to play for Northern Ireland. I did the extra training, I ate, slept and breathed football. It's the right mindset if you really want something. And I think you're ready. Do you? I mean, really?' She looked me dead in the eyes.

'I know I am.'

'Thought so.' Sadie put her hand on my shoulder, stood up and limped towards the door. I was about to head to the shower block when she turned round. 'Oh, just wondering how you got in here? You really shouldn't be in the clubhouse out of hours. It would be an insurance nightmare if something happened.'

'It was open,' I blurted out with a shrug.

'That's strange. OK, well, no more clubhouse outside practice hours, OK? And keep up the good work. Stay focused.'

I waited until her footsteps disappeared up the corridor again before running round the corner to Shane. But he wasn't there. Just an open window.

I looked at my phone.

SHANE: Sorry, had to catch the bus. Let me know what happened!

ME: I'm starting on Friday!!!!

SHANE: Fucking right!

ME: All thanks to an awesome coach ;)

SHANE: Nah, all down to you x

I waved at Sadie in the office as I walked past, a huge grin on my face. And whatever was going on between me and Niall, I couldn't ignore the fact that I wanted to tell him. I thought about sending him a text message but decided to wait. I wanted to see his face when I told him. He was the only one who truly knew how much it meant to me. Even though we weren't talking, and he was acting like an asshole, the old Niall had to be in there somewhere. This kind of news was bigger than a stupid fight.

And, even though I knew it wouldn't happen, a tiny part of me couldn't help hoping that maybe Sadie would put me forward for the Northern Ireland trials too. I drove home in a total blur of happiness, then got home to an empty house.

I watched Netflix, did some shooting practice, and ate the frozen pizza that Mum had bought before she left. Then I tidied up and checked outside for Niall's car.

Niall got home around seven, his brakes screeching into the driveway. Mum and Dad would be raging if they'd seen him drive like that.

I probably should have guessed by the way he was driving, or the way he slammed the car door and looked at the ground that he was in a bad mood. But it didn't register. I was too happy, too excited to share the news that I'd been dying to get since I started Westing FC.

He walked in the door and threw his keys on to the sideboard before starting up the stairs.

'Hey, guess what?' I said, standing in the hallway grinning like an idiot.

'What?' he said.

And I *still* didn't catch on that this wasn't the right time, that he was basically telling me to fuck off with his tone.

'I'm starting in the match on Friday.' Even my voice was filled with glee.

He didn't even stop on the stairs. Didn't hesitate; he just kept walking. 'Great.' He left the word behind, apathetic and cold. My heart shattered.

I waited to hear his bedroom door slam before bursting into tears, letting myself ugly cry at the bottom of the stairs. It surprised me how much it hurt. How much I needed him to say 'well done' or to just acknowledge the amazing thing that had just happened.

I was asleep by the time Mum and Dad got home on Sunday night, and the next morning I came down to some serious tension in the kitchen. Niall was staring into a cup of coffee and Mum and Dad were tiptoeing round him. But I'd woken up more angry than upset. I didn't even care what was wrong with him.

'Dad, guess what?' I said.

Dad's eyes lit up when he turned round. 'What?'

'Don't leave us in suspense, Lexie,' said Mum, drumming her nails on the counter.

'I'm starting in the next match. I'm on the *first team*. Will you come and watch?'

'Alexandra, that is incredible. Come here!' Dad walked towards me, arms open, and I hugged him back tightly. 'I wouldn't miss it for the world! And Niall, will you be there to watch your sister?'

Niall flicked his head up, but didn't say anything.

'You can use words, you know,' said Dad.

'Leave him alone – he's had a fight with Megan,' Mum whispered, but I don't know why because everyone could hear her.

I stared at Niall, and he looked back at me before breaking my gaze. He wasn't giving anything away. I wondered what had happened, and I automatically put my hand on my phone, about to send a message to Megan to see if she was OK. Then I stopped myself.

'Mum, leave it,' said Niall.

'Don't speak to your mother like that, Niall,' Dad said in a tone that made both of us look up.

Niall screeched his chair back and got up. 'I'm out of here. Let's go, Lexie.'

I grabbed the keys and followed him out the door, feeling

stupid but not knowing what else to do, because that was the way it had always been. Niall said 'jump' and I said 'how high?'.

I decided to broach Niall and Megan's fight about five minutes down the road.

'What happened?' I asked.

'Nothing,' he said sullenly, looking out the window.

'Obviously something happened.'

'She's going to London for uni next year.'

'What? Since when?' I was as shocked as he must have been. Megan had never mentioned going across the water.

'Dunno, since whenever.'

The hole in the pit of my stomach grew with Niall's disappointment, dark and deep and nauseous. And it made me even angrier at Megan than I already was. It was so selfish. *She* was so selfish. She was just going to leave?

'But you want to go to UUJ ...' I trailed off and my voice choked. We'd filled in our forms and sent them a couple of months ago. We were all going to go to UUJ, down the road.

'No shit.'

'There's no need to be so bloody rude, you know,' I said, because as much as I'd been saying it for his benefit, I was trying to make sense of it in my own head. 'Are you going to stay together?'

'I don't *know*, Lexie. Just give over!' he shouted.

We drove the rest of the way to school in silence.

When I saw Megan, her face was tear-stained. She stared after Niall as he stormed into school.

'London?' I said.

She turned to me. 'Yeah.' She shrugged like it was nothing.

But she wasn't just leaving Niall; she was leaving me too. And it clearly didn't matter to her at all.

So how could I tell her my news? The news that had made me swell with so much pride I thought I was going to burst. I'd know she wouldn't mean whatever reaction she managed to conjure.

So I didn't.

I avoided both of them the rest of the day and hung out with Hunter instead. And even though things should have been super awkward, he was acting like everything was normal. He sat beside me at lunchtime and showed me all the obscure football shirts he'd bought. I even pretended to be interested. I hung out with Zoe too, and let her tell me about her itinerary for the trip she was taking to New York at half-term. And I felt like a bitch, because in my head all I was thinking about was the fact that I was starting instead of her, and that Shane had rejected her offer of a V-Ball date. I'd got one up on her and I was happy about it.

18

I was meeting Shane at Victoria Square. I parked in the underground car park and practically ran up the escalator. I glanced around outside House of Fraser, then I saw him. He was in his St Anne's school uniform, looking at his phone, his shirt tail out and his tie a mess. I stopped for a second and just looked at him. I'd never seen him in anything other than a tracksuit – or boxers. And as if he'd felt my gaze, he looked up and smiled.

My whole world stopped.

I had Shane. I was starting in the match on Friday, and we were about to go shopping for V-Ball outfits that would blow everyone away. Could life get any better?

When I got to him, he smiled even harder. I kissed him, pulling his head towards mine, making sure he knew how much I wanted him. Then I scanned the shopping centre, checking there was nobody else in our uniform in our eyeline. Safe.

'What was that for?' he teased.

'I couldn't help myself,' I said.

He stepped back and scanned my school uniform. 'So this is what posh girl uniform looks like close up.' He nodded in approval. 'Pretty hot.'

I smirked and rolled my eyes. 'Do *not* call me "posh girl".' I pushed him playfully. 'And I'm loving the "St Anne's boy pulled through a hedge backwards" uniform too.' I tugged his wonky tie and pulled him closer to me again, planting a tiny kiss on his lips. Then I quickly looked around to make sure nobody had seen. I had to stop being careless, but it was hard when he looked like that.

'Where are we headed? I haven't a clue,' he said. 'Oh, and I don't have *that* much time.'

'Oh, everything OK?' I asked, hoping he would elaborate. But he didn't.

'Yeah, grand, just something I have to do.'

'Why so mysterious?' I said with a grin, keeping it light, but I really wanted to know.

'It's boring, that's all. This is way more exciting. Where are we going?' He scanned the shopping centre.

'Hugo Boss?' I asked.

'*Hugo Boss?*' He didn't hide his shock. And he looked so cute I laughed. 'I was thinking Primark or something.'

'No. Sorry. I've been thinking about how good you'd look in Boss all day.' I smiled and took his hand, pulling him towards the escalators.

'Oh really?'

'Really.' I kept checking around me. I couldn't let this get back to Niall, especially with the state he was in at the minute.

Then we were outside the shop. 'Seriously, Lexie, you can't,' he said, trying to stop me pulling him inside.

'I can. And I will,' I said stubbornly.

He rolled his eyes and let me pull him in.

I told the shop assistant what we needed. Years of shopping with Mum taught me that you need to be confident for them to take you seriously. Especially in shops like that.

She came back with a couple of different options, and we followed her to the unisex changing rooms, where I sat on the sofa to enjoy the show. I watched the assistant take his measurements and was shocked by how it triggered a pang of jealousy.

When Shane stepped out of the cubicle in the first tux, I had to stop myself from throwing myself at him then and there. I was so used to seeing him in football shirts and tracksuits, playing with a ball, that the beauty of his face sometimes took a back seat to his skills. But now? It was centre stage.

I stood up to get a closer look. I hooked my arm through his and looked at us in the mirror. 'We look good together.' I smiled. 'Well, maybe not how I'm dressed right now, but I don't think V-Ball's going to know what hit it.'

'You look amazing right now.' He turned away from the mirror and looked down at me. And then we were kissing, right there in the shop.

The shop assistant cleared her throat and we jumped apart. 'I brought another one,' she said, hanging up another tux behind us.

'Thanks,' I said and dissolved into giggles.

Shane chose the second tux. Traditional. Gorgeous.

Shane watched me try on four dresses.

I settled on a floor-length black-sequin dress with cream contrast down the sides that made my hourglass curves look even more dramatic. It was the look on Shane's face that made my final decision.

'You like it?' I asked, looking in the mirror and smoothing the fabric over my hips. I was standing on my toes, mimicking the heels I'd be wearing.

'Too much.' He smiled and pushed his hand through his hair. 'How am I supposed to get through a whole night of you looking like that? But, Lexie, are you sure it's a good idea? Me coming? I mean, what if your brother is there? Half the Westing team go to Blackport. I mean, I don't care about all that, but I don't want to make drama for you.'

But I was sick of sneaking about like he was some dirty secret. 'I don't care any more. Let them know,' I said with as much conviction as I could, ignoring the sinking feeling in my stomach that haunted me every time I thought about Niall realizing that I was going out with his nemesis. I reminded myself how cruel he'd been to Shane, to me, and how selfish him and Megan were being. Now it was my turn. Why should I have to hide the person who made me happier than anything? Even football.

'You really don't care?' I checked.

He shrugged. 'Nope. I reckon there are way more serious things to get stressed about than some other kid's jealousy. I just don't give stuff like that any space in my head.'

He'd done it again: made me see something from a different angle. He was right. And I wished I could do it too.

When I paid, I saw him look at the time again.

'I hate that I can't stay. And thank you, really. So much. I'll pay you back for it.'

'You will not!' I said, meaning it.

He hesitated and looked away, then back to me. 'Sorry, Lexie, I really have to go.' He kissed me briefly, then turned and walked away. And I just stood there watching him disappear with an uneasiness in my chest, wondering why he wouldn't just tell me what was going on.

19

By the end of the week, the assembly hall looked incredible for V-Ball. I'd laughed when I'd found out they'd been decorating for weeks, but when I saw it at lunchtime, I understood why. Fake trees, flowers and lampposts everywhere. There was even a fountain in the corner, ready to be moved to wherever Zoe wanted it.

'Looks pretty cool, doesn't it?'

I spun round to see Hunter watching me. Happy he couldn't see into my head, at how, when I gazed around the room, I was imagining tomorrow night, when me and Shane would be dancing, *kissing*, out in the open.

'Yeah, it's amazing.'

Hunter fidgeted with a fake flower he'd pulled from one of the vases. 'I hate it, you know.'

'Hate what?' I asked, confused and irritated by his presence.

'The way we don't hang out any more. Like since Niall and Megan got together.' He sounded so sad.

I let myself think back to before Niall and Megan. Did we really hang out? Or was it just that he was there all the time with Niall? He did used to stick up for me if Niall was taking the piss, and two years ago, he bought me a single rose for Valentine's Day. I thought it was because he didn't want me to feel left out, because loads of people had sent Megan roses, but now I wasn't so sure.

But the way he'd joined in when Niall was being awful to Shane. I'd never forget that.

I rolled my eyes. 'You can thank Niall for that.'

'It sucks when things change,' he said, and I smiled at him in empathy.

'Yeah, it really does,' I agreed.

I sat down at one of the tables and Hunter sat down beside me.

'Still not going to V-Ball?' he asked, raising his eyebrows.

I hesitated. I hadn't thought this through. 'I don't think so.'

'Oh, you don't *think* so? So there's doubt?' He grinned and for the first time I realized that Hunter had a really nice smile. One of those contagious ones that I had to actively try not to smile back at.

'What I really meant was, no, I'm not going,' I said, surprised at how easily the lie came out. I'd deal with that later.

'Oh,' he said, looking disappointed.

'Well, seeing that my number-one choice is bailing, I might ask Zoe,' he said, scanning my face like he was waiting for my reaction.

'That's a really great idea, she's gorgeous,' I said.

I saw a flicker of disappointment in his eyes before he stood up. I really hoped Zoe would say yes to Hunter, unless she'd found someone else to go with after Shane had said no.

'Yeah, she's cool. We'd better go – the bell's about to ring.' He held out his hand for me to stand up.

I laughed and took it, then he spun me round like we were dancing.

I tried to move away. 'Hunter, what the hell?'

'Just getting my dance now.' He pulled me into him, so we were centimetres apart.

I was rigid and he must have felt it. I don't know what he was hoping for here. A kiss? I tried to make my face neutral so my reluctance to be this close to him wouldn't be so totally obvious.

'Oh look, there's Zoe,' I said, delighted that she'd walked in. 'Hey, Zoe!' I called and escaped from him. 'There you go, Hunter, now's your chance.' I winked at him and walked towards the door.

'You two were looking pretty cosy,' Zoe said, her eyes flicking from me to Hunter. Her tone frostier than usual.

'He's all yours,' I said.

As I left, I wondered if she was pissed off that I was starting in the match instead of her. Maybe she didn't even know about it. The decision had seemed kind of last minute.

At home I ate pasta, I did stretches, I drank water. I needed to be focused.

I sent a message to Shane before I left.

ME: Wish me luck x

But there was no reply. Nothing. And I didn't have time to sit and watch my phone. We had to leave.

'Alexandra, you ready?' Dad jingled his keys.

'Always ready.' I smiled, knowing by the fact Dad hadn't called for Niall that he wasn't coming, and my stomach sank with disappointment. Yeah, he was upset about Megan, but this was the biggest thing that had ever happened to me. I'd thought that maybe he'd want to be there.

'Just us?' I asked.

Dad smiled. 'Just us.'

I was one of the first ones there. I jogged on to the pitch to stand beside Sadie.

She looked me dead in the eyes. 'Hi, Lexie. You ready?'

I forced Shane and Niall and everything else out of my head. 'Yes.'

I scanned the pitch. Floodlights, frozen breath, the sound of warm-up footballs being smashed into nets. This was it. *This* was what I'd been training for. The *first* team.

I went over all the things Shane had taught me at our extra practices. Defence tactics, the Cruyff turn, I would use them all and Sadie would wonder why she hadn't played me before.

I gazed over at the crowd hoping to see Shane. But he wasn't there. I waved to Dad, who was waving right back at me. And right beside him? Megan. She waved too, then jogged on to the pitch towards me. She wasn't wearing a Westing kit.

'I couldn't miss it. I'll be in the dugout. Good luck, Lex – show them what you've got.' She hesitated before reaching over to hug me. I melted into her for a second, before pulling away. And it shook me. My head was a mess. I wanted to hug her again, to fix everything that had happened between us, but this wasn't the time.

'You're not playing?' I asked, confused.

She shook her head. 'Sadie wants me to rest before the trials; she's worried I'll get injured. Zoe's playing my position, I think.'

I turned round to see Zoe warming up behind me.

'That's why I'm playing,' I said out loud. Of course Sadie wasn't going to play me over Zoe. How stupid could I be? Tears welled in my eyes.

'Hey, Lex, what's wrong?' Megan asked, her hand on my arm.

I brushed it off and stepped back. 'The only reason I'm playing is because you're not. I thought . . .' I stopped before I embarrassed myself.

'Who cares? Why does it matter *why* you're starting? You're starting, Lex – this is all you've wanted for so long.' She tried to grab my hands to make her point, but I moved away and she flinched.

Who was she to tell me what I wanted? Her words just sounded patronizing. Megan, who was leaving for England at the end of the summer, who didn't even appreciate being invited to NI trials.

'Why are you even here?' I said.

'To see you play,' she said sadly.

'I don't need you. I don't need Niall. I don't need anyone.' I turned away and squeezed my eyes shut for a second before I ran back to the team.

'It's going to be a tough game; this team hasn't been beaten by anyone all season. So let's make it their first loss. Lexie and Hazel, cover each other. Zoe, you're taking Megan's spot, so you do what she does. Do not stop running. Come on, girls. You can do this.' Sadie emphasized each word like she needed us to know how much she meant it.

I took one last look at the crowd to see if Shane or Niall had come at the last minute. But they hadn't. Now I had to get my head in the game. And I did. I tackled the way Shane had shown me, marked players far better than I ever had, and my passes were way more accurate. Lola scored at the end of the first half, and we were one–nil up. I was buzzing when I ran in for the team talk.

'Nice work, girls. Zoe, you're doing a great job in midfield, and Lexie, excellent work. I can see a huge improvement in your skills. Hannah, keep focused – they're going to come back strong in the second half. We can win this, girls. Come on!'

Sadie was right. The other team did come back strong. It was like they were faster, more skilful, fitter than us. They scored an early goal, and we fell apart. I couldn't concentrate. I started throwing myself into tackles, made sloppy passes and with each mistake I just felt worse. And even more pissed off.

When it went out and should have been a goal kick, I snapped. 'It's not a corner!'

The ref ignored me and pointed to the side line. 'Corner ball.'

I kicked the ground. 'It's not a *fucking* corner.'

The ref blew her whistle and called me over. 'There's no swearing on my pitch. Any more of that and it'll be a red card.'

I nodded through gritted teeth.

'Lexie, settle!' Sadie called from the sidelines.

I couldn't look at her. I'd done all this training, and I still wasn't good enough. I just didn't have it in me to be good for a whole match.

And then we were losing. Two–one.

And after wishing so hard that they'd been there during the first half, I was so glad that Shane or Niall hadn't come to see me make such an embarrassment of myself.

Zoe got man of the match and Sadie couldn't seem to stop telling her how great she was as a midfielder. And I didn't have the energy to hide my feelings. The lump in my throat was getting bigger and I had to leave the pitch before they saw me cry.

'Lex,' I heard Megan say.

Why had she stayed? I hated that she'd stayed to see that mess of a match. I couldn't even look at her. So I waited until she started talking to Sadie before I walked past them and over to Dad.

On the way home, Dad tried to make me feel better.

'That was a great pass you made to . . . What do you call her? The redhead?'

'Zoe,' I said, her name bitter on my tongue.

'And you didn't stop. The whole time, Lexie, you didn't stop running. I'm so impressed.'

It was like he was trying to think of anything positive to say. And that's why, halfway home, he ran out of words and left me alone.

I looked at my phone.

> **SHANE:** Aw shit, I'm so sorry. I thought the match was next week. How did it go?

Then I cried. Right there in the car. Silent tears, but not silent enough.

'Lexie, don't cry,' Dad said. 'Focus on the good parts. Yeah, it was a tough second half, but you were all over them in the first half. And that goal? It came from your clearance out of the box.'

I shook my head and didn't say anything because I didn't want him to hear my voice clogged with tears. Shane forgot? He knew how important it was to me.

> **ME:** It was terrible. I was terrible. We lost and at least one of the goals was my fault

> **SHANE:** No. A goal is never the fault of one person. It's a TEAM sport. I bet it wasn't as bad as you think

> **ME:** It was. I let the team down. Sadie will never want me on the firsts again

> **SHANE:** I've had awful games too

I knew he was lying, but it helped.

ME: Really?

SHANE: Really. Everyone has off days. It doesn't say anything about you. You're brilliant, Lexie, and I wish I'd been there. I'm so sorry. How can I make it up to you?

ME: Be excited for V-Ball

I knew he'd been hesitating, and so had I, thinking about how it would look. All the people who would be upset when they found out about us: Niall, Hunter, Megan, Zoe. But I wanted it, like I needed to prove something. When I walked into V-Ball with Shane on my arm, I wanted the whole school to know I was worthy of someone like that.

20

Then all of a sudden it was Saturday. V-Ball day, and Megan was at our house, before the NI trials. We hadn't spoken since the match. The one I was desperately trying not to think about; like if I pretended it didn't happen, then maybe Sadie would forget too. But I couldn't forget. Not completely. And every time it burst into my mind, it reminded me that Shane hadn't come, that Niall hadn't come, and that Megan had witnessed the car crash.

When I came out of my bedroom she was sitting half on top of Niall on the sofa while he played some game I didn't recognize. They'd obviously made up with each other. I didn't understand it. Megan was leaving for England and Niall was all loved up again?

When she saw me, she got up to go to the bathroom and left me with Niall.

Silence, except for the guns blasting from the screen.

'So you lost last night then?'

It was like a slap in the face.

'Yeah, but they were really good. Haven't been beaten all season,' I shot back.

'Meg said you didn't have a great game. So annoying when that happens.'

Something burned in my stomach. Was this some half-arsed attempt at being supportive?

'She said what?' I spat out.

'No, not like in a bad way. She was being nice. She felt bad because it was your first game with the team.' Niall stopped playing and looked at me, his shaggy blonde hair half over his eyes.

'She said I played shit in a *good* way?' I dared him to clarify.

He sighed. 'She didn't say you played shit. Jesus, Lexie.'

'Actually, everybody played terribly; it wasn't just me.' My words were running together and getting mixed up. Tears welled in my eyes.

'OK,' Niall said, going back to his game.

Megan knew something was wrong as soon as she came back. Because it was written all over my face, and I was too angry to even try to change my expression.

'What? What's wrong?'

'Ask your boyfriend,' I said, standing up.

'Niall?' Megan looked at him, waiting for an explanation.

'What?' he said. 'We were just talking about the match last night and Lexie turned into a psychopath.'

'Are you serious?' I was shouting now. 'Niall told me what you said. That I had a shit game.' And then I was crying, hot angry tears that I couldn't wipe away fast enough.

'I did not say you had a shit game. Niall!' Megan slapped him on the shoulder.

'Meg, I didn't say that. I said that you said she didn't have the best game and by the sounds of things she didn't, so why am I getting yelled at?'

'Fuck sake, Niall!' Megan looked at him, then back at me. 'I was just telling him about the game in general, that the team we were playing were really good,' she said, trying to backtrack. 'And I told him you had a great first half!' She sounded desperate.

'You think I'm rubbish. You know what? Good luck for your trials. See you whenever.' I ran into my bedroom and lay down on the bed. If I'd been thinking straight, I would have stopped the tears before they made my face red and puffy. But I couldn't. It hurt too much. And it wasn't just the fact that Megan had said it, but that she'd said it to Niall. Deep down I knew she thought that. Of course she did. How could she not?

But Niall? It was so pathetic that when I thought back to when we were kids, the times I remember feeling the happiest were the times when I did something, and Niall thought it was great. There was this time I did a trick on my skateboard and Niall said it was 'amazing' and made me show all his mates. I was on cloud nine for days.

I didn't even say goodbye to Megan and Niall before they left for the trials. I didn't wish her good luck and ignored her knock on my door. I'd also been ignoring Zoe's messages; she was asking if I was coming to Amina's because they were meeting there and getting a car together.

I spent hours getting ready: make-up, hair, fake tan, nails, everything. I needed to look perfect for Shane. I wanted to blow him away and surprise the whole school when I showed up with the hottest guy ever.

I put my dress on, sprayed perfume and slid on my heels. I looked at myself in the mirror. Satisfied. Almost.

I was meeting Shane there. Usually if I wasn't seeing him until later, like at practice or something, he would send me messages during the day. But I hadn't heard from him all afternoon. I guess it was better that way, then I could surprise him properly. We were going to meet under the flower arch outside the assembly hall.

I was driving myself there. But before I left, Mum and Dad made me stand in the kitchen to get photos taken.

'So beautiful, Lexie.' Mum looked like she was about to cry.

'Gorgeous,' Dad agreed. 'And you're meeting Zoe there?' He looked concerned.

'Yep, she's waiting for me already.' I smiled the way I knew made him relax.

'OK. Well, have an amazing time, Lexie, and no drinking.'

I reached over and hugged him. 'Dad, I'm driving. And thanks.' I cringed at the memory of Dad watching the game last night, like some horror movie stuck on repeat in my head.

I shook it off. Soon I'd be with Shane. He'd see me looking amazing, and everything would be perfect.

'Are you sure you don't want me to drive you?' Dad asked as I picked up my keys and walked towards the door.

'And show up to V-Ball with my *Dad*?' I teased.

He held up his hands in surrender, and I laughed before going over to give them both a quick hug, excitement building and hard to hide.

I waited outside the assembly hall, sitting on one of the chairs that was probably intended for the teachers, and watched groups and couples walking in, laughing, happy. That would be me soon. I watched the entrance, scanning every single male face that came through the door. I was worried I'd miss him in the sea of tuxedos, so I stood up to get a better look. But he wasn't any of them.

'Lex?' Hunter broke free from his group and came over to me. He looked confused. 'Thought you weren't coming tonight?'

I shrugged, still watching the door. 'Yeah, changed my mind last minute.'

'I came with Zoe,' he said. 'Where's Niall? It's been radio silence from him lately.'

'He's away with Megan to the NI trials,' I said, avoiding his gaze.

'You waiting for someone?'

'Just a friend.'

'Do I know them?'

And this time I looked at him. Into the brown eyes that were searching mine for an answer.

'It's actually Shane,' I said. There was no point trying to hide it; he was about to walk through the door.

'Shane from football Shane?' Hunter's eyes were wide, and he looked around like he was trying to find someone to tell.

'Yeah. Niall doesn't know yet,' I said.

'Fuck, he is not going to take that well. You're really going out with that dick?'

'Yeah. And he's not a dick,' I said, trying my best not to rise to his words, one eye still on the door.

'So why didn't you just say? I mean, I didn't like you *that* much that my whole world would end if I knew. In fact, I kind of just asked you out of convenience. Nobody actually cares. Except Niall. He'll lose his shit.' Hunter waited for me to answer.

And, whether it was true or not, his words still stung.

'It wasn't about that. It was about Niall finding out.' I felt my hands prick with sweat when I glanced up and Shane still wasn't walking through the door.

'Yeah, good luck with that.' Hunter laughed cruelly. 'I'm away to find Zoe.'

I felt like telling him that Zoe had asked Shane to V-Ball just to wipe the smug smile off his face, but I was too distracted. I went back to watching the door as he walked away, feeling sick as the crowds of people coming in started to tail off.

I looked at my phone again. No messages. Where was he? Maybe he'd got it wrong. Maybe he thought we were meeting in the hall. I sent him a message.

ME: You on your way?

I stared at the screen, waiting for the little blue ticks that would tell me that he'd read it. But they didn't come and now the hint of nausea from earlier was out of control. I felt uncomfortable standing there at the door where everyone could see me being stood up, and at the same time wondering how many people Hunter had told.

I walked into the assembly hall. It was packed with kids from school, all looking completely at home in their black-tie suits and dresses. The band played some upbeat cover I didn't recognize. Lights swirled overhead, casting sparkles and shadows everywhere. I walked around, scanning faces, touching shoulders of dark-haired, tuxedo-wearing boys, just to have them turn round and not be Shane.

The head teacher gave a speech, the dance floor filled with couples kissing, and still, no Shane. I watched Hunter dance with Zoe, who looked gorgeous in a long white satin dress. I watched him whisper to her and then they both looked at me. I felt like an idiot standing there alone, watching all these couples having the night of their lives.

The tears were coming back. I could feel them at the back of my eyes and in the back of my throat. He was supposed to be here. It was supposed to be perfect. Zoe threw back her head laughing at something Hunter had said, then someone nudged into me, spilling their drink on my dress. And that was the final straw.

The band had just started playing some slowed-up version of Coldplay's 'The Scientist' as I ran through the crowd. I needed to get out of there. It was like the room was closing in. All these people, except for the one I needed. Maybe he was too embarrassed to be seen with me after I'd told him how crap I played last night?

By the time I got out of the hall, I was a mess. Strands of hair had come out of their clips and there was no way my mascara hadn't run. I took out my phone to ring Dad, just to hear a friendly voice. But, just as I did, I heard my name.

I looked up and my heart stopped. There he was, standing at the flower arch, just like we'd arranged, in his tuxedo. Out of breath, his bow tie askew, dark hair over one eye.

'I'm so sorry I'm late,' he said.

I was already halfway to him, tears rolling down my cheeks, reaching up to pull him into a kiss because I needed him. The one person who made me feel like I wasn't a complete and utter failure.

'I sent you a message,' I said, as I pulled away, steadying my voice.

He felt in his pocket for his phone. 'Sorry, I didn't check. Everything was a bit chaotic. But I'm here now.' His brow was furrowed.

I reached up and touched it gently, watching the tension disappear. 'Are you OK?' I asked. I was worried.

He smiled and pushed his hair back off his face. 'I am now.'

I pulled him back into the hall where another slow song was playing, and led him to the dance floor.

We didn't talk. He didn't explain why he was late. He just held me as we danced in the enchanted garden and kissed like nobody was watching.

21

But everybody *was* watching. I could feel their eyes on us, and I could see couples whispering behind their hands and some openly pointing. This was what I'd wanted. For me and Shane to show up at Blackport like an explosion and for everyone to want what I had. I thought it would feel good. But it didn't. I wished I could turn back time to when nobody knew about us. When Shane pulled away, he lifted my chin gently like he'd sensed the panic.

'Are *you* OK?'

I nodded, scared to speak in case I cried again. 'I thought you weren't coming,' I whispered.

'I'm sorry. I just had some stuff going on.'

'Why won't you tell me anything?' I said without thinking.

He looked into my eyes as the music played and we swayed together, his hand tightening its grip on my back, like he was trying to work out what to say. But why was it so hard?

'I don't want to ruin it,' he said. 'You'd think of me differently, and I don't . . . I can't . . . I just love what we have – does that make sense?'

I nodded, even though it didn't make any sense at all. Then someone tapped me on the shoulder.

I pulled away from Shane to see Zoe standing there, still trying to digest what Shane had just said.

'Hi, Shane.' She smiled sweetly at him.

'Hey, Zoe,' he replied.

'So this is who you were seeing?' Zoe looked to Shane for an answer. 'Lexie?'

'Yeah, we were just keeping things quiet,' Shane said.

'Well, you know the whole school is talking about it.' Zoe looked at me. 'And Hunter said Niall doesn't know yet?' She pulled a face.

I shrugged, trying to act like I didn't care, even though every time someone mentioned Niall's name my stomach lurched. 'Not yet.'

'Well, I'd say he does now.' Zoe pulled a worried face. She showed me her phone screen. 'Amina just sent me this.'

It was a picture of me and Shane kissing, and I wanted to be sick. What did I expect?

I felt Shane squeeze my hand, and it made me braver knowing he was there. I moved closer to him and whispered, 'Do you want to get out of here?'

He nodded so I pulled him towards the back of the hall, a million eyes on us.

'Oh, Lexie?' Zoe called above the music.

I spun round. 'What?'

She smiled. 'Great game last night, wasn't it?'

And she smiled like she meant it, but how could she? The second half was a total disaster.

'I have an idea,' I said, as I walked towards the exit with Shane.

I opened the door at the back of the hall and walked out into the night. Megan had done it before with Jasper in Year Thirteen, after one of the previous Year Fourteen's had told her if you go into the caretaker's room at the back, there's a spare key to the pool in a red box on one of the shelves.

'Where are we going?' Shane asked as I took off my shoes and pulled up my dress.

'You'll see. Come on.' I ran across the grass, ignoring the buzzing phone in my bag.

When we reached the building at the bottom of the hill, the one that overlooked the lake, I pushed the caretaker's door and hoped to God it would open.

'Yes,' I whispered, as it did.

It was dark, and Shane followed me inside. We used our phones as torches and scanned the shelves for a red box.

'That one!' I pointed it out to Shane.

He brushed past me and reached up for the box, then passed it to me.

'And the key should be in . . . here.' I pulled the box open and there it was, a silver key shining at me.

We walked back round to the main door of the pool. Shane kept watch as I twisted the key in the lock, trying to be as silent as possible. I pushed the door open and pulled him in behind me.

'Is this a swimming pool?' Shane asked, inhaling the chlorine air.

I smiled. 'Maybe.'

'Are you serious? We have to use the gross one in town.'

The pool glowed turquoise with the underwater lights. I led him to the edge, and we stared down at the water together.

'What now?' Shane asked, leaning into me.

I didn't say anything. Just took off my dress and dived into the pool. And when I came up for air, Shane was staring at me with a smile on his face.

I splashed water towards him, and he moved backwards, laughing.

'Come on!'

'Sorry. Coming now.'

I watched him as he took off his suit, slowly, carefully, folding each piece of it on the bench. I ran my eyes over him standing there in his boxers. I'd never wanted anything more. My gaze stopped on his legs. Half-healed cuts and bruises patchworked on his skin.

'Jesus, Shane, your legs,' I said, treading water.

'Ah, yeah, way worse now I play for Westing. Didn't have any of that at Ferndale, unless I was playing against Oscar, who just hacks you because he has zero coordination.' He laughed and walked to the edge of the pool. Because of the light and the shadows, I could see every contour of his stomach. The outline of the muscle, the V-cut abs and the way he clearly didn't know or care how amazing he looked. He jumped in beside me. When he emerged from the water, he pulled me close and I wrapped my legs round his waist, mouth on mouth, melting into each other.

Ecstasy. My mind was one hundred per cent on Shane. Where Niall or Megan or Zoe couldn't touch it. Not even football got a look in.

After we swam, we sat on the edge in soaking underwear, leaning against each other to keep warm.

'You look amazing tonight,' Shane said, turning to me.

And we kissed again, cold wet bodies pressed against each other.

Shane sighed. 'I wish we could do this all the time.'

'Why can't we?'

'Life, I guess.' He hesitated, then said, 'Football?' He nudged me. 'How much do you love it?'

'More than anything,' I said genuinely.

'Yeah, I can tell. The way you talk about it. Actually, it's kind of made me realize how much I *don't* love it. Your eyes light up when you talk about the game, you know that?'

I looked down. 'Do they?'

And I suppose it made sense. It was the one thing that had always made me happy. Regardless of what else was going on in my life, football was the 'quiet' in my head. The one thing I loved more than anything else . . . until Shane.

He laughed. 'They do.'

'Like yours do when you talk about your dad.'

He stared at me for a second then smiled. 'God, that's so uncool. Do I talk about him too much? I don't mean to; it's just . . .'

'What?'

'Ever since I was a kid, I would have done anything to try and make him proud. And I guess it never went away.'

'Football?'

'Yeah. But how do you tell someone you've spent your whole life trying to impress that you don't love the thing they love?' He flicked the water with his feet, and we watched it splash back into the pool. 'He wants me to go pro.'

'But if it doesn't make you happy, I bet he'd understand?' I said, reaching for his hand and sliding my fingers between his.

'Yeah. I don't know. I'm not brave, not like you, the way you give everything and put yourself out there to get what you want. I'm not like that. I just want everyone to be happy.'

Brave? I wasn't brave. Stubborn maybe . . .

'That's really nice. That you want everyone to be happy,' I said, my stomach sinking.

'Don't you?' he asked with no judgement.

I thought about Niall and Megan. How I didn't care if they were happy together or not; I just hated how it made *me* feel.

'Maybe not all the time,' I admitted. 'Maybe I'm just selfish.'

'I don't think trying really hard to get what you want makes you selfish, and if it does, maybe I should be a bit more selfish.' He smiled and held my hand to his mouth, kissing it. 'You've gone somewhere,' he said with a laugh. 'Are you OK?'

I shook my head and brought myself back. 'Yeah.'

He stood up and pulled me with him. 'We need some towels.'

I pointed. 'Down there.' There was a stack of white towels all rolled up for whatever classes were in here on Monday.

I followed him and we dried ourselves before putting our ball clothes back on.

'I should go,' he said, though he didn't make a move to go anywhere.

'Already? How come?' I decided to just put it out there and ask him directly. 'Please tell me. Tell me why you're always mysteriously leaving. I'm starting to suspect you've got a second life. Like one of those internet scammers.' I tried to make light of it by grinning, but he only smiled briefly back at me.

'I promise I'll tell you, just not tonight.'

He leaned down and kissed me gently, before taking my hand and walking out into the freezing-cold night and on to the pitches. And when he didn't say anything, I filled the silence, because despite the fact there was still this roadblock between us, I wasn't ready for the night to end. 'Do you have time for one more dance?'

'What about your wet hair? They'll know we broke into the pool.'

He was right. I wasn't thinking straight. We'd already caused enough of a shock for one night.

'OK, come on.' I led him round the side of the assembly hall towards the car park.

I leaned against the brick wall and let him lift me up, so my back was pressed against it, my legs wrapped round him. And we kissed like we hadn't been doing the same thing all night.

'Lexie?'

I looked up quickly, scratching my back on the wall. Shane put me down and we both turned.

And there in the dark, staring at us, were Niall and Megan, their mouths open.

'So it's true. You know, I sort of hoped it was some kind of AI, Photoshop crap, but I guess I never was the smart one.' Niall was looking right at me. He didn't even acknowledge Shane.

Megan tried to pull Niall away, but he didn't move. 'Niall, let's go. Leave them to it.'

'Seriously, Lexie? Are you fucking kidding me?' He kicked the ground and twisted away before turning back to us with a look of complete disbelief. 'This prick?' Then he was looking at Shane and they were staring at each other like two animals before one of them pounces on the other.

And that's when I should have said something, stood up for myself, stood up for Shane, but the words were stuck in my throat, and even if I could have got them out, I didn't know what they would be.

Shane moved so he was standing in front of me, and I was so grateful. Not because I thought Niall would hurt me, but because I couldn't bear to look at him any more.

'Just leave it, man,' Shane said.

I waited for it, the moment that Niall snapped and lunged for Shane, but it didn't come. He just scoffed, took one last look at us, turned and walked away.

I thought it would feel good. Getting my own back on Niall, showing him that I was doing exactly what he told me to do. Living my own life. There I was, with my boyfriend at the school formal, showing my brother that I didn't need him, that I could do what I wanted without caring what he thought. I thought it would be liberating.

But it wasn't.

Niall's look of disgust was directed at me, not Shane. And I felt even smaller than ever.

22

Niall stormed inside the school and didn't look back. Megan hung behind, looking at me like she was going to ask something, then disappeared after Niall.

'Are you OK?' Shane asked when they were out of sight.

I inhaled, trying to slow the heartbeat that was so strong it was thudding in my ears.

'Yeah, I'm fine,' I lied. I leaned into his chest. 'I just didn't expect . . .' I paused.

'Expect what?' Shane asked, pushing wet hair behind my ear.

'How upset he'd look.'

'He kind of just looked pissed off to me.'

I gave a small laugh and stepped back from his chest. 'That's the thing about Niall, when he's upset, he gets angry. Like really angry. And he's never been that angry at me before.' I sighed and leaned against the wall.

'Ah, OK. But why? I don't get it. Is it just the football thing?'

Blood rushed to my head, and I slammed my hand against the wall in frustration.

'Hey.' He grabbed it, holding it tightly, pressing my skin to his lips.

'Maybe you should go . . .' I said, trying not to cry.

'I'm not leaving you like this.' He had concern in his eyes. 'Let's walk.'

I nodded and let him pull me away from the wall. I shivered and he took off his jacket, wrapping it round my shoulders.

'Thanks.'

'Your brother really hates me,' Shane said.

'Well, you know that stuff you said about your dad? How you want to impress him? Niall's like that with our dad too, and I guess you taking his position hurt his pride or whatever.' I shrugged. I knew exactly how much it must have hurt him.

'Ah, OK. Well, what if I stepped away? Went back to Ferndale, would that help?'

'You can't,' I said. Shane leaving would mean seeing him less.

'But if it made things easier? And you know I don't want the position. Not really.'

I took a deep breath. 'I hardly see you as it is. And you'd have to tell your dad,' I said.

Shane inhaled and looked away before turning back and staring into my eyes. 'I'd do it for you. I mean, we've just outed ourselves to everyone, so I guess that makes us official? And couples do things for each other.' He pushed a strand of wet hair from my face.

I reached up and kissed him. 'I think I might be falling in love with you,' I whispered into the night.

He smiled. 'Might be?'

I laughed. 'I *am* falling in love with you.'

And he didn't hesitate. 'I was thinking the same thing.'

I leaned into his chest, listening to the thud of his heart and replaying the words we'd just said to each other over and over. We stood like that until I started to shiver. Then I snaked my arms round his waist and under his shirt.

He jumped from the shock of my cold hands.

'Sorry.'

'You're freezing!'

'I know, my dress is soaking.' My teeth started to chatter.

'Ah Lexie, you need to get home.'

'I'm fine.'

He laughed. 'Let me walk you back to your car.'

I let him lead me towards the car park. 'Do you want a lift home?'

'From my girlfriend? Sure. Thanks.'

He grinned and I smiled back.

We held hands the whole way to the car, and when I drove, his hand was on top of mine as I moved the gear stick.

'Did you have any girlfriends at St Anne's?' I asked, a bit scared of the answer. I knew if he said yes, I'd be jealous, even though that wasn't fair. But I wanted to know how experienced he was.

'Nope, it's always just been school and football,' he said. 'I never met anyone I really liked. Not like this.' He squeezed my hand. 'What about you? How many posh boys have you been out with?'

I laughed. 'None. Same, school and football, and hanging out with Niall and Megan.'

'Are you guys still not talking? You and Megan?'

I took a deep breath. 'Nope, and now I guess it'll be even worse.'

He sighed. 'Aw, Lexie. I'm sorry I'm making such a mess of your life.'

I wanted to stop the car right there in the middle of the road, grab his face and show him that all he'd done was make my life better, despite all the other stuff. 'You're not. Not at all. I've spent so long just being this other part of Niall, I didn't even think about what could be beyond that. And you've given me that. You know what I mean?' I looked over at him and for a split second I thought I saw his eyes glisten.

He looked down at his knees. 'Yeah, completely.'

'You make my life make more sense.'

Shane coughed. 'Jesus, I think that's the nicest thing anyone's ever said to me.'

I laughed and turned to him. He was staring at me. 'You make my life make more sense too.'

I turned up the music and treated Shane to a concert all the way to his house. But when we pulled into his street it was like I could feel the tension come back. The same tension that showed up when I pushed him for answers that he didn't want to give me.

I pulled up at the kerb outside his house.

'Thanks, Lexie, for an amazing and kind of weird night.'

'Always here for amazing and weird.'

He pecked me on the lips before getting out of the car and didn't even turn round before he walked into his house.

On the way home I played the song we'd been listening to on repeat, pretending that he was still there, trying desperately to forget the strange tension and the way he left without one last goodbye.

Mum and Dad were still up when I got in.

Dad looked confused when I put my keys down on the kitchen island. 'Is your hair wet?'

'Don't ask,' I replied.

'Are you OK?' he asked, still looking at my hair.

I smiled. 'Yeah, I'm absolutely fine.'

'Megan's trials went well I heard. She's been asked back for the next round,' Dad said. 'Niall phoned us after they ended.'

And my happiness dissolved. Just like that.

'Great.'

'Stephen,' Mum said, warning him not to say any more.

Dad looked at Mum in confusion. 'What?'

She shook her head and turned to me, wine glass in hand. 'How was V-Ball, Lexie? And why on earth *is* your hair wet?' She laughed, trying her best to lighten the thundercloud that filled my head.

'It was great,' I said, smiling, 'and I *might* have gone for a swim.'

Mum had always been good at dragging me out of my head.

She looked shocked but happy. 'What? They let you swim at these things?'

'Em, yeah?'

Dad looked horrified. 'Lexie!'

'You're only young once.' Mum chucked a packet of crisps at Dad's head. 'I remember when your father and I were at school . . .'

'Georgina!' Now it was Dad who was warning Mum not to carry on.

'Fine, fine. Glad you had fun, love. Have you heard from Niall?'

My stomach dropped. 'Nope.'

'Oh, that's a shame. You and Niall don't seem as close any more. Has something happened?' she asked.

'He's just busy with Megan,' I said. 'But I'm kind of tired, so I'm going to go to bed.'

'OK, night, love.' They said the last part together.

When I got to my room, I couldn't stop thinking of the way Shane kissed me, the way his fingers traced my skin and made me want him. Then I remembered the look on Niall's face. The disgust. The betrayal. And the good thoughts were dust.

It was getting almost impossible to get up now. All the extra training I'd been doing meant that I was exhausted every morning, even if I wasn't getting up early to meet Shane.

I forced my eyes open, then pulled the duvet over my head as I remembered last night. I could have just kept it all a secret, but now? Everyone knew and now I'd have to deal with it.

I checked my phone.

SHANE: Good morning x

And then it all felt worth it. The complicated mess of my life didn't matter when I had Shane. He'd said that he *loved* me.

ME: I heard Thunderland is back in town. Date night?

SHANE: Tonight?

181

ME: If you're free?

SHANE: I'm there. But . . .

ME: But?

SHANE: I'm terrified of fairground rides

ME: I'll protect you

SHANE: Meet you there at 8?

ME: Can't wait. I can pick you up if you like?

SHANE: Sure, thanks

'Morning, Lexie,' Mum said when I eventually got up. I was dressed for training and planned to get a couple of hours in on the pitch outside. 'So, tell me about last night; now your dad's not here. You can tell me all the good stuff.' She grinned, then took a sip from a cup of coffee.

'It was great,' I said before I could think. But she'd already seen my smile. 'I'm kind of going out with someone . . .'

I let the comment hang in the air and enjoyed seeing Mum's face light up.

'What? How did I not know? Is this new?' She put down her cup.

'I guess. Kind of . . .'

Mum tapped the seat beside her. 'Sit!'

I sat down.

'What's his name?'

'Shane.'

'Shane. That's a nice name. What school does he go to?'

'St Anne's.'

She smirked. 'Excellent school.' Mum had gone to St Anne's. 'Where did you meet him?'

'Football.'

'When can I meet him?'

I glanced at my phone that was sitting on the table. Message after message asking me about Shane. I didn't have the energy for it. Some messages were even from numbers I didn't recognize. Apprehension churned in my stomach.

I forced out a laugh at Mum's question and got down from the seat to do some stretching, then walked towards the French doors.

'Lexie, you're not training *again*, are you?' Mum asked, concern on her face.

'What's wrong with training?'

I was used to her telling me to stop doing so much, but I'd never actually asked her why.

'You can do too much is what's wrong.'

'How would you know?' I snapped back and felt immediately bad.

She inhaled and looked at me for a second. 'Can I show you something?'

I was itching to get outside – like my muscles were on a timer – but she'd already left the kitchen to get something, so I stood there waiting, staring at the clock.

She came back with one of those lever-arch files I used at school. 'Come, take a look,' she said.

She set the file on the kitchen counter and opened it. It was full of tennis articles.

St Anne's eleven-year-old tennis superstar Georgina Callow wins again.

Child tennis prodigy Georgina Callow showing huge promise for the future.

'Wait. What's this?' I looked at Mum, and then back to the file. 'This was you?'

She nodded.

'But why didn't I know this? You were some kind of prodigy?'

Mum shook her head. 'I wasn't that good. But that's the point. My parents had me training so hard, six days a week, tennis, tennis, tennis, and I lost out on so much, on friends, on a social life, on anything that wasn't related to tennis. And guess what? As soon as I got to about fourteen it was clear to everyone that I wasn't good enough to become professional.'

My stomach lurched. 'And you didn't tell me because . . .'

'Because I didn't think it would be helpful. I could see how seriously you were taking your football, and I don't know, I thought it might give you extra pressure, like you had to prove something. That you could do better. And I don't want you to miss out on life like I did. Lexie, life is a million different things, it's not just one hobby. Life at your age should be having fun, kissing boys, or girls, laughing so hard with Megan that your stomach hurts, or playing that stupid Xbox with Niall. It should be trying to figure out who you are. Of course it has to be exams and all the boring stuff too, but it's so, *so* much more than just a sport.'

I shook my head. I couldn't take it in, whatever she was saying. 'I can't believe nobody told me. Does Niall know how good you were?'

'Do I know what?' Niall walked into the kitchen looking exhausted.

'That Mum was some kind of tennis sensation and she didn't tell me to try and save my feelings because I'll never be as good.' I didn't mean to cry, but I couldn't help it.

'Lexie, you're completely missing the point,' Mum said, putting her hand on my shoulder.

I shook it off. Humiliated.

'Of course I knew. Everyone in Seaport knows. If you type any of our names into Google, it comes up. And of course nobody wanted to tell you, Lexie; nobody wants to tell you anything because of the way you react, like it's some huge conspiracy against you –'

'Niall,' Mum cut in.

'And another thing,' Niall said. 'Do you really think Mum wants to talk about it? You think she wants to go over that again? Did you even think about how hard it must have been for her to tell you? Or how hard it was for Megan when you found out about us? And I bet you didn't even think about it, going out with the bloody baller, knowing how it would make me feel. Lexie, you're so selfish it makes me sick.' Niall abandoned his words in the kitchen and left me standing there with Mum.

'Is it true?' I asked Mum.

She nodded. 'I suppose it is. It's difficult to talk about, and I don't know if it's fair, but I blame my parents for a lot of it, and I promised myself that if I had kids, I'd never put that pressure on them. But, Lexie, you put that pressure on yourself, and I just don't want the same thing happening to you. I can see it, the look on your face when you play. It's more than just a hobby. And I'm so glad you've met a nice boy and are enjoying things that aren't football.' She reached out to take my hand and I thought about pulling it away, like I usually would, but at the perfect moment, the way Shane saw things from a different point of view came back to me. Like the way he'd done with Megan and the trials. I made myself think like Mum. If I had kids, would I want them to try as hard as I did?

'He's really nice,' I said, my voice choked with tears.

'Oh, Lexie.' Mum pulled me into a hug. I breathed in her familiar perfume and let myself cry into her shoulder.

'You know that's not why I didn't tell you. The things Niall said. I know how deeply you feel everything. And it's a beautiful thing. I just couldn't bear to see you hurt.'

'I know,' I whispered.

'There's so much more to life than sports. Like boys,' Mum teased. 'Oh, and if you want me to stay at home instead of going away with your dad over the next while, will you tell me? Just say the word and I'm here.' She smiled.

'Thanks, Mum, but I'll be fine.' I didn't need a babysitter. I needed time alone, to think about everything.

I went back up to my room to daydream about Shane.

23

I stayed in my room the rest of the day, talking to Shane.

> **ME:** Found out today that my mum was actually some tennis prodigy when she was a kid

> **SHANE:** Wow, that's so cool! So she's the reason you're so good at football then?

I smiled at his message. Before Shane I would have pushed back on the compliment if anyone had said something like that, but I felt like I didn't have to with him.

> **ME:** Maybe ☺ But the thing is, she never told me. She kept it a secret my whole life. Even Niall knew. She said she didn't tell me because she thought it would put pressure on me

I sent him one of the links about Mum.

SHANE: I think it's really nice that she'd think that way. Are you OK? That she didn't tell you?

ME: I don't know. Am I difficult to talk to?

I put it out there, hoping it would trigger him into telling me his secrets.

SHANE: I think you're the opposite

I left his message there for five minutes, staring at the hypocrisy, hoping he'd type again, telling me everything. But he didn't. So I decided to suck it up and ask him something I'd been terrified of asking since we'd started going out.

ME: So what are your plans for next year?

As soon as I hit send my heart raced. The thought of him disappearing across the water like Megan made me feel sick. Having to stop whatever this was before it had even started? It wasn't worth thinking about. But I guess I needed *something*. Something to prove that I wasn't some brick wall people couldn't get past.

SHANE: You mean uni and stuff? It's not for me. Don't fancy getting into debt for something I won't even know if I like. What about you?

ME: Sports science at UUJ. Hopefully anyway. So that means you're sticking around?

SHANE: Yep :) Are you OK after last night? It was kind of intense

ME: Yeah, I'll be fine. I mean, I don't know if me and Niall will ever talk again, but I had a nice chat with Mum so at least I have some allies, even if she's on Niall's side too

SHANE: And me. I'll always be on your side. But like I said, I can leave Westing if it makes things easier

ME: Thanks :) But let's talk about it later? I need some time to get ready

SHANE: Bet you look amazing right now anyway

I sent him a picture with my face screwed up and my tongue sticking out.

ME: I don't. Here's some evidence

I spent ages getting ready. I wanted to look perfect for him. My favourite Man United shirt, that he'd say he'd hate, my favourite jeans, the ones that were tight in all the right places, and the new parka Mum had bought me for the winter.

'Bye, Mum. Away to Thunderland,' I called to her before I left.

'Who are you going with?' she asked with a smile.

I grinned back. 'None of your business.'

'Well, have a lovely time, and don't be too late – the roads will get icy.'

'OK, Mum. Bye!'

I parked outside Shane's house and sent him a message. Part of me was hoping he'd invite me in, but he didn't.

But even though I was disappointed that he didn't ask me to come in, I couldn't help but smile when he came out. Even his coat was sporty. A black Nike puffer one that looked so inviting that I couldn't wait to get my hands inside it.

191

'Hey,' he said when he got in.

'Hey,' I replied and leaned over to kiss him.

He smiled. 'What was that for?'

'I missed you.'

Then he kissed me again before we drove across town.

I parked about half a mile away from Thunderland. The Ferris wheel was glittering silver and green in the night. I followed the lights, not feeling the cold because of the warmth that rushed though me every time I stole a look at Shane.

We stood at the entrance, high on the smell of popcorn, fried onions, and the sound of music and exhilarated screams from high above. Before we went inside, I turned and slipped my hands under his coat and round his waist, looking up at him.

'You have no idea how happy I am to see you.'

He kissed my nose, and I closed my eyes, trying to capture this exact moment so I could keep it forever.

'Probably not as happy as I am to see you.' He smiled, but it was tinged with something else. Sadness maybe.

'Everything OK?' I asked, hoping this was when he would open up about whatever it was that he was keeping from me.

'Oh yeah, grand. Better now. Let's go.' He grabbed my hand and I tried to ignore the momentary sinking in my stomach. Because the thing was, it never lasted long with him. Everything else was too good, too special. He made me forget all the bad stuff.

He held up my hand, laughing. 'Are you wearing mittens?'

'What's wrong with mittens?' I held them up in front of my face. 'I love a good mitten.'

'They're cute.'

'OK, what are we going on first?' I put my hands on my hips and waited for his answer.

'The teacups?'

'Are you kidding me?' I pushed him with a mitten. 'OK, seeing as you're scared, why don't we try the Ferris wheel first? It's super slow and almost never gets stuck.'

'Almost never?' He raised his eyebrows.

'I mean, there was this one time Meg had to climb down a few carts but she was fine.'

'What?'

The shock on his face was hilarious.

'I'm sorry! It was too tempting! I'm taking the piss. I promise we'll be OK. Do you trust me?'

'I really don't know now,' he replied.

I pulled him towards the Ferris wheel anyway and we sat in one of the little carts. I pulled the bar down slowly.

'I feel sick,' he said.

I pulled off a mitten. 'Do you want to hold my hand? We can get off if you want, you know, if you really don't want to.' He looked so scared I'd started to feel bad.

'No, I'm doing this. It's time.' He laced his fingers through my de-mittened hand and held on tightly.

And we wouldn't have had time to get off anyway because right then it creaked forward, the music started, and we floated into the night sky.

'So if you're not going to uni, what do you want to do next year?' I asked, curious because uni had always been the only option for me.

He shrugged. 'I dunno. Stay at home, get a job. I'm not actually sure. I kind of thought about getting into coaching.

'Of course! That makes so much sense, and I happen to know first-hand that you'd make an amazing coach.'

He looked so genuinely pleased, his eyes as wide as his grin, his lips just asking to be kissed. So I kissed him, releasing my hand from his and tracing the outline of his jaw with my fingertips.

'Hey, look,' I said.

I pointed across the lough. A perfect moon was shining on the water like it had been the night of Zoe's party.

He looked at me instead. 'I can't.'

'It's really beautiful,' I said.

'Not as beautiful as what I'm looking at.'

I smiled a big dorky, open-mouthed smile that made me want to punch myself in the head.

'You have the most expressive face I've ever seen,' he said. 'I love it.'

I didn't see any more of the view on that time round. Or the next one, nor the next. And he was right – what could be more beautiful than this?

'Well?' I asked him as soon as we got off, leaning into him as we walked aimlessly, undecided about where to go next.

He laughed. 'It wasn't that bad.'

'Wasn't *bad*?' I said, mock outraged.

'The kissing helped,' he admitted.

'Oh really?' I stopped him right there, where the fairground music blasted in our ears and people rushed past us. 'Where next?'

'Over here,' he replied, grabbing my re-mittened hand and pulling me towards one of the millions of stalls.

It was one of those basketball things – throwing them into the hoops and winning prizes.

'Aw no, I'm so bad at this,' I said.

'I'm not,' he said with a smile, as we queued. 'I still remember my dad taking me to one of these. He was amazing at this stuff, and I'd come home with like, three of the giant teddy bears and a huge bucket of candyfloss and my mum would go mad because there was nowhere to put them.

'That's so funny. My parents never took us to fairs.' I gazed around at the lights and breathed in the smoke and popcorn. 'I only ever went with Niall and Meg, and now I'm wondering if they were into each other even then.' I rolled my eyes.

'But it's not like they wouldn't have wanted you there.'

'I don't even know any more.'

Shane put his arm round my shoulder and pulled me close. 'I want you here.'

'Thanks,' I said with a smile, and he kissed my head.

'Have you ever been to Liverpool?' I asked, changing the subject, and hoping the hole in my stomach would disappear. The one that always showed up when I thought about Niall and Megan.

'Never,' Shane said with a sigh.

'How come?'

'Ah, my dad doesn't like to go back. Too many bad memories.'

'Football?'

He nodded. 'Yeah. It hit him really hard, he said. I mean, he'll talk about it and all, *loves* talking about it, but I think it's just easier when he's in a different country or something. It doesn't actually make any sense to me.' Shane shrugged.

'Does he have a Scouse accent?' I asked, and Shane nodded. 'I *have* to meet this man. It's only my favourite accent ever. "Look over there, lad," I said in my best Liverpudlian accent, pointing at some kids who were far too young to be smoking behind one of the tents.

Shane burst out laughing. 'That's the worst accent I've ever heard.'

I gasped. 'How dare you? I'm going to do it for your dad, see what he thinks. What about your mum? What's she like?' I wanted to know everything.

'Ah, she's great too. She works really hard. Obsessed with the Pogues.'

I laughed. 'What?'

'Yep. On constantly in our house.' Shane rolled his eyes affectionately.

'Hold on a minute. Is that why you're –'

'Yep,' he said, cutting in, as we moved up the queue. 'Named after Shane MacGowan. She even wore black for a week when he died there.'

'Amazing. Can definitely think of worse people to be named after. I was named after Alexandra the Great.' I put my hands on my hips and smiled.

He laughed. 'Yep. That fits.'

I loved making him laugh because you knew he meant it. You couldn't fake a sound like that.

'Shane.'

He looked down at me. 'What's up?'

'You can talk to me, you know . . .' I left the words hanging in the air, watched as they landed and waited to see what he would do with them.

He smiled easily, tugging my hand gently to start walking again. 'I know.'

I didn't move. 'I just wanted you to know that, in case you thought you couldn't talk to me or something . . .'

'No, I know I can.' He tried to keep walking again, but again I didn't move.

And maybe it was the conversation with Mum that made me even more sensitive to the fact that he was keeping secrets, but I'd suddenly had enough. I didn't have any more patience.

'So why then? Why won't you tell me why you keep disappearing?' I hated that my voice shook and my eyes welled up. I *hated* it.

'Lexie, it's nothing to do with you, I promise.' He took both my hands and squeezed them, his face serious in the flash of the fairground lights.

'But I don't understand. Why can't you tell me?'

'Because you *wouldn't* understand,' he said, raising his voice above the screams.

And everything stopped. It felt like I was falling head first into some kind of black hole. The same place I went when I found out about Megan and Niall. The same place that swallowed me whole when I found out about Mum. All these secrets, all these people deciding how I would react and what I would or wouldn't understand.

I snatched my hands from his grip and wiped them across

my face, hard. I stepped back, still watching him. The boy I loved, breaking my heart into pieces.

'I'm sorry, Lexie. I didn't mean . . .'

'You said you loved me.' My words were choked.

'I do.' He stepped towards me, arms reaching for me. 'I *do* love you.'

I shook my head. 'You don't. You can't. If you love someone, you share everything. There *are* no secrets.'

He pushed his hands through his hair and winced like he was in pain. 'Lexie, I *can't*. You need to just accept that or –'

'Or what?' I demanded and immediately wished I hadn't. But I wasn't about to let him say it. 'You know what? I'll save you the bother. We're finished.'

I just about got the words out and turned away before bursting into ugly tears, chest heaving, nose running.

'Lexie, wait.'

But I didn't wait. I ran back to my car and drove home, my eyes blurred, leaving him in Thunderland with his stupid secrets.

24

'Lexie, what happened?'

It was like Mum had been waiting for me. She jumped up from her chair and came towards me. But this time I didn't want to talk to her about Shane. I thought about how happy I'd been before I left. Humiliating. So I ran upstairs to my room and threw myself on to my bed.

I heard a gentle knock at the door. 'Lexie, love?'

I didn't answer. And Mum didn't come in.

'What's for you won't go past you,' she said.

She loved that phrase. As if it made anything better.

Ten minutes later there was another knock at the door.

'Lexie? Can I come in?' It was Megan's voice.

And I had no more energy, so I didn't say anything when the door opened slowly, and Megan poked her head into my room.

'Lex,' she said, *her* voice shaking.

I shook my head into the pillow. Then I felt her get on to my bed beside me, lie down and stretch her arm round my back.

'What happened?' she whispered.

I pushed myself up and looked at her. 'What's wrong with me, Meg?'

'What do you mean? There's nothing wrong with you; you're amazing,' she said.

I hiccupped. 'He wouldn't tell me. And you wouldn't tell me, and even *Mum* wouldn't tell me. Why won't anyone let me in?' I said, knowing I wasn't making much sense.

'He wouldn't tell you . . . ?' She cocked her head and pulled her knees into her chest.

'And you, you didn't tell me about you and Niall. Why? Because I'm such a mess that I couldn't handle it?' And when I came out with it, I realized it was true: I *couldn't* handle it.

'Because I felt guilty,' she said simply. 'It wasn't to do with you. Well, it was, because I didn't want to hurt you and I knew how close you guys were. So it was just easier, not telling you.' Megan shrugged, her wide eyes looking like she was about to cry. 'I never meant to hurt you.' And then she *was* crying. 'I miss you so much, Lex.'

'I miss you too,' I said.

She leaned over and hugged me and I breathed in the familiar fruity smell of her hair.

'Maybe it's the same with Shane? Maybe he's keeping secrets because he's scared?' she offered.

'Of me?' I said, ready to cry all over again.

'Of your reaction,' she corrected.

'I never even asked about the trials,' I said, filling the silence that followed.

'Oh my God, so boring.' Megan rolled her eyes. 'You would

have loved it. So many drills. But, yeah, they want me back for the next bit.'

The usual rage about Megan not caring enough about football didn't show up in my gut like it usually did. I just felt happy for her.

'That's amazing,' I said. 'Tell me you're going to go.'

'Maybe,' she said with a smile. 'Niall's just as bad as you, you know. It's so weird, you're practically the same person. Which kind of freaks me out.'

I shook my head. I wasn't ready to talk about Niall. Forgiving Megan was one thing, but Niall? No way.

'Oh, and, Lexie? Sadie phoned me yesterday. There's going to be a scout at the game on Saturday. They were actually coming to see Shane, but they saw me play a couple of weeks ago apparently and want to watch again.'

I sniffed and wiped leftover tears from my face. 'Are you serious?' I let the thought settle. I'd barely thought about the game on Saturday. 'That's amazing. Are you excited?'

'Yeah. I mean, it's pretty cool, but I'm actually kind of worried about what happens if they're interested . . .'

And even though it hurt to think of Shane right then, I remembered what he'd said. That it's only great if it's something you want.

'You can always say no, you know, later, if you want?' I said, and she looked at me with surprise in her eyes, like she couldn't believe what I was saying.

'You're right. Thanks, Lex, but look at me, acting like I've already been chosen or something. Let's talk about you. I've missed you so much. Will you tell me about Shane?'

And I did. From the very beginning. The night we met, Zoe's party, the extra training, the night at my house, the funfair.

'Shit, that's really intense. Oh Lex, I've never seen you like this. But Niall was saying that Harrison had a word with him about me, that he hates when personal lives get mixed up in football. Like a warning or something, so maybe you dodged a bullet there?'

I could feel all the emotion coming back. In waves so strong they made me feel sick. But I didn't want to cry again, so I shook Shane out of my head.

'Megan?'

'Yeah?'

'Do you really think I'll ever make the firsts? Like to start?' I was too upset to care that I'd just asked a question whose answer terrified me.

But she didn't hesitate. 'Of course I do. You deserve it, Lexie. More than anyone.'

I forgot that about Megan, that she could make me feel like I was so much better than I was. And sometimes I just needed to hear it.

'Do you want to do some practice?' she asked, and I nodded. Then my phone rang.

'It's Sadie,' I said, and we both stared at it vibrating on my bed.

'Answer it!' Megan said, picking it up and shoving it towards me.

'Hello?'

I could barely hear what Sadie said beyond 'Can you play

on Saturday?'. My ears were ringing and I just about stopped myself from bursting into tears on the phone. I saved those for after.

Megan was staring at me the whole time, trying to work out what was happening. I hung up and clamped my hand over my mouth, as if that would stop the tears streaming down my cheeks.

Megan looked panicked. 'What? What happened?'

'She wants me to play on Saturday.'

Then Megan's arms were round me. I held on to her, wishing it was Shane I was holding on to. I wished I could send him a message to tell him I was on the team. That I'd be there too, when the scout was coming to watch him and Megan. But instead I went outside with Megan, and we trained until we were exhausted.

'Meg, you want to watch a movie?' Niall called from the kitchen door.

I looked at her, expecting that to be the end of our training session.

'Can't, sorry, babe. Just doing some training with Lex,' she shouted back, passing me the ball. 'Can I sleep in your room tonight?' she asked me.

And I felt nothing for Niall as I heard the kitchen door slam.

25

The dynamic shifted again now that me and Megan were talking. I started giving them lifts to school and Niall went back to his usual spot with his earbuds in. But it was still weird. I had to be careful about what I was talking about. No Shane, not that I wanted to bring him up, even though he was right there in my head, taking up every inch of space in my brain. This morning I'd gone into WhatsApp and hovered on his name for what felt like forever, debating whether I should send him a message or not. As soon as he came online, I locked my screen and put my phone face down, my heart beating hard, as if he could see me. I missed him. And every time I thought about how I'd ruined everything with my temper, I made myself think about the fact that he was hiding something from me and I'd given him a million chances to tell me.

'We should celebrate,' Megan said, putting on lipstick in the car mirror.

'Celebrate what?' I asked, confused.

'Being friends again.'

I couldn't help smiling at her enthusiasm. I was happy too.

It was like part of the weight that had been crushing my chest had been lifted.

'How should we do it? Extra practice after school?' I stuck out my tongue at her as she closed her eyes and pretended to snore. 'Fine, fine. What's your suggestion?'

She side-eyed me. 'Party?'

'Where?' I didn't really like house parties. But this time I was on board. A party was exactly what I needed to stop thinking about Shane and his stupid secrets. Although I don't even know if that would work. I was torturing myself with images of Shane with other girls. And there was nothing to prove anything, but my mind wouldn't leave me alone, telling me repeatedly that the big secret was that he already had a girlfriend.

Megan looked at me. 'Aren't your parents going away this weekend?'

I laughed because it was such a ridiculous suggestion. 'Are you serious? My dad would go mental,' I said, glancing in the mirror to check that Niall still had his earbuds in.

'That's what Niall said. But it would just be a *little* party.' Megan fluttered her eyelashes at me.

Niall being against the idea made the suggestion so much more attractive.

I smiled. 'I'm in.'

Megan squealed. 'You have no idea how glad I am to have my friend back.'

'Me too. Meg?'

'Yeah?'

'Do you think Shane has another girlfriend? And that's the secret?' It hurt to say it.

'No. No way,' she said immediately. 'I mean, that would be a total dick move. Did you get any of those vibes?'

'No. I mean the only thing was that Zoe was really into him and I saw her talking to him one night before practice.' The feelings from that night were back. The jealousy, the anger. 'And she asked him to V-Ball.'

'Zoe? No way. But sure, Zoe talks to everyone. There's no chance he'd go for someone like her.'

'But she's really pretty.'

'She *is* pretty, but so are you. And you don't walk around smiling like some AI simulation.'

I burst out laughing. 'That's true, I guess.'

'And think about when he had to leave her party? Would it make sense?' Megan asked, in full detective mode.

He had left Zoe's party early, so I guess it didn't. But that was my head at the minute. A complete and utter mess.

'Yeah, you're right. But there's something else. I've seen someone called Grace messaging him a few times, and he's never mentioned who she is.'

Megan gave a disapproving snort. 'Ugh, maybe he *is* a fuckboy. Do you really need that drama in your life?'

I winced at the word she'd used, never thinking it would be used in the context of Shane. I shook my head sadly.

'And we can have the best night ever on Friday. I'll help you forget all about Shane.' Megan reached over and squeezed my hand on the steering wheel. 'And the match on Saturday isn't until midday, so it'll be totally fine.'

'Yeah,' I agreed. Outwardly anyway.

Megan got to work as soon as we got to school, telling

everyone about the *little* party, that was turning into a definitely not little party already.

Niall didn't find out until break time, when he came up to me with a face like thunder. 'Lexie, what the hell? A party? I'm not taking the fall for it. You can explain that one to Mum and Dad yourself.'

'Nice one, twins.' Hunter slapped Niall on the back. 'Sounds like you're going to be a bit of craic again finally.'

Niall forced a smile. 'Yeah man, but here, don't be telling too many people, OK?'

'You have my word,' said Hunter. 'You're not bringing your boyfriend are you, Lexie?'

My stomach lurched. 'No, he can't come,' I said.

I could feel Niall looking at me. Megan mustn't have told him about our conversation last night. I was touched.

Niall's expression softened. 'Good,' he said.

'Aw, come on, man. She's upset that her boyfriend won't be there,' Hunter said. 'Don't worry, I'll cheer you up at the party. I'll bring a keg. Ryan can get me one.'

Hunter was way too into this already. And usually I'd be panicking, but, fuck it, I needed it.

'Yeah. Niall, chill out,' I said and smiled sweetly at him.

Megan came over. 'OK, Zoe's going to tell her lot, I'll tell the football ones tomorrow night, and Hunter's already told half the school. It's going to be a total rager.' She grinned, then her smile disappeared when she saw Niall's face.

His mood lasted all day. When we got home, he came into my bedroom.

'Get out,' I said when he walked in without knocking.

'You need to cancel this party; it's getting out of control. I'm getting messages from Birch High kids who want to come.'

I shrugged. 'So tell them they can't.'

'Lexie, what the hell has got into you? And there's a match on Saturday. You planning to play with a hangover?'

I rolled my eyes. 'Not all of us plan to get as drunk as possible at every opportunity.'

'It's your funeral,' he said and slammed the door behind him.

Whatever. I didn't care what he thought. I was done thinking about Niall all the time. Football and fun, that's all I wanted to think about from now on. Definitely not Shane.

I looked perfect on Tuesday night for practice. Hair washed, make-up on. My favourite perfume, my wee shorts. I'd show him what he was missing. And I played my heart out. Megan cheered me on, pointing out all the good things I did and making excuses for my mistakes.

Out of breath, I hung around, trying to catch a glimpse of him, to see if he was as devastated as I was. But in the crowd of boys, I couldn't see him. Anywhere.

'Is he here?' Megan was beside me now, her breath completely back to a normal rhythm.

'I don't see him.'

'That's weird. Hold on, look. Harrison's telling them something.'

He'd gathered all the boys in the corner of the pitch.

'Come on.' Megan pulled my hand and led me to the edge of the pitch so we could get closer. Out of sight, but we could hear everything.

'Some news, boys. Shane has left us. He's gone back to Ferndale United.'

The boys started talking between themselves.

'It's going to be a bit of a blow to the team. I tried to convince him to stay, but he's decided that Westing isn't for him. It's not for everyone. But now I know what kind of team we can be, I want to see extra effort from now on.'

Harrison's words blurred into something inaudible.

'Lex, are you OK?' Megan was staring at me with concern.

I shook my head because I didn't know what else to do. He was supposed to be here. He was supposed to see how great I looked and want me back.

'He left?' I said.

'Yeah, he mustn't have liked it here.'

'Because of Niall and Hunter,' I said, desperately trying to stop tears from coming.

I remembered how he'd said it would be easier if he left.

Easier for who? Not me.

And if someone had told me he wasn't going to be there tonight, I'd have said I didn't care, that he could keep his secrets and I never wanted to see him again. But it would have been a lie.

I didn't expect the pain. The physical pain that seared through my chest and made me want to throw up.

26

I ignored all Mum's requests to reduce my training. I did the opposite. I didn't need Shane. Every morning that week I was outside, running laps and doing drills before school. I needed it, to get him out of my head.

Everything reminded me of Shane. The beach, catching a glimpse of my clarinet, even the cutlery in the kitchen brought me right back to that perfect night. But thoughts like that made me run harder.

'Miss Ryan, are you awake?'

I jerked my eyes open to see Mrs Skillen staring at me.

'Sorry, yeah, I just . . .'

'Fell asleep?' she finished for me.

'Yeah. Sorry.'

She held me behind after class. 'Alexandra, I'm worried about you. Your grades have slipped quite significantly and falling asleep in class? That's not like you. Is everything OK? At home?'

Mrs Skillen was nice. One of those gentle teachers that most kids took advantage of.

'I'm fine. Nothing's wrong, I've just been doing a lot of football training lately,' I said. And part of me wanted to leave it there so she'd think I was something special. Like I was Megan or something and a seriously big deal.

'Maybe you should pull back on the training and try to concentrate on your schoolwork for a while? I don't want you to fall behind, not just before your exams.'

'I'm fine, promise. I can do it all,' I said, standing up.

'I'm here, Alexandra, if you want to talk,' she said as I left the room.

At least I knew he wouldn't be at training on Thursday. Then I could tell myself that I was just there for me, to show Sadie what I could do, so she wouldn't regret her choice to play me on Saturday.

'OK, girls, huge game on Saturday. A scout will be there to watch Megan, but you never know, stranger things have happened, maybe someone else will catch her eye. I want you all there for warm-up at eleven thirty. And I want you all to get early nights. We're playing Barn United. They're a good team and they'll put up a fight, so be prepared for that. See you all on Saturday.' Then Sadie smiled. Well, as close as Sadie can come to a smile.

I went for a jog when the boys' practice was on, even though Megan begged me not to. But I couldn't stand there watching. Not when that was where I first saw him. Haunted by the night we met.

Mum and Dad left that evening. And as I stood there in

the hallway waving them off, I could see the doubt in Niall's eyes, trying to decide whether he should out me or not. But he didn't. He didn't say anything at all.

Megan came over as soon as they'd left. She said she'd told her parents she was studying with me, even though they weren't stupid and knew she was going out with Niall.

'Thing is, if I keep talking at them about things, they get really irritated and just want me to leave, so that's what I did.' Megan smiled. She was in my room, sitting on my bed, the way it used to be. Sort of.

'They'll miss you when you go to uni,' I said quietly.

Megan looked at me like she didn't know what to say.

'*I'll* miss you when you go to uni. You could have told me, you know . . .'

'And this?' Megan waved her hand in front of my face. 'It makes me want to cry. I know I should have said, but I hate seeing you upset more than anything. Forgive me?'

She cocked an eyebrow and I laughed. 'Suppose so. But you need to promise that nothing will change between us again.'

She held out her little finger and I hooked mine round it. 'Promise. But on to more important things: what are you wearing tomorrow night? Something low-cut, best tits in Belfast?'

I laughed. 'Maybe. What are you wearing?'

'I'm going all out. Little black dress. I'm so excited.'

'Me too,' I said, trying to convince myself. A tiny part of me wished I'd asked Mum to stay, and that the party wasn't happening.

I couldn't sleep that night. The smell of the ocean pulled me out of bed and outside under the glow of the moon. I started running, even though I was exhausted, and my muscles screamed for me to stop. I ran until I couldn't think any more and Shane wasn't haunting my thoughts.

The next day, school was insane. Every second person who talked to me was asking about the party, even people I didn't know. But I didn't care. All I cared about was the fact I wouldn't have to think about Shane all night.

'This is a mistake,' Niall said on the way home.

'It'll be fine,' replied Megan. 'We'll get up early and clean the place and your mum and dad will never know!'

'We'll see,' Niall said.

Hunter showed up first, rolling a keg of beer in front of him.

'What the hell?' I said.

He stopped rolling and looked at me. 'Lexie, you look amazing.'

'Thanks,' I said, and was surprised when my cheeks flushed with heat. 'Kitchen?' I pointed at the keg.

And that was only the start of it. Kid after kid showed up with more alcohol than I'd ever seen. There were already ones from the year below kicking a ball about on the pitch and a group of girls vaping outside.

Megan grabbed my hand and squeezed it. 'Oh my God, Lexie, this is going to be amazing.'

She looked incredible. I was so used to seeing her in a football kit and her baggy jumpers, so now that she'd made an effort, she looked like a different person. I watched

Niall's face when he saw her, like something from a cartoon: mouth open, imaginary smoke pouring out his ears. And I thought of Shane then, how much I loved it when he ran his eyes over me, and that electric current rushed through my veins.

'Shot?' Megan dragged me over to the kitchen island where Hunter was handing out shots of something blue.

'Sure?' I pulled a face when I looked at it.

'Get it down ya,' said Hunter. I swallowed it.

'How come Shane isn't coming?'

I turned round to see Zoe studying my expression. I wished she hadn't said his name. Hearing it coming out of her lips felt worse than the constant reel of his face going round in my head.

I smiled and reached for another shot. 'Just busy.' I wished so hard that my lie was true, that he was playing football or something, that we hadn't had that fight, and that my heart wasn't shattered.

'Hey, Hunter, don't forget me, your date,' Zoe said with a grin.

They were going out now?

Hunter handed her a shot. 'Sorry, babe.'

In the kitchen, Niall was already picking up rubbish. But a couple of hours later he'd obviously abandoned his efforts, because there were crisp packets, empty bottles and pizza boxes everywhere. My house looked like a bomb site.

The music was so loud that it made my ears ache. There were people everywhere. Every room I went into had people kissing, people laughing, people just hanging out. I'd never felt so lonely.

The shots had gone to my head. But I liked it. The woozy, blurry feeling softened the edges of all my thoughts of Shane. So I drank another.

'You good, Lexie?'

I looked up to see Hunter smiling at me.

I smiled back. 'I'm good.'

'Can I show you something?'

I laughed. 'In my own house?'

'Yeah, in your own house. Actually upstairs.'

I sighed and shrugged. I wasn't doing anything else and could definitely use a distraction.

'Come on.' Hunter nodded his head towards the staircase.

I swallowed another shot. They'd actually started to taste nice now. I followed Hunter upstairs to the games room, where he sat down on the sofa. There were only a few other kids up here. Well, there could be some in my bedroom, but I wasn't about to check.

He turned on the Nintendo.

'You wanted to show me the Switch?' I said, confused.

'Just wait. You're so impatient.'

I watched as he turned on *Mario Kart* and went on to one of the Bowser's Castle levels. 'Just watch. Next time you play Niall, use this cheat.'

I watched as Hunter cheated with Toad, my favourite character.

'Amazing,' I said. 'I'm definitely going to use that. Thanks, Hunter.' And because I wasn't thinking straight, I was just enjoying not thinking about Shane, I was back in time, playing Nintendo with Niall, when losing a Grand Prix was the biggest worry I had. And I was too late. For everything. It was like a slow-motion car crash that I couldn't stop.

Hunter put down the controller and turned round. He put his hand on my leg and leaned towards me. But my head was spinning, and although I knew I wanted to get out of his way, whatever signal that went from my brain to my legs wasn't working properly. So I just sat there as he kissed me.

'Lexie?' I heard.

I pulled away from Hunter, pushing his chest away from me at the same time. Then I turned towards the stairs, and I have never hated myself more.

Shane. Standing there in his tracksuit, quarter zip up to his chin, pain in his eyes. And right beside him? Zoe.

Shane was staring at me in utter shock and Zoe looked like she was about to burst into tears.

'Shane,' I said, horrified.

He shook his head, turned round and walked down the stairs.

'Hunter, what the fuck?' I looked at him, then pushed his shoulder. 'Why did you do that?' I stood up and walked towards the stairs. Zoe had disappeared. 'You're with *Zoe*. And I'm . . .'

'You're what?'

I didn't want to waste any more time on him, so I ignored his question and stumbled down the stairs to find Shane. How could I have been so stupid? I knew what Hunter was like. I pushed past people on the stairs and scanned the hallway, looking for Shane.

As soon as I reached the bottom step, Zoe was in front of

me. Amina's arm round her shoulder, tears streaming down her face.

'You just couldn't help yourself, could you?' She looked pissed off and on the verge of tears.

I felt so sick. 'What?'

'You knew I wanted Shane and then you took him, and now I can't even have Hunter? Niall told me you were upstairs, so I was just showing Shane where you were. I didn't ... Just why, Lexie?' She could barely get the words out through her tears.

'I don't want Hunter. He kissed me,' I slurred. Then I walked away. I needed to find Shane.

I went outside into the freezing night and shouted his name so loudly that my throat hurt. Then I phoned him. Again and again and again. No answer. I didn't even try and stop the tears. I walked back inside, grabbed the closed bottle of whatever spirit was on the sideboard and took a huge swig, bringing it back outside with me.

Then I went to the beach. There were kids all over the garden, but I hoped nobody would be there. I breathed in the salty air, hoping it would calm me down, but only the bottle of vodka in my hand had any chance of doing that. I walked over rocks and seaweed and headed straight for the water. I walked in, still wearing my trainers, and thought about the night here with Shane.

'I'm sorry,' I said into the night. I looked at the stars and then I was back at Zoe's house, where everything was new and exciting, before this mess.

'Lexie, what the hell?'

I spun round, almost falling into the water to see Niall staring at me with fear on his face.

'What?' I asked. 'Want some?' I held up the bottle.

'No, Lexie, what are you doing? You don't drink.' He walked towards me, splashing through the freezing water in his jeans. He took the bottle from me and I snatched it back, taking another drink to prove him wrong.

'I do now.'

'You and Hunter now?'

'What, Niall? Why do you even care? And no, I'm not with Hunter. He's an idiot. It's Shane, I wanted Shane. And I've ruined everything.'

'Nah, ruining things is my job. Come on.'

I didn't fight him as he led me back to the house, then upstairs. He told the people on my bed to piss off and waited while I lay down on top of the covers and closed my eyes.

But he was gone when I opened them again. I jumped out of bed and ran to the bathroom where I threw up everywhere.

I slept on the bathroom floor, the cold tiles soothing against my hot face. And despite how ill I felt, I wished it would get worse, *anything* to mask the pain of what I'd just done.

27

I woke up with a dry mouth, a sore neck, a thumping headache and a blanket over me. Still on the bathroom floor. And for a few seconds that's all it was. A hangover. Until it hit me, and the tears were back, my chest was heaving as I lay there on the floor curled up like a wounded animal.

Eventually I pulled myself off the tiles, got undressed and stepped into the shower. The same shower that we'd used that perfect evening.

When I got out, I looked at my phone, hoping for a missed call or a message. And I almost threw up again when I looked at WhatsApp, at the messages I'd sent Shane.

> **ME:** Hpnter kissed me i don't like him

> **ME:** I love u Shane. Im sry for t other nite I just want to no your secrts cos I love u

> **ME:** U hav a grlfrend? Who is GRae/

> **ME:** I feel sik I wish u were here

He hadn't replied to any of them.

There was a knock at my door. 'Lexie?'

Megan walked in before waiting for an answer. She took one look at my face and rushed towards me, pulling me into a hug and the tears started all over again.

'I tried to move you last night, but you wouldn't budge, so I just brought a blanket. I should have stayed in here with you.'

I shook my head as I cried. 'I don't deserve it. Shane, he saw.'

'Saw what? The Hunter thing?'

I nodded.

'But, look, he came to see you. Came to your house when the whole team were here, the ones who hate him, who were saying horrible shit to him! That has to mean something.' Megan had her hands on my shoulders and was looking into my swollen eyes.

'But I ruined it.'

Megan shook her head. 'You weren't together. And you had a good reason to break up with him. Stop blaming yourself for everything, Lexie. Look. Get dressed for football, let's tidy the house and then later on we can chill out and make a plan? Yeah?'

I couldn't speak so I just hugged her.

'Football. Shit.'

Megan laughed. 'Yeah. At least one of us was sensible last night. See you when you're ready.'

Then I was alone again. I got dressed in shorts and my Westing shirt. I'd almost put on Shane's zip top just to remember his smell, but even picking it out of my drawer made me cry all over again and I couldn't bring myself to put it over my head.

When I emerged I saw bodies everywhere. On the couch, on the floor, the smell of alcohol thick in the air.

Fuck.

I walked downstairs and it was the same deal: kids everywhere, half-empty beer bottles on every surface. I looked at the wooden floor and saw pools of alcohol and abandoned bits of food. I couldn't even think about Shane right now.

Niall walked out of the kitchen with a half-full bin bag and a face like thunder.

'Happy now?' he asked and looked at me with so much disdain I couldn't speak. 'Have you seen this place? It's an absolute mess, Lexie.'

I opened my mouth, but nothing came out.

'Seriously? You've *nothing* to say? *Nothing?*'

And I didn't. I didn't even want to think about it, never mind talk about it, so I went outside and started to run.

I ran despite the nausea and the headache that got worse every time my feet pounded the fake grass. Desperate to feel anything that wasn't Shane.

By the time we'd cleared everybody out and filled a few bin bags, it was time to leave.

*

We were playing at Blanchflower Stadium.

Through the nausea my stomach was filled with butterflies. A real-life scout was going to be there. I knew they were there for Megan, but I still wanted to impress them. And they were still coming, even though Shane had quit.

Niall was driving. Megan was in the front, and she wasn't talking very much. Was she nervous? I never thought Megan got nervous about anything.

'You excited for the scout?' I asked.

'You know, I think I am. I keep telling myself I don't want it, and I don't care, but then I think about how good I look in a Man United kit.' She laughed and I watched Niall reach over and squeeze her leg. And it didn't make me want to throw up this time. Now that I'd made up with Megan, the whole relationship didn't seem as bad. I still didn't like it, but it didn't have the same effect on me any more.

When we got to the pitch Sadie was already there. She was talking to a woman in a black coat and baseball cap. The scout. The butterflies in my stomach were going mental. The rest of the team had started to arrive, and we walked over to join Megan and Sadie on the pitch. Niall went to watch from the stands.

'OK, girls, this is it. Forget there's anyone watching – just play the way you always play.' Sadie took our warm-ups.

'Anyone heard from Zoe?' Sadie asked afterwards.

She wasn't there. I'd been too distracted to even notice.

'Nope, sorry,' said Megan, sharing a look with me.

I shrugged. 'She's probably just running late.' I wondered if she was too upset about Hunter, and even though I wasn't Zoe's biggest fan, I felt kind of guilty.

'OK, we've only one sub now,' Sadie said, and she looked me dead in the eye. A silent 'You can do this'.

I nodded, trying to suppress the excitement that was exploding inside me.

I tried not to smile too hard so I wouldn't look like a psycho, so I gazed at the ground instead, watching my new pink boots as I ran to the dugout to take off my jumper.

More of the boys' team was there now, laughing on the sidelines. I noticed Hunter watching me and I looked away quickly.

'Good luck, Meg,' I said.

She threw her arm round my shoulder and squeezed. 'Thanks.'

I forced myself to push Shane out of my head. There was an actual scout here and I was starting. This is what I wanted more than anything. I didn't need to think about him.

And from the first whistle I was on fire, tackling all around me, sending balls up the wing to Katie, to Megan; in fact, I definitely contributed to the first goal. And what a goal it was. Megan, of course, hard and low into the bottom-right corner. And when she scored, she scanned the pitch and then ran to celebrate with me.

Megan scored again. And again. The scout could not have picked a better match.

At half-time I felt like I was going to throw my guts up in the best way. I was shattered. Megan looked like she'd barely broken a sweat.

'You're doing great out there; keep up the good work,' Sadie said before taking Megan off to the side to tell her something privately. And this time there was no jealousy. Megan deserved all the attention. She was incredible.

'Still no Zoe?' Sadie scanned the stadium. 'Lexie, brilliant job out there!'

I grinned. 'Thanks Sadie, loving it!'

'You're doing great.'

The second half was even better. I ran harder, pushed harder, tackled harder and tried to ignore the hangover nausea that was getting even worse.

'Calm down, Lexie!' Sadie shouted from the sidelines.

What was she on about? I threw myself into another tackle, but I was too slow; she moved the ball and I twisted and then heard a snap. And the pain was like nothing I'd felt before – burning in my leg from my ankle, right up my calf.

I screamed.

'Lexie!' Megan ran over and kneeled down beside me.

The whistle blew, but I could barely hear it. My ears were ringing, and I leaned over and threw up because of the pain.

'Oh my God, Lex, are you OK?' Megan said, panicking beside me.

I couldn't answer. The pain was so bad I couldn't think. I couldn't hear. Then Megan's dad was by my side examining my leg gently.

'Probably a tear, given the amount of pain she's in. Definitely best to get it checked out to make sure. Ambulance is on the way.'

And then I was on a stretcher and being carried off the pitch towards an ambulance.

They were about to close the doors when Niall jumped in to come with me.

28

Niall took my hand in the ambulance, and I let him. They'd given me painkillers, so as the world became gradually visible, I could think again.

'It hurts.'

'I know,' he said. 'Should have heard your scream. I felt it, Lexie. Like it was happening to me too.' He was holding on to my hand even more tightly now.

'Always trying to steal my thunder.'

He laughed. 'Meg wanted to come with you, but I made her stay for the scout.'

I nodded through the pain as a realization sank in. 'I'm not going to be able to play for ages.'

Then the tears started. Thick and fast.

'Players get injured, Lexie. It's no big deal.'

'No big deal?' I repeated. 'It's literally the most important thing in my life.' I choked the words out.

Niall let go of my hand to play with the tubes that were attached to me.

'Don't you think you were doing a bit much? Didn't you listen to what Mum said?' Niall said gently.

'I just wanted on the team,' I said and broke down again.

Niall was silent for the rest of the journey, just sitting beside me as I cried and thought about how much of a disaster this was.

I had an X-ray, but nothing was broken. Dr Evans was right. I'd torn my calf muscle, so I definitely wouldn't be playing football for ages. I'd need loads of rest and then physiotherapy. I couldn't even cry. It was like it was too unbelievable. But all of it, *all* of it, was my fault. Shane, the injury. They'd all told me not to do too much. What an idiot.

They gave me a prescription for a load of medication I'd never even heard of and lent me a pair of crutches.

Niall phoned a taxi and helped me into it, then into the house when we got back.

I'd forgotten about the party. The house was still a mess and stank of alcohol.

I sat down in the living room and looked at my phone. Missed calls from Megan and two messages.

MEGAN: Are you OK?

MEGAN: Call me!!!

I phoned her and she almost cried when I told her that her dad was right. And then *I* cried when she told me what had happened at the end of the match.

The scout wanted to see her play again. They were really impressed. So not only did she ace the NI trials and get into the training programme but she was also on the radar of a Premier League scout.

I was so happy for her. Yeah, I thought about how it would feel if it had been me, but being happy for her felt good.

Despite the painkillers and the ice that Niall had brought me, my leg hurt so much.

I had no idea how Niall was going to sort the house out by himself. But he tried. I've never seen him do so much cleaning in his life.

We didn't talk. I sat there while he went from room to room, picking up more bottles and scrubbing bits of carpet.

Megan showed up in the evening.

'I can't believe you tore it. Does this mean you can't . . . ?'

'Play football for ages,' I said, finishing her sentence and bursting into tears. It was like I'd been holding it in all afternoon, and now that some of the painkillers had worn off everything felt even more unfair.

She leaned in to hug me.

'That's amazing news about the scout, Meg.'

Megan just listened as I cried, about the pain, about the fact I couldn't play football, about Shane.

'She's OK,' I heard her say.

I pulled myself from Megan's shoulder and looked towards the door. Niall was standing there staring at me with a look of horror on his face. Megan pulled away and walked over to him. They left the room and I could hear them whispering outside.

I took out my phone and checked WhatsApp again, just in case I'd accidentally turned off notifications and hadn't noticed that Shane had sent me a message. But nothing. He'd read the ones I'd sent last night, but no reply. I thought about sending him a picture of my leg, but that wasn't fair, so I flicked on to his Instagram. To the page that he barely updated. Some old photos of kids playing football in mismatched green kits. I looked at the picture carefully and spotted him. He was laughing at something, and he looked so happy. I ached to be near him again. Maybe I could forget it all, everything that had happened, just to have him back. And then it hit me how much I wanted him to tell me all his secrets, when I hadn't actually told him all mine. Yeah, he knew that I loved football, but he didn't know how it had completely taken over my life, that I was willing to do so much that an injury was inevitable.

Niall walked back into the room. 'Mum and Dad are coming back,' he told me. 'Sorry I didn't tell you – you were out of it, and I kind of freaked out. I phoned them earlier to tell them what had happened. I figured they'd want to know. They'll be back in about an hour.'

Panic rushed over me. The house still didn't look the way they'd left it. There was no way they wouldn't guess.

'But the house,' I said.

'I'll do some more now, but I think we're just going to have to wing it.'

Niall and Megan worked their arses off, trying to make it look like we hadn't had a huge house party last night. They even opened all the windows and doors in a useless attempt to get rid of the smell of alcohol.

Niall dropped Megan home before Mum and Dad got

back, so for about fifteen minutes it was just the two of us again. But this time without the chaos of the hospital.

'You need more painkillers?'

'Yes, please.'

I swallowed the pills.

'Lexie . . .'

Niall hesitated when I turned to him, my face tear-stained. 'What?'

'Nothing, it doesn't matter,' he said.

And then the front door opened.

'Oh my goodness, Lexie.' Mum's voice sounded shaky, like she'd been crying. She rushed into the living room and had my face in her hands in seconds. 'What happened?'

'Calf muscle,' I said, and fell apart again, feeling about ten years old. 'I tore it.'

'It's OK, love, it'll be OK. It's just a setback and it'll force you to have a good rest.'

I shook my head. I didn't want to rest. I never wanted to rest.

'We'll get you better, pet,' Dad said from the doorway. I could tell he was stressed about something. 'Niall, a word?' He motioned for Niall to step into the hall.

I tried to listen to what he was saying, but I could barely hear over Mum telling me all the things she was going to do to make my recovery as quick as possible.

'I'm sorry,' I heard Niall say. 'It was only a few people.'

My blood ran cold. How had he figured it out already?

'You've had too many chances, Niall. I'd hoped by now I could trust you, but it's clear that I can't. Get out of my sight.' Dad's voice was clipped and cold.

I heard Niall disappear up the stairs and my heart sank.

'How you feeling, love?' Dad came in, his tone immediately warm.

'OK,' I said.

'A party, Georgina. Niall had a party here when we were gone.' He looked at Mum and shook his head in disgust.

'No, he wouldn't have. He knows better than that,' she said.

'An empty beer can in the plant pot by the door was the first indication. He admitted it when I asked. I haven't even looked through the rest of the house for damage.' Dad scanned the room, looking for evidence.

'Lexie, you tell us. What happened?' Mum looked at me, desperate to hear that it was all a lie and we'd actually just sat and watched TV together when they were gone.

But I couldn't do it to him. Dad's face. The disgust. I knew how much it must have hurt him. I was touched that he hadn't thrown me under the bus, but it wasn't his fault.

'It wasn't Niall who had the party.'

Dad looked right at me. 'There's no point lying, Lexie. He told me everything.'

'It was me. He didn't want it. He tried to stop it.'

There was silence.

'Oh, Lexie,' Mum said beside me.

And I burst into tears again because I was such a mess. On top of everything else, I was a crap daughter.

'I didn't expect this from you,' Dad said. 'You'll be paying for any damage to this house, regardless of the injury.'

'OK,' I said quietly.

'OK, let's just forget about the party for now. We need to

focus on getting you better.' Mum put her arm round me and Dad left the room with another piece of my heart.

'You know, I've been away too much recently. I'm going to stay with you guys from now on. And I don't want you to worry about the house. Dad is over the top about it. It's only stuff,' she said.

'Thanks, Mum,' I choked out.

I felt terrible. For so long I'd seen Mum as this kind of superfluous part of our family. Like she was just there to be nice. But I couldn't have been more wrong. I thought back to when she'd told me about her tennis and for the first time, I truly understood how hard it must have been to tell me, and how she'd just been trying to protect me.

Wrong about Mum, wrong about Niall, who actually still seemed to care about me. What else was I wrong about?

29

Mum came into my room the next morning and opened my blinds.

'Morning, love. I gave one of the girls from yoga a call. She's a sports physio and she's going to come out and help you next week, but for now you need lots of rest and ice.'

I winced at the pain in my calf.

'I brought you painkillers,' Mum said, and I reached for them. 'If you need any help getting dressed, let me know,' she said, before leaving.

I pulled on shorts and a Man United shirt. I opened my laptop and turned on Aitana Bonmatí's best moments, but I had to turn it off. It was too depressing.

A knock on my door.

'Can I come in?' Niall's voice.

'Yeah.'

He walked in and sat on my bed, looking at his hands rather than me. 'You didn't have to tell them, you know.'

'The party? Of course I did. I couldn't let you take the fall for my stupid decisions.'

'I've been kind of worried about you,' Niall said. And

then he did look at me, his forehead creased, his expression sincere.

'Worried? Why?'

'The way you've been acting. The training, it was so much. It was part of the reason I didn't want to tell you about me and Megan. I knew it would drive you crazy. I'm sorry. If I've done any of this, I'm sorry.'

I shook my head, as all the feelings I'd been holding on to for so long came bubbling thick and fast to the surface.

'It's not you. It's not anybody. It's *me*. Do you know how hard I try? For everything? It's fucking exhausting. And still, *still*, I'll never be as good at football or as clever as Megan. I'm a fucking failure in every single part of my life. That's what's going on with me and I guess I feel like we drifted apart or something.' I moved my leg and recoiled in pain.

'Lexie, are you serious? Do you know how many times I've wished I was more like you? How much you try? I just get to a certain point and then I quit. And you might be jealous of Megan, but I've been jealous of you for a really long time. The way Dad looks at you? How well you do at school? I wish I could stick at things the way you do. And I guess, I dunno, I felt like I've been losing you too.' He shrugged, embarrassed, and looked away again.

'Jealous of me?' I asked, so confused.

'Yeah, Lexie, jealous of you. Jealous of your boyfriend. I was going to really try this year, so Dad would think I was class, but then he showed up and blew me out of the water.'

The mention of Shane made my heart sink. 'You were horrible to him.'

Niall nodded his head. 'Yep, I was. And it wasn't me. Like, it didn't feel like something I would do, be a dick to someone I don't know. I just wanted to feel better than someone or something.'

It was sad seeing Niall like this. Hating himself. That feeling was usually reserved for me.

'Well, he's gone now, so you don't need to worry about that.'

'Megan told me what happened between you two. I'm sorry. I guess you really liked him?'

I didn't have any warning. More tears spilled from my eyes, and I couldn't stop them. 'I loved him, Niall. I loved him and he's gone. He wouldn't tell me why he had to keep leaving. Am I that hard to talk to? What's wrong with me?'

'Nothing's wrong with you. Everybody loves you and nobody wants to hurt you. Maybe he was worried about how you'd react if he told you whatever it is. Because he didn't want to make you feel worse than you clearly do.'

I wiped my eyes and stared at the crutches that were leaning against my bed. 'Was it that obvious?'

'Even to me,' he said.

I stayed in my room when Niall left, thinking about all the things he'd just said. How it had been so painfully obvious to everyone that I was falling apart and keeping secrets had just been their way of protecting me. And I felt OK about it. Because for the first time, I understood.

A week later, my calf was starting to feel slightly better. I'd spent the last seven days spaced out on painkillers and sadness, and I couldn't take it any more. The silence. So I sent him a message.

ME: Hey. Can we talk?

ME: Please?

I watched as the little ticks turned to blue, so I knew he'd read it, but there was no reply.

Then the physio came to the house, with grey hair and a smile that was trying its hardest to make me smile too. But I couldn't. Not when I'd just reminded myself how much Shane hated me.

'Nice to meet you, Alexandra. So football's your poison?' She laughed good-naturedly.

'I guess,' I said.

She showed me exercise after exercise – and they all hurt.

'Every day. You need to be doing these every day multiple times. Do I have your word?'

I nodded.

'I'll help.'

I turned to see Niall watching me do the exercises.

'Brilliant. Always great to have family members who are willing to lend a hand. Come and watch how to do these properly.' She waved Niall over and he watched intently as I completed each exercise.

My heart swelled. This was the old Niall, the one who was part of my team.

When Annie left, Niall sat with me, and we watched *Back to the Future*. Our old favourite movie.

'So, Megan then . . .' I was ready. Ready to talk to him about it. 'Do you love her?'

'Yeah,' he said without hesitation. 'I don't know what I'm going to do when she leaves,' he said sadly.

'You can go and visit her. And anyway, seeing as the scout's interested, she might not even be in London.'

'She'll still be in England.'

'I wish I'd applied somewhere over there now,' he said. And I wished the same. Now I didn't have Shane, I didn't want to be here. I'd just got Niall and Megan back and now I was going to lose them all over again.

I remember when we'd made the decision to stay at home. We didn't want to split up, and even the idea of going to different universities felt ridiculous.

'You could always transfer?' I suggested. 'I bet they do sports science degrees in loads of places.'

'You wouldn't mind?' he asked, his eyes lighting up at the prospect.

I sighed. 'I think it's weird, maybe kind of cringe, but even though you were right about having separate lives –'

'I felt really bad about saying that.'

I shook my head. 'It's fine. I just meant that even though we're our own people, I think we'll always have that connection, and even if you're on the other side of the world, I reckon we'll still be in each other's lives. So you weren't *totally* right.' I stuck out my tongue.

He shrugged. 'I never thought about it like that . . . You're right. It *is* cringe.' He laughed. 'But true.'

'But, yeah, the Megan-in-England thing, you should think

about it anyway. She clearly loves you too.' I rolled my eyes and laughed.

'Do you still love *him*?' Niall asked, and my breath caught in my throat.

I nodded, too scared to speak. Unsure how my voice would come out. 'So don't mess it up with Megan, you need to make it work, at least one of us should be happy and not screw up everything.'

We watched the rest of the movie in easy silence. When it was almost over, my phone buzzed.

> **ZOE:** Hey, I heard about what happened. Are you OK? ♥

I stared at it for a few seconds. When I saw her name flash up on my phone, I was expecting some essay of hate, so it took me a while to get my head around the kindness.

Niall looked at me with concern. 'Who is it? Is it him?'

I shook my head. 'Zoe.'

Niall pulled a face. 'Oh shit.'

'It's fine. She's asking how I am.'

> **ME:** I'm OK, won't be playing football for a while, though ☹. How come you weren't at the match?

> **ZOE:** Honestly?

> **ME:** Go for it

ZOE: I was too upset about Hunter

ME: Can I just tell you again that it was him who kissed me, and I didn't want it at all . . .

ZOE: It wasn't just him. I think it all got on top of me. Hunter, Shane and even Megan

ME: Megan? Why?

ZOE: You guys have such a great friendship. I've never had that and it looks like so much fun. But seriously, I am glad you're OK

ME: Maybe we could hang out when I'm back at school?

ZOE: Sure, I'd like that :)

Over the next few days and weeks Niall kept to his word. He helped me do my exercises every day. He was enthusiastic, he measured my progress, and it felt like I'd got my brother back. Mum was super attentive and one day she sat with me for hours watching *Modern Family*. And it was nice, knowing that with her I didn't have to do anything. I didn't have to be the best at anything. She loved me anyway. Even Dad had chilled out. When he wasn't working, he'd started hanging out with Niall, just the two of them, going to the cinema or out for dinner, and one night Mum *and* Dad played *Mario Kart* with us, and I hadn't laughed that much in a really long time.

Megan helped too, making me laugh when I was falling back into my own head and thinking about football or Shane. She'd pull me out with some stupid joke or dance.

Sadie came to visit one afternoon. The same afternoon Niall and Megan had gone out on some mystery date.

'How are you doing, Lexie? That was some injury.' She pulled a face.

'I'm OK. I've got physio to do and painkillers.'

She nodded. 'I've come to give you something. You know the awards ceremony that we have in the summer?'

I nodded while she looked for something in her bag.

She pulled out a trophy. 'This is for you. Manager's player. For the player who tries the hardest, who always gives one hundred per cent. An absolute credit to the club.'

She held it out to me, and I took it. My eyes welled up as I read the inscription.

Manager's Player

Alexandra Ryan

2024–2025

'Thank you,' I said, my voice quiet. These awards weren't usually given out until the end of the season.

'No, thank *you*, Lexie. I haven't come across a player as determined as you for a very long time and it's given me hope that there are more of you out there somewhere. You are an absolute joy to coach, and we'll be there when you get back to full health.'

She sounded like she was going to cry. Sadie was not an emotional person. I tried to swallow the lump in my throat.

Mum came in to say hello properly, then she saw the trophy and her face lit up.

'You've got some daughter, Mrs Ryan.' Sadie stood up, getting ready to leave.

'Don't I know it.' Mum winked at me, then showed Sadie out the door.

Mum came back in and put the trophy gently on the mantelpiece.

I stared at it and my chest swelled with pride.

'See, what did I tell you, Lexie? What's for you won't pass you.'

I'd been feeling like such a failure, for failing to get a proper place on the team, for pushing myself so hard I got injured . . . for Shane. And it wasn't like the award fixed everything, but it coloured in a tiny corner of the black hole I'd been living in.

30

Walking into school with crutches meant *a lot* of people asking what had happened. And I didn't mind the questions. I just didn't want the attention.

Niall and Megan had class at the other side of the school, so I was by myself, and of course the first person I saw was Hunter, on his phone in the doorway. When he saw me, he put his phone away and gave me a grin.

'Lex!' He came towards me and wrapped me in a hug before I could get away. 'How are you? I wanted to visit, but Niall was being weird about it, so that's why I didn't, in case you thought I didn't care. I was going to bring you flowers and everything.'

I hadn't actually thought about it at all. I hadn't been expecting him to visit, and if I had thought about him, it was only brief thoughts of panic that I'd have to see him again after that kiss.

'I'm fine,' I said, wriggling out of his hug. 'Where's Zoe?'

'Dunno. We're not together any more. That was short.' He laughed and I screwed up my face.

'Yeah, because you messed things up.'

'The heart wants what the heart wants,' he teased, and I kept my face the way it was.

'Pretty sure that night was nothing to do with your heart. You really hurt her, you know.'

'She'll get over it,' he scoffed.

'Yeah? So will you. Fuck off, Hunter,' I said the words simply, but inside I was burning with rage at how he'd treated Zoe, and how he'd treated me. I couldn't believe I hadn't seen it before, but I guess he'd been part of our lives for so long that it was easy to excuse the way he acted as 'Hunter being Hunter'.

I limped away and ignored him calling after me.

I walked into the corridor and there was Zoe, leaning against a locker and talking to Amina. When I walked over, they stopped talking.

I smiled. 'Hey.'

I watched as Amina looked at Zoe like she was waiting for her reaction.

'Hey, Lexie.' Zoe smiled back warmly, and Amina looked confused.

'You have English now, don't you? Want to walk together?' I asked hopefully.

'Sure.'

'Ugh, I have chemistry. Chat later, bitches,' said Amina, and she walked the other way with a wave.

For once I was happy to see Zoe's trademark smile.

'I think you smile more than anyone I've ever met,' I commented.

Zoe laughed and touched my shoulder. 'I guess it's from

when I was a kid. My mum always said, "You catch more flies with honey," so she told me to smile all the time and people would like me.' She shrugged, her voice slowing at the end like she was embarrassed. 'I guess it just became such a habit I don't even know I'm doing it any more . . .'

'You have a great smile.'

She grinned. 'Thanks. My mum's always been kind of OTT about me making friends. Obsessed with me being popular, being good at everything, blah, blah, blah. So weird. I mean, did you see her that night ages ago after practice? Total cringe.' She pulled a face. 'I was so embarrassed.' I could see some pain in her eyes, and it hit me how hard that must be and how grateful I was for my own mum, who was the total opposite.

'To be fair, you're always talking to people, so I guess her wish came true. I probably should have tried to be more like that. Stupid only having one really good friend.'

'Oh my God, no! I would kill to have a best, best friend. I mean, Amina's cool but she's more into TikTok than talking to me most of the time, and I think everyone else just talks to me because I'm rich and pretty,' she said seriously.

I burst out laughing. 'Zoe!'

'What? It's true. I'm not even saying I have everything. Hunter couldn't even stand me for a month. And he didn't even ask me to V-Ball until the day before.'

We were almost at class, and I slowed down more than I had to.

'Hunter's an asshole. It's nothing to do with you. And, hey, he made us friends, so not all bad.'

Zoe stared at me. 'Really? Like proper friends? Like, do you want to come over to my house sometime and come out on our boat?' Zoe's smile was off the charts.

'That sounds great.'

Niall met me after my last class and took my bag for me. 'How's it going?'

'Fine,' I said.

But it wasn't fine. The whole day I'd been thinking about Shane, replaying the moment I looked up at the party and saw him staring at me in horror. I reminded myself that we'd broken up because he was keeping secrets, but it didn't make me feel any better. I let myself think about our training sessions, how much we laughed, covered in sweat, and how much I'd wanted him.

Niall shared a look with Megan.

Megan walked slowly beside me. 'Hey, the NI Senior Women's match is coming up. Let's all go together?'

'Sure,' I said sadly.

'You're totally not fine,' Megan said to me in the car. We were sitting in the back. 'Shane?'

I nodded. 'Yeah.'

'Did you talk to him?'

I shook my head and held back tears. Megan took my hand and held it the whole way back to her house.

When we got home Niall turned to me in the back seat.

'Want to go down to the beach?'

I hadn't been down to the beach with Niall in years.

Niall put our bags in the house, and we walked to the shore, where I abandoned my crutches and held on to Niall to steady me. Then I sat down and stared out at the waves while Niall chucked stones into the water.

'You know me and Meg are always here if you want to talk.' He kept chucking the stones and my heart swelled for him.

'I just wish I hadn't messed everything up.'

'But did you?'

'I broke up with him because there was something he wasn't telling me. And then he showed up and saw me kissing Hunter, even though I didn't kiss him. *He* kissed *me*.'

'Hunter's a fucking idiot,' said Niall. 'But, like, I don't have any secrets from Megan. It shouldn't be like that. You did the right thing.'

And because it came from Niall it felt like maybe I *had* done the right thing, even though my heart still ached.

'What's that annoying thing Mum always says?' Niall turned to me, and I looked at him quizzically. 'What's for you won't pass you. That's it. Yep, it works here.'

He turned back to the lough, and I thought about it. He was right. If it was meant to be, it would happen. There was still hope. And if it didn't happen, it wasn't supposed to be. I pulled myself up and limped over beside him. I picked up a handful of rocks and started throwing them into the water, balancing on one leg.

I picked up a piece of polystyrene that had washed up on the sand. 'Hey, want to make a boat?'

Niall laughed. 'Obviously.'

31

Over the next few weeks my mood plummeted. Mum and Dad didn't even mention the party any more. It was like, despite what Dad said, they'd just given me a clean slate after what had happened with my calf.

Niall and Megan did their best to cheer me up, but I couldn't shift the black cloud that had settled right over my head. Even Zoe came to visit one afternoon after school, but nothing helped. All I could think about was the fact that everything had blown up in my face. I wasn't even studying, despite the fact my exams started soon. So I'd probably fail those too.

At night I'd scroll through Shane's Instagram to see if he'd posted anything else, so I could get a tiny glimpse into his life. I'd been doing it since we'd broken up, trying to hang on to a sliver of his life. But there was nothing. On WhatsApp he was hardly online. I hovered over his old messages and didn't even try to stop the tears that came when I did.

'You need to do your exercises,' Niall begged me one evening.

'What's the point?' I replied, pulling the duvet over my head.

Niall sat on the end of my bed. 'The point is, you could be left with a permanently rubbish leg if you don't.'

'I don't care,' I replied. And I didn't. Because even if I had a working leg, I still probably wouldn't make the team and I still wouldn't have Shane.

'What would Sadie think?' Niall went there.

'I don't care,' I said with less conviction. I'd be mortified if she saw me like this.

'Lexie, what can we do to help?' Niall sounded desperate now.

'Nothing,' I said. 'Nobody can do *anything*.'

And then my phone rang. I held my hand over my mouth. It was Shane. Shane who hadn't spoken to me since we'd broken up. Who'd ignored all my messages and phone calls, who made my heart stop.

I looked at Niall in panic. He nodded at the phone.

'Answer.'

I picked it up before it rang out. 'Hello?'

'Lexie,' Shane said.

He sounded different. Quieter, like he was tired, or like he'd been crying.

'Are you OK?' I asked, my heart thudding in my ears, forgetting everything else when I heard the pain in his voice.

'I want to explain what happened. Everything. I need you. I'm at the hospital, the Royal. Can you come? I'm sorry, I just can't do this by myself.' He sounded panicked now, his voice shaking.

'Shane, are you OK? What happened?' And now I was panicked too.

'It's my dad. I'll explain when you get here. I'll meet you in the cafe.'

'OK, see you soon.'

I hung up the phone and Niall stared at me, waiting to be filled in.

'Can you drive me to the hospital?' I asked him.

'Shit, what happened?'

'Something to do with his dad. He sounded really weird.' My eyes welled thinking about the pain in his voice and the growing fear in my gut.

I tied my hair up in a high ponytail and didn't bother putting on any make-up.

'Mum, I'm just going out with Niall,' I said, when I made it downstairs.

She studied my face. 'Lexie, are you OK? Did something happen?'

'I'm fine. I just need to meet a friend,' I said. 'I'll tell you everything later, I promise.'

She just nodded and opened the door for me.

Niall drove quickly to the hospital. 'Give me a call when you're done.'

'Thanks,' I said, then reached over and hugged him. It had been years since I'd hugged Niall, but I was so thankful for everything. How he'd helped with the recovery, how he'd gone back to being the Niall I knew and loved.

'Do you want me to come in?' Niall asked, concern on his face.

I shook my head. 'Thanks, but I'll be fine.'

I got out of the car and made my way through the hospital,

up the escalator, into the lift and looked for the cafe. I didn't have to look too hard. He was sitting in the window, his Adidas jacket zipped right up to his chin, staring into the cup his hands were clasped round. I could barely breathe.

'Shane,' I said.

He looked up and his face was as blotchy as mine.

I sat beside him, and he looked at my crutches.

'What happened?' He looked horrified.

I shook my head. 'I'm fine. I'll tell you later. What's happened to *you*?'

'My dad. He had a fall. I wasn't there. It was my fault.'

'Your dad? What was your fault? Why?' I lifted the cup from his hands and took them in mine instead. He turned to look at me and my heart ached. He looked so broken.

'I never told you. That was the thing I couldn't tell you.'

'Told me what?'

He inhaled. 'Dad, he can't walk. He had an accident when I was wee, about seven or something. He's a quadriplegic. Me and my mum, we're kind of like his carers.' He took his hand away and pushed it through his hair, hard. 'I mean, sort of. We do the best we can. And Mum never wanted to ask anyone else for help, so we didn't. And then I met you and, Lexie, you were like a drug, and I became so selfish. Like I spent so much time with you when I should have been at home, but I couldn't help it. I loved it. I loved you.' He looked like he was going to cry again.

'Oh, Shane. I'm sorry it was so hard to tell me,' I said, emotions forcing their way to the surface again. The story of my life. I wished right then I was better, that I was warm and open, so that everyone could just tell me whatever they wanted. I wished I didn't have this stupid wall that people found impossible to break through. I inhaled, trying to steady my emotions. This wasn't about me. 'I wish you'd felt like you could tell me.'

He shook his head. 'It's not your fault. The way you talked about my dad, the way your face lit up when I told you all that great stuff about him, I wanted him to have that. I wanted someone else to think of him the same way I did. He's class, he really is. And I should have been there,' he said, 'but I was at Ferndale, talking to Raj at training, and I stayed late, and I even told Raj it was OK, that Mum was there, but I knew she had to leave to go to work. I was supposed to be back. Stupid. So stupid. I should have been there.' He shook his head.

'Oh, Shane.' I squeezed his hand and just let him talk in rapid emotional bursts.

'If I'd been there, it wouldn't have happened, he wouldn't have hit his head.'

'It's just you and your mum?' I asked gently.

He cried then. He let go of my hand and shoved his hands into his eye sockets. I put my hand on his hair, stroking it, knowing that there was nothing I could say to make anything better.

'Will he be OK?' I asked, terrified of the answer.

'They think so. It's just so much more complicated because of his condition.'

'Of course,' I said.

I felt ridiculous then, selfish and stupid. Here was Shane

dealing with all of this, and I had been moaning about not being able to play football for a while. I disgusted myself. But maybe I could help him. I noticed as soon as I got there, his haunted eyes softened slightly, like a weight had been lifted.

'I should have told you,' Shane said. 'It was never that I thought you wouldn't understand. I was just enjoying being a normal teenager for once. And you were so focused on your football. I didn't want to give you any other distractions.'

Is that how it had looked to him?

'But I knew, that night at your house, and at the funfair, when you let yourself relax, that you had that easy side too, and I meant it when I said I loved you. You made me so happy, Lexie. That night at your house? Best night of my life. It's just been so hard the last few years with school and everything, and nobody really seems to understand. It felt easier to keep it to myself, instead of putting it all on somebody else. I thought I was helping you.'

I shook my head. 'How could it help me? I love you, Shane.'

He looked like he was going to cry again so I leaned into him, and we hugged, with my head in his neck, filling my lungs with his scent, and desperately thinking of anything to make him feel better.

'I love you too,' he whispered.

'And that kiss. I didn't kiss him. I wouldn't. I would never . . .' I pulled away so he could see my face and how much I meant it.

'I know,' he said. 'When I calmed down and thought about it, it didn't really make any sense.'

'No sense,' I agreed.

'But what happened to you?' He moved his chair back so he could get a good look at my leg.

'Tore my calf, like, pretty badly,' I said.

'Jesus, Lexie.' He leaned down and stroked my leg. 'That must have been so sore.'

'It was. But I'm OK.'

'And when can you play again?' He looked at me with so much worry that the gravity of my injury faded. Like I could see beyond myself and how it was just an injury that would get better; not like his dad who had to live with a disability for the rest of his life.

'Not for a while,' I said with a shrug.

It hurt to say it, but not as much.

'Oh, Lexie,' he said, knowing what that meant.

'I don't know who I am without football,' I said sadly.

'Football is the least interesting part of who you are,' he said without hesitation. 'You're clever and funny, and I know it might sound like a lie, but I've never told anybody else all the things I told you. Like about Dad's depression and how I'm not that into football. You're so much more than football, Lexie.' He twisted his fingers through mine and stared right into my soul.

When I didn't know what to say, he continued. 'Would you ever think of joining Ferndale United with me?' He looked at me, gauging my reaction.

I cocked my head in thought. I'd never have considered it before. Westing was all I wanted. Westing was what I *needed*. But what if he was right? Maybe football wasn't all

I was? I thought about the times I'd left a match upset, left training upset, the hours I'd spent planning how to get on to the team. I wouldn't have to do that at Ferndale. They were in a division way below Westing, and I don't know, maybe it could be fun?

'I'll definitely think about it,' I said.

'Yeah?' he asked. And to see him light up a bit, through his despair, gave me hope. Maybe it wasn't any of the other stuff that mattered, but this – these moments that made us laugh and cry and hold each other when nobody else would do. Because being here right now, as a crutch for Shane, felt better than any award I'd ever won or any compliment on my football skills. And that thought was mind-blowing.

'Can I meet him?' I asked. 'I mean, not now or anything, but some time when he's feeling better?'

'Yeah, I think he'd like that,' said Shane. 'He keeps asking about you.'

I felt a rush of love when I realized that meant he'd told his parents about me.

'The whole football thing, it was always for him. He was mad keen on me getting scouted and trying to go pro, that's why I joined Westing, even though we can barely afford it.'

'You should tell him,' I said gently. 'That you've gone back to Ferndale.'

'It'll break his heart.'

I squeezed Shane's hands like he'd squeezed mine. I bet his dad would only want him to be happy.

Then a woman came into the cafe.

She was thin with greying hair and was wearing a long

dress with a cardigan over it. She looked over at us. 'Shane? He's awake. He's asking for you,' she said.

I could sense him relax beside me.

'Thank God,' he whispered.

'I'll see you soon?' I asked, standing up.

Shane waited until his mum had walked away before standing up too. He leaned down and kissed me gently on the forehead.

'Definitely,' he said. 'And, Lexie?'

'Yeah?'

'Thanks. For everything. Can we maybe . . . try again?' He looked at me like he was scared I was going to say no.

How could I? When he'd come back into my life like sunshine after months of rain.

'I'll do better,' he said. 'I promise. No more secrets.'

'I'll do better too,' I promised.

I was quiet on the way home with Niall. Not in a bad way, just thinking about the logistics of moving to Ferndale United. But the more I thought about it, the better an idea it seemed.

'You OK?' Niall asked.

I inhaled. 'I was thinking about joining Ferndale United when I'm better.' I liked how it sounded out loud, and I loved the relief that came with it.

'What?' Niall almost ran a red light. 'Ferndale, are you serious? They're shite.'

I pushed his arm. 'Hey!'

'It's just facts. But why?'

'I have a feeling it will be way more fun than Westing and, let's face it, I'm never getting scouted. I'm barely even getting on the team,' I said.

'Lex . . . but . . . well, maybe it *is* a good idea. Maybe both of us get too stressed out with football.'

'I think you're right,' I agreed.

'Do it,' he said.

32

Six weeks later, my leg was better, and I couldn't wait to start training at Ferndale with Shane. And because I'd done my exercises religiously, the physio had agreed I could play a match.

Shane's dad was in hospital for another few weeks, so we hadn't seen each other. Between school, football and hospital visits, there hadn't been much time. But Shane had woken something in me. Something I didn't think I even had. It spurred me on to do my exercises and get back to me. But not the old me. Shane had made me realize that I was more than football. It was like he'd lifted a veil. One I'd been shrouded in for years, one that had stopped me from seeing beyond my obsession with football. But now it was like I could see everything more clearly, and I didn't have this constant twisting in my chest and an awful voice telling me I was worthless.

We messaged each other every day, morning and afternoon, and we FaceTimed every night before we went to bed. I even talked to Mum and Dad about him. Mum had stopped asking after the night I'd come home upset, obviously putting two and two together. Now she was obsessed with me inviting him for dinner.

At Westing the pitches were perfect – 4G, newly painted fences, floodlights that worked. Ferndale was a different ball game altogether. There were only two pitches and they were both surrounded by broken fences. One pitch even had a burn mark in the middle of it. I parked my car and got out to look for Shane. I checked the time. Ten to six. Kick-off at six, and I'd thought I was going to be late. At Westing we had to be there at least thirty minutes before the whistle.

'Lexie?'

I turned round to see Shane jogging towards me, and there it was again, that slow-motion, breath-stopping, words-caught-in-my-throat feeling that made it impossible to move. And then he was there, right in front of me, like the last couple of months had never happened. I threw my arms round his neck and breathed him in.

We'd agreed not to see each other. Shane had wanted to concentrate on his dad, and I put all my efforts into studying and getting better, so this moment was everything. Part of me was scared that it wouldn't be the same. That the rush of magic that had made everything so special was only the way it was because we'd had to sneak around. What if the spark was gone?

'Hey,' he said with a smile. And the electricity was back, rushing through my veins like adrenaline. He pulled me towards the clubhouse, so we were semi out of sight.

'Hey,' I replied.

'I've missed you, Lexie.'

'I've missed you too.'

I leaned into his chest as he stood against the wall, déjà vu from the night at the Dub. He didn't take his eyes off me.

I reached up and pulled him towards me by his football shirt because I needed to feel his lips on mine, the lips I'd been dreaming about ever since our last kiss.

It was just like I remembered. Except better. A spark that grew into a raging fire, my hands twisted in his thick dark hair, tugging gently to remind myself what it felt like. Letting myself feel every feeling, his tongue on mine, his hands on my waist, finding the space above my shorts and under the green shirt I'd borrowed from Niall that was far too big.

I pulled away, hearing voices in the distance.

'Isn't kick-off now?' I looked at the time on my phone.

'Yeah, don't worry, we always start late. Here, come on and meet Raj!'

Shane pulled me in the direction of the pitch, where kids had started to congregate, an array of green T-shirts. Some with numbers, some without.

I let Shane lead me to a man who was leaning against the broken fence watching the team do a warm-up, cigarette in his hand.

'Raj, this is Lexie, the one I told you about.'

'Ah, OK. So *you're* the famous Lexie.' Raj gave me a huge smile, white teeth luminous against his brown skin.

I smiled. 'Yep, that's me.'

'Defence?'

I nodded.

'Thank God. Poor Oscar needs all the help he can get. You're starting.'

A smile burst across my face, and I grabbed Shane's hand in excitement. 'Amazing!'

'You're not at Westing now, Lexie,' said Raj. 'Shane, you're up front, as usual.'

Ferndale had so few players that girls and guys were on the same team. Shane had been back playing for Ferndale for a few weeks now.

Raj sucked on his cigarette and blew the smoke in rings above us. 'Are you ready to play for a real team?'

'I can't wait,' I said. And I was genuinely excited. Yeah, part of me was sad that I wasn't still with my old team, just because it was easier when you knew everyone, but I wouldn't miss the stress of every practice and the constant overthinking about whether I'd get to play or not.

Then there was a girl standing beside us. Younger. About thirteen, maybe. She looked nervous and she was staring at me.

'Are you Lexie?' she asked. She was about a head smaller than me, elfin, with short red hair and a million freckles.

Shane stepped in to clear up the confusion. 'Lexie, this is Grace. She's been torturing me for ages to come back to Ferndale and I told her that it was you who gave me the balls to do it.'

Grace.

I smiled at her because I didn't know what to say, and because I was still enjoying the relief of finding out who she was.

She laughed, her face now bright red. 'You have no idea how happy we are. Shane is the best coach ever!' Then she ran off to the other pitch to join her team.

'Best coach ever,' Raj muttered, rolling his eyes.

'She seems nice,' I said.

'They're all nice.' Shane smiled.

'What about you, mate? How are you doing with everything?' Raj's tone was low, serious.

I looked at Shane to catch his reaction.

He hesitated for a second then burst into life. 'Ah yeah, man, all good. I've got some support now.' Shane elbowed me and I leaned into him.

'I'm glad to hear that. Oh, and the under-nines have been asking for you now that they know you're back. Sorry, you know I can't lie. They've a match after and are asking if you could stick around?' Raj looked at Shane apologetically. 'They really missed you coaching.'

'You coached kids?' I said.

Just when I thought I couldn't love him any more.

'Yeah, just a bit. I wasn't very good at it,' he said.

'Don't talk shite,' said Raj, laughing. 'You were the best coach we had. Didn't you hear what Grace said?'

'Of course I'll hang around,' Shane said.

'Thanks, mate, they'll be buzzing.'

'Is that OK with you? I know we were supposed to hang out after. Would you stay too?' Shane asked me.

'Of course.' I couldn't wait to see him coaching.

He grinned at me, and I had to stop myself from kissing him again. 'Should we start this warm-up then?'

He took my hand, and we walked over to join our new team.

33

I have never laughed so much in a football match. Correction: I'd never laughed in a football match. And we lost. Nine–nil. But it had never been more fun. Nobody cared if you messed up. Missed a pass? They just laughed at you and tried to get it back. Own goal? They took the piss. But it was all in good humour, no side-eyes or straight-up balling someone out for missing a chance. And when the game was over, I couldn't shake the grin from my face.

Shane slung his arm round my shoulders. 'Have fun?' he asked into my hair, sending electricity the whole way down my spine.

'It feels wrong to say yes,' I replied and wiped sweat from my brow.

'Nah, that's what I loved about it here. Winning, losing, it didn't matter. Everyone here just loves the game, even if they're crap,' he said and laughed.

But I barely got to talk to Shane because about six eight-year-olds had swarmed around him.

'*Mister! You're back!*'

'Are you going to be our coach again?'

'Raj is shite at coaching; we need you back.'

I laughed. Shane was laughing too, trying to calm them down.

'I'll be back when I have a bit of time, wee man. And maybe my friend Lexie will help me.' Shane looked at me, his eyes sparkling.

The gang of kids looked at me. Sizing me up, scrunching up their faces.

'But she's a girl,' one of the boys said.

Shane pointed to our teammates who were lying exhausted on the ground. 'She's better than any boy on that team.'

It was nice of him to say it, but I was still buzzing over how much I'd enjoyed the match.

'Fine then,' the boy said.

It was beautiful watching Shane coach the kids' team. He was so invested, telling them where to stand, encouraging them, giving them team talks at half-time, and you could see how much they loved him.

But not as much as I did.

We went for a walk after the matches. Hands twisted in each other's, we walked into Ferndale.

'Oh my God, is that a milkshake bar?' I spotted it a mile off. Fairy lights all round the door frame with a big luminous 'Maggie's' sign glaring neon-pink.

Shane shrugged. 'Yep. The Birch High kids kind of claimed it as theirs. I never go in.'

'Until now,' I said, pulling him towards the door.

'Until now,' he repeated, smiling.

The place was packed! It was full of teenagers, in groups, in couples, staring at phones, laughing over the music. Niall and Megan would love this place. I reminded myself to tell them.

As we stood in the queue, I read the noticeboard, my eye falling on a poster of some kid with a top knot. Massive smile.

Reigning Champion of Maggie's Challenge
Michael Crawley

'This guy has tried every flavour of milkshake. Every single one.' I scanned the never-ending list of flavours.

'Very impressive,' Shane agreed. Then I noticed him look at his phone, read something, then put it away again. He saw me looking. 'Oh, that's just Mum asking when I'll be back, but she said no rush.'

'Shall we get them to take away?'

'Sure, thanks.'

We left with my winter berry milkshake and Shane's sugar cookie.

'So where now? Do you want to go home?' I asked.

'No, I want to show you something first.'

I thought right then that I'd follow him anywhere.

We walked down the street and then Shane turned us up an alleyway where we went into an arcade.

'I love arcades,' I said.

'My dad used to bring me here all the time when I was a kid. He used to give me loads of two ps and let me work away on the machines. It was, like, my favourite thing.'

'Let's do it,' I said. I changed a tenner into pennies and

Shane stood behind me as we put coin after coin into the machine, losing every single one.

'I'm usually better than that,' he said.

'What are you trying to say?' I asked, outraged. 'That I'm bringing bad vibes to the party? Maybe, Shane O'Connoll, you can't be good at everything.'

He laughed. 'I'm definitely not good at everything.'

I rolled my eyes. 'Had me fooled. Dodgems! We're doing it,' I said and pulled him towards the back of the arcades. 'Get in, you're driving. I've had enough of being everyone's chauffeur.' Also, using the car pedals hurt my calf a bit. It was technically 'better' but it still twinged now and again, especially after the match.

'Yes, sir,' he said and pretended to look scared.

We didn't do much driving. It was too dark and there were two other couples who seemed content with crashing into each other, so nobody noticed us kissing in the corner.

We spent the next hour walking around Ferndale, hands twisted together. We walked through the park and towards the fountain that reminded me of that night at Zoe's. We sat down on the edge.

'Will you come to my house to meet my parents?' he said. 'They'd really like to meet you. Properly.'

I'd dreamed about this moment before. I'd thought about how nice it would be to see where he came from, to be part of his world.

'I'd love to,' I said, and he looked relieved. 'Did you think I was going to say no?'

'I just worry, you know. Dad, it's such a big thing for some people. I've seen people's reactions to him sometimes, making excuses to leave, awkward smiles; it's really sad to watch, because I know how much he loves people.'

'I'm more worried about what he'll think of *me*,' I said. And I meant it.

'He'll adore you, Lexie. Just don't tell him you support United.'

I laughed.

'Oh, and I still haven't told him I've gone back to Ferndale,' Shane said, sounding guilty.

I squeezed his hand. 'How come?'

'It just never felt like the right time, you know? He was so sick, and then he was better, but everything's still such a struggle and I couldn't face disappointing him, not after all that.'

'I get it. Does your mum know?'

Shane nodded. 'She thinks it's great. She never wanted me to leave. And she said Dad would be fine with it. But I'm still worried, you know?'

'Yeah, I get it. Don't worry, we can come up with a plan to tell him, I'll help.'

'Thanks.'

'You still OK to come over tomorrow for dinner?' I asked and my stomach flipped. I was so excited to show him off.

'Wouldn't miss it.'

34

I only spent about thirty minutes getting ready. Not the hours I'd usually take if I had a date. Shane made me feel comfortable, like I didn't *have* to be perfect. But I still wanted to look good, so I did curl my hair and put on lip gloss, but I wasn't meticulous, and I definitely wasn't perfect. But that was OK.

When I'd finished getting ready, Megan knocked on my door.

'You read–' she said as she walked in, stopping mid-word as she saw me. 'Lex, you look amazing. How do you expect him to chat to your parents when you look like that?' She sat down on the bed.

I laughed. 'I'm sure he'll manage. But you think this is OK?' I gave her a spin of my new Barcelona shirt that I'd tucked into my favourite shorts. The ones Shane loved. Megan gave me a very enthusiastic thumbs up.

'How do you think it'll go? Think your parents will like him?'

'I think so?' I cocked my head in the mirror. 'Mum's just so excited I have a boyfriend, I'd be really surprised if she didn't like him.'

'Yeah, I mean, he's super likable . . . and super hot.'

I threw a pillow at her, laughing. 'Well, I hope she *doesn't* think that!'

Then I turned to her and inhaled. 'What about Niall? How do you think he'll be?'

On the face of it, the old Niall was back. The Niall that I knew and loved, who played *Mario Kart* with me, who took the piss out of teachers with me and watched football clips on YouTube with me for hours. But Shane hadn't been in the picture. Not properly. And I deliberately didn't talk about him in front of Niall. I saved all that for Megan. I'd even been opening up about it to Zoe. She'd been so sweet about everything, even though I knew she probably still liked him. And it's not like I brought it up or anything. She did. Turns out, she really wasn't the girl I thought she was.

Megan was lying on her stomach on my bed now, her chin in her hands, shiny brown hair tied up in a ponytail. 'You know what? We don't really talk about it that much. I tried to bring it up before, but he totally shut down and then I just didn't push it. So I think he'll *probably* be fine, but I really can't be sure. Sorry.' She sighed.

'It's not your fault. Ah well, guess we'll just have to go for it and see what happens.'

Megan sat up and sniffed. 'What's that smell?'

'Mum wanted to cook.' I rolled my eyes. 'Mum can't cook.' I made a crying face. 'And Shane's, like, really good at cooking. He's going to be horrified.' I put my hands on my face. I'd thought about asking her to get takeaway or something, but she was *so* into it that I couldn't bring myself to disappoint her.

'What's she making?' Megan asked.

'Lasagne,' I said.

'OK, that's *fine*! How wrong can lasagne go?'

I laughed. 'That just tells me that you've never tried my mum's cooking.'

'Lexie?' I heard Mum call from downstairs.

'Oh my God, she heard us,' Megan whispered, and I laughed.

'What?'

'Shane's here.'

And then my stomach was in my throat. I took a last look in the mirror. I was happy. I looked good, I smelled great, and I couldn't wait to see him.

'Go for it,' said Megan.

I smiled at her and walked downstairs. And he was standing there in the hall in a pair of jeans, trainers and a black jumper. I ran down the last few stairs, into his arms and breathed him in before anyone saw me.

'I didn't want to wear a tracksuit,' he said as I pulled away. 'Mum got me these jeans. I never wear jeans.' He sounded nervous, and I quickly looked towards the kitchen to check Mum and Dad weren't coming before reaching up to kiss him.

'You look so good,' I said. 'But a tracksuit would have been fine too.'

'Oh, hey,' Shane said, looking behind me.

I spun round to see Niall staring at us. There was no way he hadn't seen the kiss.

It felt like thirty minutes instead of three seconds before Niall spoke.

'Hey, man,' he said.

I let out a breath.

'Nice house,' Shane said.

I felt for him. What was he supposed to say when Niall was just standing there making him feel awkward?

'Do you play *Mario Kart*?' Niall asked.

I almost laughed with relief.

'I don't have it, but yeah, I've played.'

'Grand Prix?' Niall asked and nodded upstairs.

Shane looked at me, like he wasn't sure what to do. 'Sure?'

'Let's do it,' I said. I took Shane's hand and pulled him upstairs after Niall.

Megan was playing too. We all chose our characters and were squished together on the sofa.

Niall then Megan, then me, then Shane.

'Hey, before we start, can I say something?'

Mario Kart music played in the background, and everyone looked at Niall.

'Sure, yeah,' said Shane, clearly even more nervous now.

'Sorry for acting like a dick when you joined Westing. Don't know why I did that. Can we be cool?' Niall reached over for a fist bump.

'Yeah, man, sounds good,' Shane said with a smile, and I shared a look of relief with Megan.

I was so grateful to Niall right then.

'Nice one. You're not beating me at this, though. Or you're dead.' Niall laughed.

But Shane didn't win. *I did.* And then I did a victory dance, which was cut short when Mum came up the stairs.

'Dinner's ready. I think I did a really good job this time.'
She smiled and looked so proud.

'Thanks, Mum.'

We went downstairs and Mum had set the table like it was Christmas or something, with a centrepiece and candles and the good cutlery. So embarrassing.

'Look at the lovely flowers Shane brought.' Mum pointed to the carnations in the middle of the table, and I looked at Shane, who'd gone bright red.

'So, Shane, sit down, tell us about you,' Dad said. 'Lexie has already told us bits and pieces, but I'd love to know more. Then maybe I'll understand why my daughter is walking about with a grin on her face all the time.'

I wanted to die. 'Dad!'

Shane talked about football and school *and* his family. He talked about everything that had been going on, starting with his dad's accident. I hooked my foot round his under the table.

'Oh, Shane. That's a lot to deal with at your age. If there's anything at all we can do to make things easier, please tell Lexie and we'll do whatever we can,' Mum said. I was hoping she wouldn't cry when Shane was talking, because she looked like she was about to. But she didn't. Instead, she got up and opened the oven. 'It's ready!' she sang.

Nobody said anything when she set the lasagne on the table. We just stared at it. Black congealed cheese round the edges, dried out sheets of pasta that hadn't been covered in sauce.

Niall burst out laughing. And then everybody laughed, including Mum.

Dad got up and squeezed Mum's shoulders behind her. 'Shall we get some pizza?'

She nodded through tears of laughter, and later, we sat in the living room eating pizza and trading stories about school.

Then Mum came in to ask us all a question. 'I have a challenge for you all. We'd love to take you on holiday this summer. Shane, we can work around you and whatever you need, but I need you all to come up with somewhere to go. Anywhere.'

Megan gasped and grabbed Niall's hand. I looked at Shane, scared it was too much and that he would run right out of my house.

He just smiled at Mum. 'That sounds amazing, Mrs Ryan. I'll speak to my mum and see what could work.'

'Brilliant.' Mum looked so happy.

When Shane had to leave, we stood in the hallway again. This time we were actually alone.

'You know, you don't have to come on holiday, if it doesn't work with your dad or whatever. I can say no for you. Or maybe I'll just stay at home.' I shrugged.

'I'd love to go, Lexie. Aunt Tammy has promised to help out even more than she does, and Mum has been saying that I need more time to do my own thing.'

I reached up and kissed him. Then I felt his hand slip underneath the bottom of my shirt, and find that space at the top of my shorts. Our space.

My whole body was fizzing with electricity when he left.

35

Shane came to my house loads after that. After school, at the weekend after football. But now it was my turn. I still hadn't met his family. But today was the day. What would I say to his dad? Would it be awkward? I'd bought some of the expensive cupcakes from town and I asked Megan a million times if my outfit looked OK. I was wearing jeans and a Nike jumper, keeping it sporty, but not one Man United logo in sight. Niall dropped me off outside.

I knocked on the door with my brown box of cupcakes, and waited, butterflies about seeing Shane, nerves about meeting his family.

Shane's mum answered the door.

'Hi, come on in. You must be Lexie.' She smiled and waved me in, and I heard Niall drive off.

'It's so nice to meet you,' I said. 'Oh, these are for you.' I handed her the cupcakes.

'How lovely. Thank you, Lexie. I'm so sorry – I've just had a call from work, someone has phoned in sick and I have to go, but I just wanted to say that you're very welcome here, any time. Anyone who makes our Shane this happy is always welcome.' And this must have been how Shane felt when Niall asked him to play *Mario Kart*. Welcome. She smiled a tired smile and squeezed my shoulder before leaving.

Shane's house was tidy, and it had pictures everywhere. I glanced at them as I walked past. There were ones of Shane playing football and others that I assume were of his dad.

'In here, Lexie!' Shane called.

It was a small house, so I followed the voice easily into a little living room, which had been made even smaller by the bed in the corner. Shane was sitting on the sofa, football on the television, and there was his dad, watching from a wheelchair in the corner.

Before I even said hello to Shane, his dad looked up and broke into a grin.

'So, you're Lexie,' he said, half raising a hand in a sort of wave. His voice was slurred, but there was so much warmth in it.

'I am! And you must be Mr O'Connoll.' I walked over and shook his hand. 'It's so nice to meet you. Shane has told me so much.'

'Good things, I hope,' he said.

'Oh my God, the best things.' I sat down beside Shane. 'So tell me about the football. From the very beginning. I want to know every detail. I bet Shane left some stuff out.'

'Shane, why don't you make Lexie some tea?' his dad said.

'Yeah, Shane, tea,' I said.

Shane smiled at me as he got up.

I spent the next hour listening to Shane's dad tell me the most amazing stories about how he was scouted, all the players he met, how intense it was, and then he told me about the accident. I held back tears when he told me about the surgeries and how his sister couldn't visit him for weeks because she was so upset. And I got it. If something like that happened to Niall, I don't think I'd be able to deal with it.

'Spinal injury,' he said.

Shane played with his hair beside me, and I moved closer to him so our legs were touching.

'I'm sorry that happened,' I said.

'It's just life,' Shane's dad replied.

'I guess it is.'

Then Shane cut in. 'You know, Dad, Lexie's going to join Ferndale United.'

'I thought you were at Westing?' his dad asked me, confused.

I nodded. 'Well . . . I hardly ever got to start.' I sighed. 'But Shane took me to Ferndale, and it was so much fun.'

'Well, I suppose it depends on what you want from it. Our Shane wants it all, don't you, lad?'

Shane was quiet.

I stared at the TV. Some old World Cup match.

'I don't,' Shane said quietly.

I pressed my leg against his. A leg of support.

'What do you mean?'

'I don't want Westing. I don't want to be scouted. I want football to be fun again.'

His dad was quiet. Then: 'I thought you loved it? I thought it was what you wanted? For your future.'

Shane shook his head, and I slid my hand into his. He squeezed it. 'I want to play for fun. And I think I want to be a coach.'

I was so proud of him for being so brave. And after seeing him coach those kids, it made total sense. He was a natural.

'But I thought you loved it,' his dad repeated.

'I'm sorry.' Shane looked at his lap.

His dad shook his head. 'Don't be sorry. I should be sorry.'

I excused myself and went to the bathroom while Shane and his dad carried on talking in low voices. But when I heard them laughing, I knew it was safe to return.

'Do you need anything before I go upstairs, Dad?' Shane asked.

He stood up, and when his dad said no Shane squeezed his shoulder.

I followed him upstairs to his room. It was small, tidy and, like the rest of the house, smelled like fabric conditioner. I sat down on the bed.

'How much do you actually do? For your dad?' I asked. I didn't know how he managed to fit it all in with school and football.

'Ah, you know, most of it is second nature now. Helping him to the bathroom, cooking, sorting his medicine; that's why I learned to cook something other than spaghetti bolognese,' he laughed. 'Going out is always a bit of an event, so there's that. Cleaning, that sort of stuff.'

He laughed at my mouth hanging open.

'But how? How do you fit it all in?'

He shrugged. 'I just do. I mean, everything else suffers a bit, but I wouldn't have it any other way, and my aunt, you know the one who came to the Glentoran match?'

I nodded and he continued.

'Well, like I said to your parents, she's going to start coming to help us more too. She was talking to Mum about how I should have more time. And it's not like I asked for it or anything, I don't mind doing all that stuff for Dad, but I guess some extra free time might be nice. And I told them about the holiday. Honestly, I thought they'd say no right away, and that would have been fine, but they didn't. They really want to make it work for me.'

He'd been dealing with so much, and he was right, it *was* complicated. I squeezed his hand. 'You're amazing.'

He laughed. 'Ah, no I'm not. My A levels will be a joke.'

'Fuck the A levels. You will make an incredible coach. And it was so brave telling your dad about Ferndale.'

'Thanks, yeah, decided just to go for it while you were there. Felt easier. Turns out I should have done it ages ago,' he said, sitting down beside me. 'But if I didn't join Westing, I never would have met you.' He tilted my chin and kissed me. And then it was back: electricity, fireworks, and a relief so strong that I could feel tears building behind my eyes.

'So tell me more about coaching,' I said. 'It's such a brilliant idea.'

'Yeah, I was actually thinking, what if I could coach a team of kids that are all carers? I mean, I know there would be so much to organize and it's complicated. It's a stupid idea . . .'

My heart swelled. 'Shane, it's the opposite of a stupid idea,' I said genuinely.

'You think? I had this idea about using the Ferndale grounds early mornings, like when we did our training because I always helped out Dad at seven a.m., and I bet there are loads of kids who do the same. And it really helped me. Those few hours cleared my head, and being with you made me happier than I've been in years.' He couldn't stop smiling.

'I love you,' I said.

'I love you too,' he replied.

And I thought my heart might burst all over again.

36

Officially joining Ferndale FC was much less complicated than Westing. There was one form to fill out instead of a million and not that it really mattered to Mum and Dad, but it cost half the price. And it didn't matter when Shane couldn't come to some of the practices; he wasn't kicked off the team or made to feel guilty about it. Raj knew his situation, so it was totally cool.

'Oh, I was thinking about your idea,' Raj said to him one day at practice. He glanced over at me. 'You know Shane's idea to set up a football team for young carers?'

I nodded and he continued.

'Well, I spoke to the club, and they said they'd be happy to let you use the pitches two mornings a week.' He took a drag of a cigarette I hadn't even seen him light. 'As long as I come too. Something to do with insurance, but I'd stopped listening by that point.'

Shane's face lit up with a grin. 'Are you serious?'

Raj nodded.

'Thanks so much, man.' Shane slapped his shoulder and Raj flashed him a smile, before walking away.

I felt such a rush of love for Shane. 'It'll be amazing. As

long as you don't teach them all the secret skills you taught me,' I said with a wink, pulling Shane's hand and leading him towards the back of the clubhouse. This time I leaned against the wall. Both of us out of sight.

'I do miss our private coaching sessions,' Shane said.

'Maybe we should restart them,' I said, pulling him towards me and I got lost in Shane for the next five minutes before practice.

Practice with Ferndale was amazing. Half the kids weren't even dressed for football. One girl was even wearing jeans.

Afterwards I went back to Shane's house for dinner, where he cooked for us all.

I was in awe of him. How much he did. How much he could do. And I was so comfortable there with his family, chatting away to his dad like I'd known him forever.

'Oh, we have our first league game with Ferndale this weekend. Do you think you'd maybe want to come?' Shane looked across the table at his dad. 'I could help get you down and everything; we could get a taxi. I mean, don't worry if it's too hard. I know it's not easy,' Shane waved away his suggestion.

'We'd love to come,' his mum answered for him.

I watched her squeeze Shane's dad's hand. And then I looked at Shane, who had the biggest grin on his face.

'And Tammy will want to come too,' said his mum. 'I think she loves it more than your dad.'

When I got home, I told Niall and Megan about the game. 'Actually, we kind of need another couple of players if you fancy it?'

They looked at each other on the sofa, then back to me.

'Sure,' Niall said. 'Why not?'

'Amazing. OK, just wear something green. Anything. I'll let Raj know you're coming.'

On the phone to Shane that night I described the sea again, looking out at the lough.

'Don't you think it's weird how much we don't know about the sea?' I said.

'I think it's exciting,' he said. 'It's like you. I find out something new about you every day. I mean, I never knew you could do such a good moonwalk.' He laughed. 'And that you've no shame doing it in front of my parents.'

I burst out laughing. 'It's not right to hide your talents.'

'It's kind of strange having Tammy here so much,' Shane said. He sounded nervous.

'Is she nice?'

'Aw, yeah, she's really nice, and she's been around all my life. It's just different, you know, after it being me and Mum for so long. It's hard to think that someone else will be doing some of that stuff. I think I'll kind of miss it,' he said. 'I know it sounds crazy.'

'It doesn't at all. It's obvious how much you love your family, so of course it's going to be weird bringing someone else into the mix. But just remember it's what your dad wants,' I said as gently as I could.

Shane hesitated. 'Yeah, you're right, he does. And it's so amazing that they're coming to watch the match on Saturday.'

'It really is,' I agreed.

We talked for hours. About everything and nothing and I

didn't hang up until Mum came into my room and asked if she could talk to me.

When I went downstairs, Niall was already in the kitchen with her.

What had happened now?

I swallowed nervously and shared a look with Niall, who shrugged. 'What's going on?' I asked, sliding on to a bar stool beside Niall.

'Look, you two.' Mum's expression was so serious that I thought she was going to tell us that one of them had cancer.

I moved even closer to Niall. 'What is it?' I asked, panicking.

'It's about the holiday. Look, your dad is going to try and influence you, make you try and choose somewhere with loads of historical sights –' she rolled her eyes – 'but I was watching this drama last night set in Iceland.'

Niall and I laughed.

'Did anyone die?' I said.

'Oh yes, loads of people. It was a massacre. But the scenery was particularly beautiful,' she said. 'We don't need to decide yet, and you've both exams to get on with, but just keep Iceland in mind.'

I'd actually been thinking of somewhere even closer, somewhere that if Shane needed to get back to his family, he could do it in a couple of hours. 'What about Donegal?'

'Yeah right, Lexie,' Niall scoffed.

'Well, look, we don't have to decide yet. Now, shush, don't tell him,' Mum whispered.

Dad walked into the kitchen. 'Did you know you can go and see the Bayeux Tapestry in Normandy?'

I looked at Mum.

'I told you,' she mouthed.

'Oh, Dad, we're playing a match on Saturday at Ferndale if you want to come?' Niall asked. Things between the two of them were so much better now. In fact, from the outside you might even think that Niall was Dad's favourite. If you didn't know any better.

'We'll be there,' said Mum, and I was happier than I expected. Mum had been way more interested in my football since I stopped playing for Westing. She asked about training and match fixtures all the time.

'Great,' I said, smiling.

I'd got into a routine with Shane. Some days he'd come to my house after school, but some days he had to go home and help his dad, so I went there and kept him company. It didn't matter where we were. I just loved being near him. And when I wasn't hanging out with Shane I was with Megan. We'd even reinstated our Sunday-night movies. And in the in-between times, when there was nobody else there, that's when I hung out with Niall, trying not to think about the fact that him and Megan would be gone after the summer.

The NI Senior Women's match was coming up, and Megan had asked her dad for a few extra tickets, so Shane, Zoe and Amina were coming too. Hunter was totally out of the picture after all the drama he caused at the party. And even though he'd been his best mate for ages, Niall didn't seem that upset about it. He said he'd been annoying him for a while. And

I guess everyone else felt the same way, because they didn't even mention him at all.

It was a shame it would all end, that Megan and maybe Niall would be going across the water. If anyone had asked me a few years ago about the prospect of me and Niall living in different countries, I would have accused them of insanity. But this was the new me, who had ripped up her lists and was no longer obsessed with football and perfection.

So I was OK with it. It was just a new chapter. Sports science at UUJ and helping Shane with his coaching on the side.

Shane would be here, with me, and that's all I needed.

37

I was actually kind of nervous before the Ferndale match. Not because I was scared we wouldn't win or that I'd play badly, because, let's face it, we were never going to win, but because my parents *and* Shane's parents were coming to watch.

Niall drove me and Megan, and Mum and Dad drove themselves. When we got there Shane was already at the far side of the pitch talking to his dad, with his mum and his aunt talking to each other.

I jogged over. 'Hi, Mr O'Connoll, Mrs O'Connoll, and Tammy, it's so nice to meet you, Shane has told me so much about you.'

His aunt stepped forward and took my hands in hers, smiling. 'Thank you for being so good to our Shane.' She looked like she might cry.

I shook my head. 'He's amazing.'

'He is that,' she agreed.

'Are Niall and Megan ready for the match of their life?' Shane asked, coming behind me and wrapping his arms round my neck.

I turned and smiled at him, and he kissed my head. 'I think

we might struggle today,' I said, scanning the other team, who were practising shots and scoring every single one.

'You ready?' Shane whispered and it sent a shiver right down my spine.

Megan and Niall were walking towards us, and I saw Mum and Dad coming over carrying huge boxes. They were talking to Raj, who then turned and ran on to the pitch where the rest of the team were standing.

We walked over to join them.

'OK, guys, we have some help today. Megan here has been picked up by a Prem scout and will be heading across the water soon. She is also in the Northern Ireland training programme, so do your best to get the ball to her, Shane, Niall and Lexie.'

I don't think anyone was listening. They were all staring at Megan with open mouths.

'But, look, at the end of the day, who cares! Just go out there and have some fun, and Lexie's parents have brought a ridiculous amount of donuts that we need to eat afterwards, so use that as your incentive to burn as many calories as possible. And, Oscar?' Raj looked at all six foot four of him.

'Yeah?'

Even though he was looking straight at Raj, it looked like his head was in the clouds.

'Please, for the love of God, pass it to *our* team this time. Green shirts. *Green.*'

Oscar gave Raj a thumbs up. 'Got it.'

'God help us,' Raj said.

'Donuts? And nobody cares if you mess up?' Megan slung her arm round me. 'Screw the Premier League.'

'I swear to God, Megan . . .'

She'd been winding me up about it ever since she'd decided that she was definitely going to go. And I fell for it almost every time. Old habits die hard and all that.

'Kidding,' she said. Then she ran backwards to her position.

Niall turned and called down the pitch to me. 'Don't push it too hard on that leg, Lex.'

I flushed a deep red, but at the same time I was touched by how much he cared.

'Go Lexie, go Niall!'

I turned to see Mum jumping and clapping. Dad looked at her in horror.

I tried to ignore them and just looked ahead. At Shane's perfect silhouette right in front of me.

Just as the whistle blew, he passed the ball to Niall, then looked at me, his lip curled into a half-smile.

And, like it always did when he looked at me like that, the whole world stopped.

Acknowledgements

As ever, a million thanks to Ruth Knowles, whose editing skills constantly amaze me. To everyone at Penguin who has worked on this book, I will never not be thankful to you. To Janelle Barone, who has once again perfectly illustrated my characters.

To my lovely agent, Joanna Moult, who is always on the end of the phone when needed.

To the NI Arts Council, I am ever grateful for the funding that helped buy me time to write this masterpiece, and to Jo and Chris at the Secret Bookshelf – thank you, as ever, for all the support.

To Fi and Julia, I am so thankful for our friendship. Especially the fact that you both pretend to not be jealous of my superior writing skills. To Helen, Kelly, Jill, Vicky, Morna, Mairi and Jacqui, our meet ups quell my stress and anxiety even better than a shot of tequila ever could (I imagine . . .).

Clairsie, thanks for the help with the plot (and everything else you've helped with over the last few years).

I would never have guessed how big a part football would play in my life. And what's even more of a surprise is how much I love it. From the joy of standing on Baltic sidelines in parts of Belfast I never knew existed, to being brought almost to tears because the commentators aren't being nice enough about Ipswich Town, and everything in between.

To all the coaches at Barn United (old and new) who give up so much of their time. It is so, *so* appreciated. A testament to you all is how much my kids love training. It's strange, and if I'm honest, a little bit disturbing. I was under the impression that sports training was something to 'get through' just to play the fun matches. Maybe that was just me. But your effort and enthusiasm do not go unnoticed. To the Barn United 2013 Girls, Lyla couldn't have found a better team. I think you're class.

As always, to my parents, thank you for your endless support. To my mum for definitely not still making some appointments for me because I hate phone calls, and to my dad, who started Sunday football all those years ago. It's one of my very favourite memories.

To Chris. I see first hand how much time you put into coaching, and didn't even complain when I suggested that you start taking Sunday football too. I don't know how you do it. It's very impressive. Watching you coach has been one of my very favourite things about the last few years, coming in just after publishing these books, and going to the Era's tour (obv).

Lyla, my favourite daughter. You constantly surprise me in the best way, and I can't wait to see what you do with your life. I adore you. I wish your personality was in fact *my* personality. I wasn't joking when I said you should start replying to my emails for me. ⚘ ♥

Rory, the best son. I don't know anyone more thoughtful, or

anyone with a more wonderful brain. I'm so excited for your future. Spending time with you is pure joy. ♥

Thank you both so much for bringing football into my life in such a profound way. There is nowhere I'd rather be than standing on the sidelines watching your games. Love from your number-one fan.

To everyone who reads this book, thanks a million. I know we're all time poor. It doesn't escape me how much of an honour it is when people spend any of their precious time reading my words.

Love Jenny x

Read on for an extract of

THE
F**I**RST
MOVE

SHE DESERVES
TO BE A QUEEN,
NOT A PAWN –
BUT NOW THEY'RE
PLAYING GAMES ...

ILLUSTRATION BY
JANELLE BARONE

JENNY IRELAND

Girls like her don't get their own
love stories ... or do they?

1

Juliet

There should be a disclaimer at the beginning of teen movies:

CONTENT WARNING:
REAL LIFE IS NOTHING LIKE THIS. WE
ACCEPT NO LIABILITY WHATSOEVER FOR
THE UNREALISTIC EXPECTATIONS THAT
WILL ARISE FROM WATCHING THIS FILM.
VIEWER DISCRETION IS ADVISED.

Seems fair. People *should* be warned that the whole 'guy meets girl, they hate each other (or pretend to), they get forced together, and – BAM – they fall in love' thing is total bullshit.

And yeah, I know it's fiction. That none of this stuff is *real*. But I still get sucked in. Every. Single. Time. I even get *butterflies* when they stare at each other the way I stare at my hot-water bottle and painkillers after a day of too much standing up.

And you know which movies are the worst? The ones set at Christmas. Teenagers with above-average good looks, festive jumpers and mistletoe, Tiffany boxes and fake snow, wrapped up with perfect smug smiles.

Don't even get me started on Disney movies. Targeting five-year-olds with their happy-ever-afters? It's sickening.

Here's a spoiler. Real life doesn't work like that. Real life is a first kiss with *way* too much saliva, with someone you barely know, behind the sports hall at breaktime. Your best friend is keeping lookout and whispering that you're taking too long, when you're only trying to figure out a polite way of stopping the slushy horror show. Real life is your other best friend doing *way* more than kissing, with someone else, at the same time, a few metres away.

Real life is the doctor handing you disgusting grey crutches and telling you that you'll need to use a walking aid for the foreseeable future.

Real life is staring at yourself in the mirror and trying not to despise your new reflection.

In real life, all your problems aren't solved over the course of ninety minutes. There is no witty voice-over, no strategically placed plot points, and *definitely* no over-emotional soundtrack telling you exactly how to feel.

Because real life is *nothing* like a stupid movie.

Michael was already outside. I could hear music blasting from his car. I threw off my crutches, letting them slide down the stairs, almost taking out Jeffrey, our Chihuahua-Chewbacca cross.

Mum was in the hall beside the front door, watching me come down: one step, two feet.

'Maybe we should keep the other pair downstairs, so Jeffrey doesn't have to fear for his life every morning?' Jeffrey hid behind Mum's legs as she joked, gauging my mood with a smile that didn't quite reach her eyes.

'Yeah. Would probably be easier.'

Why don't we just get it over with and put some in every room?

'How are you feeling this morning?' Mum asked.

I didn't look up. I didn't need to. I could practically see the crease of concern in her forehead deepen.

'Fine, Mum. Completely, one hundred per cent fine.' Fake smile.

'Jules.'

'Mum.' I met her gaze and smiled, properly this time. And when I did that, the forehead crease disappeared for a second.

'It's the first day of your final year, love. It's going to be great. And nobody's going to notice the crutches.'

'Yeah, I know.' *Of course* everyone was going to notice the crutches. That wasn't the issue. The issue was what they were going to say about it.

She leaned over and kissed my head.

'Ready to take on the world, kid?' Dad came out of the kitchen holding a coffee.

'Something like that.' I looked down at my new trainers. Black Nike Air Force 1s. Not exactly Birch High regulation uniform. As if I needed another reason to stick out. But shoving my feet into leather school shoes hurt too much nowadays.

Dad kissed my head too. 'Promise me a game later? I've got a new move up my sleeve.'

'Sure.'

Mum opened the door. *And there endeth the leaving ceremony.* Thank God for that.

'Hey, Mrs C, Mr C!' Michael walked into the hall and headed straight towards the kitchen. He appeared two minutes later, his mouth full of one of Mum's home-made back-to-school blueberry muffins and another one in his hand.

'Juliet is the sun. Arise, fair sun, and kill the envious moon,' he intoned, bursting into overdramatic life. *Way* too much energy for this time in the morning.

He took my school bag from me, and we walked down the driveway. 'Your hair is on point today.' He kissed his fingers, then nodded at my crutches. 'And I *love* the new accessories.'

'I'll cut you.'

'What? I'm serious. They totally give you something extra. And are those new kicks? Watch that Princess Peach doesn't try and rob them off your feet.'

He nodded towards Tara, sitting in the back of his car. Michael picked her up at the crossroads every morning. He offered to pick her up from her house, but she always said she liked a little walk in the morning, something to do with the air making her skin glow. She was smiling at her phone as we approached.

'Bye, Jules,' Mum called.

God. Why have they followed us outside?

'All will be well, my friend. I promise.'

Easy to say if you're Michael. I'd never met anyone so comfortable in their own skin. Then suddenly his smile disappeared and he looked serious. It amazed me how expressive Michael's face was, like it was impossible to hide the thoughts in his head. 'Actually, though, how are you? The new look can't be easy.'

'Seriously, I'm *fine*. We don't need to talk about it. Wait – is that a top knot?' Michael's dark hair had been pulled back off his face into this tiny bun on top of his head.

'Yeah, it is. Do you like it? My dad was watching Italian football last night, and what can I say? Something he watched finally appealed to me. Don't you think it makes me look like an Italian stallion?' His movie-star smile almost blinded me.

It was impossible not to smile back at Michael.

He squeezed my bag into the back seat with Tara and helped me into the passenger seat of the car. His parents had bought him a new black Audi over the summer.

Some of us got crutches, some of us got an Audi . . .

'Is that a muffin, Michael? I'm starving – did you bring me one?' Tara asked.

'No, sorry. You should've come in instead of sitting on your phone.' He shrugged.

'Ugh, whatever. Oh wow, you're actually bringing them to school?' Tara eyed my crutches like they were carrying some infectious disease. Michael slid them into the back seat beside her, next to my bag. 'Ouch, Michael! Watch where you're sticking those things.'

'Yeah. Remember what I said? Dr Patel –'

But she wasn't listening. She was on Insta. 'Oh my God, Hana got a *lob*. What do you think?' She pushed her phone through the space between me and Michael, and there was

Hana, head cocked, lips parted, peace sign in the camera and her black hair cut into a long bob with a blunt fringe. Gorgeous. It was pretty much the reason Tara decided to be friends with her in Year Ten. 'Hot people have hot friends,' she'd said.

She used to say that about me.

'She looks amazing,' I said.

Michael sighed. 'Yeah, looks fine.'

'Well, *your* hair looks ridiculous, Michael,' Tara said. 'Love your shoes, though, Jules – are they new?'

'Yeah, Dad bought me them yesterday.'

'Ugh, lucky bitch,' she said as Michael started the car.

'Just get yourself a disease.' I smiled.

'Do you think I could pull off crutches?'

To be fair, she probably could.

'Oh, you know that *thing* we were talking about last night, Jules? Hey, Michael, turn down the music, will you?'

I noticed Michael grip the steering wheel more tightly before reaching for the volume control.

Tara and I had spent an hour on WhatsApp last night. She'd decided she wanted to go for it. To lose her virginity this year, and we were basically going through all the guys at school, trying to find the perfect candidate. We hadn't found one.

'Yeah?' I said.

'Well, there's this party next Friday. You know, Daniel from St Anne's?'

No.

'Yeah?'

'Well, I figured that might be the perfect opportunity –'

'Am I missing something?' Michael asked, looking at me.

I shrugged and looked at Tara. I wished she'd just tell him. I hated the weird tension.

'It's kind of a "best friend only" thing.' She smiled at the back of Michael's head, and I tried to soften his side-eye by pulling a stupid face.

Michael had never liked Tara. Well, that's not true. We all used to hang out in this big group: Tara, me, Michael, Hana, Luke and Charlie.

Michael and I had met on our first day. We sat beside each other in English, and he passed me a note saying, 'Please, sir, can I be your friend?' I laughed, then we both got told off, and he's been making me laugh ever since.

Michael and Tara actually used to get on, for a few years at least. Until she told him that her second favourite ex-One Direction band member was Louis and not Zayn (first was Harry, obviously). He said that made him suspicious of her as a person. Michael took his stanning of One Direction really seriously and never trusted her after that. That's what he said anyway when I asked why he didn't like her. There are loads of other reasons now, but that triggered it. *Apparently.* He just never went into details.

They were best friends. Until they weren't ...

'Romance with substance'
Irish Times